Sasha's Way

Payback?........ Justice!

Scott Haskins

UpStream
Publication

Published by **UPSTREAM PUBLICATIONS**
A division of *A&B PUBLISHERS GROUP*
1000 Atlantic Ave.
Brooklyn, NY 11238
(718) 783-7808

ISBN 1-886433-79-8 paper

COVER ILLUSTRATION: © *André Harris*
TYPESETTING & INTERIOR DESIGN: *Industrial Fonts & Graphix*

Manufactured & Printed in Canada

10 9 8 7 6 5 4 3

my parents

**James William Haskins, Jr.
and
Janie Louise Moore-Haskins**

Acknowledgments and special thanks.

First, and foremost I thank God for the words. I thank him for his blessings. However, coming in a close second I have to give my heart to my editor, Jiton S. Davidson. You Believed in Sasha as much as I did. JD, "I love you man!!!" Kwame Alexander, for your belief. Walene White, my ace, thanks for listening and never minding me waking you up at all hours of the morning. Dennis "D-Lee" Lee, we been through some shit, partner. Robert Wallace, my mentor in the writing arena. Oh-six! Robert Murphy, the guidance and advice that you gave and always give are invaluable. Margie Jackson, at Brown and Associates in Columbia, Maryland. You never once got tired of me complaining about LIFE! I appreciate all your help while I was writing. Earl "Earlston" Bell, Jr. You were the only person who asked to be in the book when I first started writing. Your presence added a dimension that I never would have thought of. I thank you for believing in me. A special thanks to my early supporters: Llauryn Iglegart-Howard, Robin Woodlon and Leonard Anderson. If I don't mention my siblings I'll never hear the end of it. Affectionately known as the Haskins Clan: Lisa, Karen, Laura, Sondra, Iona, and my main man Ronald a.k.a. Ronnie Luub'. I love y'all to death. To Ms. Frosty: Much love and respect to you and your incredible talents. My wife Felicia, my son Scott II and my daughter Narcissa.

The completion in my circle of life.

To all who read this, I hope you enjoy Sasha's Way. Peace be unto you!!!

Session I

1

Sasha

"For the last time Cecil, stop the damn car and let me out!"

"Look Sasha, I got half a mind to let you out, while the car is still moving!"

"Yea, but you'd still be half a mind short of having good sense."

"Smart Ass!"

"Thank you!"

"Trust me baby sis, this is the best thing for you. I know what I'm talking about."

"Who the hell put you in charge of what's best for me anyway?"

"Me!"

"You?"

"Yeah! Me. Besides, as far as I am concerned you only got two choices. A lawyer. Or a shrink."

"Well then dammit, take me to a lawyer."

"Shiiit. After five minutes of talking to you, he'll send us straight to a shrink. So we might as well cut out the middle man. Get my drift?"

"Go to hell, Cecil."

"I love you too, Sasha."

"Is this so-called Doctor friend of yours a man, or a woman?"

"Does it matter?"

"Most definitely. I don't think there's a man alive who can empathize with my pain."

"Your pain!?"

"Yeah. My pain."

"Right. Well this Doctor won't have any problem empathizing with you. She'll be able to relate to you just fine. Plus, you're both in the same field, so you should get along."

"Is she black or white?"

"What difference does it make?"

"None."

"Good."

"One last question, oh Guardian Angel so-called big brother of mine."

"You have permission to speak, darling."

"Why do you have to come?"

"To make sure you don't try to slide out the back before your time is up. That's why. Now, out of the car."

"You sure are bossy. And you're getting on my very last nerve."

"Hello, Cecil. Hi. You must be Sasha. Please. Come in. I am Doctor Davis."

"Hello, I'm Doctor Timms."

"Have a seat. Make yourself right at home."

"Can I go home, and make myself at home?"

"You were right Cecil, she's a feisty one allright."

"I would appreciate it if you didn't talk about me as though I weren't in the room, Dr. Davis."

"I apologize. Look, call me Evelyn. Let's relax and just talk. Okay?"

"Fine."

"Sasha, I know you have a lot to say. A lot on your mind. Let it all out, you'll feel better in the morning. I guarantee it."

"Are you positive you want to hear what I have to say? My brother claims I need help."

"You damn straight you need help, baby girl, plenty of it!"

"Mr. Rock, that will be the last outburst from you. I agreed to let you come, but for now, you can wait in the lobby. I'll call you in when I need you. Fair enough?"

"Sorry. Fair enough."

"Bye-bye, Cecil!"

"Be nice, Sasha."

"Tell you what Sasha, take your time, be yourself. Talk to me. Start from the beginning. Introduce me to Sasha. Tell me everything and anything that's heavy on your mind. Okay?"

"I don't know if you're ready, but you asked for it!"

My name is Sasha Timms. I am very, very, very, proud to say that I have been a black woman all of my life. Beautiful Black Woman! Five foot ten. What I must confess, a perfectly proportioned body. Although I must admit, my ass received a few extra helpings. Thirty-six, 24, 38 of 100% black woman. Voluptuous, perfectly rounded breasts. The kind that would make any man wish he was a baby breast-feeding all over again. I know because I've been told more times than I can count.

Honeycoated brown sugar. Perfect skin tone. Long, firm, femininely, muscular legs. Earned on the aerobics circuit, where else! Jet black hair. Shoulder length. Full. Styled to perfection. I never have bad hair days. My face, the epitome of Black Beauty. Almost goddess-like. A smile that welcomes friendship, compassion, and understanding. White teeth and just a little gap in the front to cap off the finished product—me, Sasha Timms. I am not vain. I am self-confident. I am self-assured. I am self-employed. And, as I discovered, a **Murderess**!

We, that's me, Coleman-my shining black knight and husband, and Demetrius-the apple of my eye, cherubim adorable ten-year-old son, lived in the Philadelphia suburb of Lower Merion, Pennsylvania. I love the 'burbs because I have a refuge away from the big city. I can get in when I want and leave when I want. I always have a safe hospice to call home. A place away from the hustle and bustle of city life, Philly style. Away from homeless vagabonds begging for every nickel I earn. Away from the type of nauseating rush- hour traffic that makes me wish for the days of horse and buggy. Away from crackheads; girls, sixteen and often younger, selling their bodies and offering fifty-cent blow jobs so they can get their next high. Away, away from it all. I'm only near it on my terms, which is how I live my life. On my terms. Away from trash, graffiti, and overall filth. Filthy-delphia. The City of Slovenly Love. A great place to visit. The Philadelphia Art Museum, Franklin Institute, Fairmount Park, West River Drive, Liberty Bell, The Gallery, downtown, South Philly, a myriad of great spots. However, I wouldn't want to live there! I could go on for days!

Anyway, Coleman, my dearly beloved husband of eleven years, gave me the type of shock that surely had the angels in heaven crying for me. The type of trauma that would have made Jacko's skin turn completely white. The kind of gut-wrenching, mind-boggling, hair-raising, world-shattering, temper-tantrum-having trauma that would make the Pope curse the bejesus. I could go on for days. Coleman, handsome as any man that ever sauntered the good earth. Coleman, six-foot-two, body that would make Bo and Hershel wish they put in more hours in the gym. Dark, dark, dark, rich skin. Voice, baritone. Smooth and rich. Made me wet the first time I heard him call my name, *Saashaa*.

However, my darling husband evolved into someone I didn't know. Coleman, no-good, low-life, sorry-assed...anyway, not fit to be called a black man. The type of heartless being that was going to receive exactly what was coming to him, and then rot in hell.

Heartbreak was a feeling I never wanted to experience in a relationship. That's why I put all of myself into being an excellent wife and mother. I never knew how I would handle it. And I didn't want to find out. Just the same, Coleman caused me to experience heartbreak and heartache.

It was, Monday, February 22, 1993. I left the office early. I counsel women who are or have been in abusive situations and/or relationships. I just wanted to come home and unwind before Coleman and Demmy got home. As I entered the cul-de-sac of our single family, overpriced, very beautiful, suburban home, I noticed a foreign car in our driveway. Suddenly, the leather interior of my red 1993 Lincoln Towncar started to get a bit warm. Shit, why get excited. Coleman's Black BMW was also in the driveway. He and a buddy probably were shooting pool in the basement or engaged in some other type of manly sportsmanship. I parked on the street since our guest had my space in the driveway. As I entered the house I notice Demmy's bookbag in the middle of the floor. Why was he home from school so early?

Oh, that's right, every Monday Coleman and Demmy have father and son time. Coleman says he has to make a more positive effort to relate to his son. My husband has a hard time accepting the fact that his son is autistic. Coleman knows he's in there, inside his own little world. Sometimes I think Coleman thinks he can bring him out of it. He gets frustrated, but he never stops trying.

So, where are the fellas? Kitchen? Nope. Basement? Empty. Family room watching TV? Nothing but air. I was starting to get a little anxious. Reluctantly, I ascended the oldest Stairmaster in America. Counting as I went. Eleven, 12, 13, 14, 15... Jesus, I think we'll buy a rancher the next time we move. Stair climbing and anxiety just don't go hand in hand. I started towards Demmy's room to see if he was napping or playing that damn Genesis, only to catch a sound that I will never forget. The sound of passion coming from the master bedroom. The same master bedroom that belonged to Coleman and me. The very room where Coleman and I made love. Where Coleman and I did the Nasty. Where we fulfilled all of our lovemaking fantasies. Where our son was conceived. The sounds. Hot, heavy and very, very, very, intense. Sounded like passion. Passion that's reserved for me and my shining black knight. The type of passion when two people, like Coleman and I, collaborate to make the miracle of life. Passion that I suddenly realized I was not participating in! Hairs on the back of my neck started to stand at attention. Sweat formed on my brow. Tiny beads of perspiration, tantalized my spinal cord by easing, teasing, down, touching every disk, just long enough for me to feel the descent over and over, again and again, settling in a pool of nervousness on the hump of my rump.

I reached for the brass doorknob. I was never once prepared to face my Coleman with another woman. Coleman was the perfect husband. Coleman was the perfect father. Still, he had one skeleton in his closet that was going to cost him dearly. My sweet Coleman. Coleman, body of a God. Cole...

The turning of the doorknob, something I have been doing all of my life rather easily, took what seemed like an eternity. Anxiety. Anxious. Anxiousness. I entered. What I saw I couldn't have imagined if I spent the rest of my life trying. Coleman. My Coleman! Face down, butt-naked getting rammed up the booty by a white man. No white man that I knew, but a white man, shit, make that man regardless. Coleman, my king of kings, was not only a loving, caring, and compassionate husband and father, but also a fudge-packing, man-loving, worthless, low-life, mutha... I stood wavering in the doorway. Wanting to scream. Needing to cry. How? What? Why? Do I or could

I even accept any answers from this man I had called my husband for eleven years?

Off to my right, out of the corner of my eye, I encountered the second biggest shock of the day. Okay, I confess, of my life. Demetrius Timms, my ten-year-old son curled up in the corner, transfixed on the activities before him. Nothing he would ever see in show-and-tell would ever compare to this. Why Coleman had him in the room watching him and Mister white man I will never know, because I never bothered to ask. What answer could he possibly give that would allow me to say, "Oh, now I understand." Demmy never noticed me and neither did the fudge packers. I backed out of the room and made my way to Coleman's office down the hall. A twenty-foot walk, maybe. Seemed like the door kept moving farther and farther away. I was drenched in perspiration. That's because real women perspire, they don't sweat! Anger, hurt, and betrayal swelled inside of me awaiting to erupt when I said it was time. Betrayal! Betrayal! This man had all that I ever had to offer. Love, loyalty, companionship, trust...I could go on for days. That day Coleman betrayed me twice! The first and definitely last time! First thing I noticed when I entered Coleman's office was our family portrait taken in Martha's Vineyard during our last vacation. Coleman Timms, Sasha Timms, Demetrius Timms. Now, let's see. Closet. Left side, floor. Ahh, there it is. Hunting rifle.

I knew the return trip to the master bedroom was going to change life as I knew it. Life for Demmy would never be the same. Life for Coleman and Mister white man was never going to be the same. I stopped five feet from the door. Maybe I'll just shoot them both in the ass, I thought. Take Demmy and move away from this awful experience forever. NO! This was my home. My suburb. My life! My way! Anything short of death and eternal damnation was too good for the booty-bonin' warriors. My husband and Mister white man were making some grotesque form of love and they were going to die for their actions.

The grunting and groaning still hadn't concluded when I re-entered the room and placed the barrel against Coleman's head. Coleman, my sweet shining black knight. The light of my life. I shot Coleman first because I didn't want to see his face. I had no desire to hear any explanations; piss-poor unacceptable excuses, or "Baby, I'm sorry. I didn't know how to tell you." Coleman's head exploded like a cantaloupe that had been hit off the bat of Hammerin' Hank. Mister white man stopped his ass-pounding just long enough to say hello to the barrel, and good-bye to his pathetic alternative lifestyle. Like two million snow flakes with no duplicate, that was all that remained of Mister white man's head.

I looked over at Demetrius. Still innocent. Still curled up in a little ball. Still beautiful. He must have gotten his gorgeous looks from Coleman's side of the family. Still with a head full of jet black curly hair. Still the apple of my eye. I asked Demmy did he want to go have lunch. I called the police. Asked for my big brother, Sergeant Rock. Yeah, he was a rock all right. His rock-hard upper body gave way to a soft, slightly overhanging tummy.

Which created a Pseudo Sampson body mystique. I told Rock to come to my house and prepare for the shock of his life. I would hook up with him later so we could talk. Believe me, I told him, you're going to want to talk.

Demetrius and I went to HoJo's on City Line Avenue for lunch. That's me! Sasha Timms. Doing it the only way I know how. **MY WAY!**

2

Rock

"Cecil, you can come in now. Sasha, don't go far."

"You're the boss, Evelyn. Thanks for letting me speak on my sister's behalf. Not to make excuses for her, but she has had a rough life. Please, call me Rock."

"Is that a cop thing, going by your last name?"

"Everybody calls me Rock, my last name. Mainly because I'm not too fond of my first name, Cecil. Sasha calls me Cecil for spite. But she's always been a pain in my ass that way."

"Okay, Rock. Start where you want."

Monday morning was one of those rare, almost perfect mornings. You know how it is when you wake up and just a tiny glint of winter sun hits your face. Warm, loving sun. Lets us know that God says it's time to get up and live this day. The kind of morning when every crevice of your English muffin has just the right amount of butter in it. Teasing your taste buds with every bite. Delicious. The newspaper's on the porch for a change. Dry! And untorn. The f-i-n-e, fine, sister I met last Friday, actually called and left a message, wanting to get together real soon. Car turned over on the first try. Didn't have to shoot anybody on the way to work. Made all the lights all the way to work. Nobody ate my favorite, jelly doughnut, even though it was the last one. Even Captain Arnetti was in a good mood, which is about as rare as snow in Jamaica. Shit, I love my job. Sergeant at a fairly young age. Heaven! Heaven! Heaven!

"YO! Rock! Pick up on line two. It's your baby sis."

Crash boom thud! Trouble with a capital T! What started out to be utopia immediately turned into havoc and chaos. Shit was gonna hit the fan. How did I know? Sasha Timms, my darling little sister, never called me at work unless shit had hit. I had no idea that this was going to be the "mother of all mothers." Because I had such a beautiful morning, I figured the afternoon would go just as well. Ha! Judging by Sasha's tone I knew she was serious about me having the shock of a lifetime. I just didn't know how many volts. But knowing Sasha, I knew it would be a doozie. Sasha and I were as tight as any two siblings on earth. Siamese twins tight. Our lives revolved around loyalty to family. When I say loyalty I don't mean the everyday dictionary type of loyalty. As Webster would say, faithfulness or devotion to a person. I'm talking about the, "I'll do anything, say anything, use any means, fair or unfair, to ensure that our safety, honor, family name, whatever, remains perfect and unblemished, especially if either of us have any control over the outcome." The revolution of our family begins and ends with each other.

Since our parents were shot down like dogs in the City of Brotherly Love, Sasha and I have clung only to each other. Knowing that the person responsible for my parents' death was still walking the streets was too much for me to handle. I didn't want another family to go through what we've been through. I guess that's why I became a police officer. Nobody will get away with anything as long as I wear this blue uniform. Sasha and I are tight. I will die for my baby sis if I have to. And I will kill anyone who attempts to do her wrong.

I drove my Civic to Sasha's. A city patrol car in Lower Merion might draw too much attention. Knowing Sasha, I didn't know exactly what I was up against. Thousands of thoughts went through my mind. I was searching for answers and I didn't even know the question. Like what the hell happened. I was already formulating an alibi. Even though I still didn't have a clue. My thoughtful, loving sister, the one with the gap in her front teeth, never, ever had these type of thoughts because she was confident, 100% no questions asked. She never had a doubt in her mind that I, Sergeant Rock, officer of the law, big brother was, as usual, going to save her backside!

I had to admit, Sasha and Coleman had a '*phat*' crib. Much better than any single family in Wynnefield, my stomping grounds located on the west side of the big city, including the newly renovated duplex I purchased two months ago. As I parked in front of her house my attention went immediately to the two cars parked in the driveway, Coleman's beemer and the gold Lexus with the black trim. I was almost sure I knew the owner of the Lexus but figured my imagination was just getting the best of me. There was no way. No fucking way! Totally, absolutely, under no circumstances whatsoever would he, of all people, be in the middle of some shit with Sasha and Coleman. No way, Lord, I said to myself, don't let my day get any worse!

Living in the safe surroundings of Lower Merion must have been the reason Sasha left the front door to her house unlocked. I placed my keys back in my pocket and just had to smirk at my sister's self confidence and downright sauciness. Sis was a trip and she knew it!

"Coleman! Coleman! Yo, dude, it's me Rock!" I called out in my most professional-sounding policeman's voice. But all I got back was an echo, empty and hollow. Didn't have to be no super-sleuth to know that this was not good. Two cars; not a soul in sight. Shooting pool in the basement, just didn't hear me? Yeah, that's it, I thought. Basement! Nope. Empty. Out back. Nobody. Family room? Air! Sun room? Just me and the plants. I headed up the one flight of stairs, two at a time. A climb that was going to change my life. To what magnitude I didn't know at the time. Coleman must be in his office working. Maybe discussing a business deal with Kyle. Gong! Wrong again! Like the master detective that I am I successfully ruled out every room in the house where Coleman and Kyle might be, except the master bedroom. The master bedroom? The master bedroom! I had to confess, if Sasha didn't have that extra thick, plush-ass carpet on her floor, I'm not sure my head would have survived the fall. My entire body went limp and collapsed in a heap. The sight was beyond horrifying. I had to grab my nuts and squeeze tight just to make sure I didn't piss right at that moment. Coleman. I mean it looked like Coleman's body. He was always showing off his tight abs and rock hard body every opportunity he got. Something, however, was missing to positively confirm identification, like his head. Oh, and his clothes. Not a stitch on his body. As I moved closer to the bed I rubbed my eyes so hard I almost popped them out of their sockets. Seeing another man, a white man, on top of Coleman with his johnson in Coleman's ass was hard to grasp. My brother-in-law. Mr. lover man. Husband of my little sis. Second handsomest man I knew, was nothing more than a back-stabbing, adulterous, cheating, betraying, no type of father figure, faggot! I don't have nothing against any-one's sexual preference, except if you're married to Sasha Timms, my sister, and the father of my main man Demetrius. I attempted to identify mister butt-fucker. The body size looked about right. He, too, was missing a large portion of his head, so I needed to find his pants to corroborate my suspicions. I tell you, that Sasha really had style. Pants? Got 'em. Wallet? Got it. Driver's license. Oh boy! ID? Kiss my black ass! Shit was too deep to swim in. I wouldn't wish this job on my worst enemy. I knew I should have went back to the Superfresh to work, I said to myself. Shit, $6.50 an hour goes a long way if you know how to budget properly. So I might be riding the bus instead of driving. So I might be renting an apartment instead of owning my own home. So I might never have been able to afford to go on vacation to Rio like I did last year. So, so, so, so, so... At least I wouldn't have been standing there holding the driver's license of Kyle O'Grady. Better known as Kyle O'Grady, son of Rozen O'Grady, Mayor of the city of Philadelphia!

I staggered to the kitchen and put on a pot of coffee.

I had to think. I had to make this right so the city of Philly accepted Coleman and Kyle's deaths as nothing more than another in a long line of formidable city tragedies. This particular scene was going to have to be airtight. About as tight as Coleman's ass was before he started getting banged in it. Airtight. No leaks. I needed to think. I decided to take my time. Sat down, had a nice pot, or two, of coffee. I knew I could figure it out. Sasha knew I could figure this out. That's why I was there and she wasn't. What can I say? I have an unnatural, unequaled level of devotion to my only living sibling.

3

Sasha

Rock called me on my car phone around four thirty. Demetrius and I had been driving around the city for what seemed like days. I sure didn't have a place called home to go to anymore. He said to meet him at his house Wednesday evening. That he would need a couple of days to take care of the situation. Before he hung up, he said, "Lord knows if there wasn't but one ass in the entire Negro population that needed saving I am completely sure it would belong to no other than Sasha Timms!" Click!

I always enjoyed visiting my brother at his home in Wynnefield. Wynnefield was more like a suburb to West Philly. A little more peaceful, a little less violent, a little less dirty, a little less city. One thing I never had to worry about when Demetrius and I came to visit was having something for Demmy to do while Rock and I talked. Rock loved those damn video games with a passion. He had more games than any child could imagine. Atari 2600, Atari 5200, Intellivision, Sega Genesis, Super Nintendo, Sega CD, super this, fx chip that, bigger graphics, more memory. He's had every system out at one time or another and has at least three hooked up in his game room at any given time.

It was around seven in the evening when we arrived

at Rock's. His car was in the driveway and as usual, the light in the upstairs game room was on. I swear, whenever that man is stressed or just has some free time, he is up there shooting and killing some type of alien or monster. Demmy flew up the steps while I waited for my brother in the living room.

"Sasha! This has been one chain of events I will gladly and readily cast into the sea of lost memories." We hugged, tight and loving. I could feel the tears welling up in my eyes. That had been the first time I actually stopped to think about everything that had taken place the last couple of days. The power in Rock's hug reassured me that he had taken care of everything. His strength always allowed me to live my life with the confidence that comes from knowing somebody has my back.

"I love you, Rock" was about all I could mutter without my voice cracking too hard. "Rock, before you tell me how you took care of this, I have to tell you one thing. Can you believe that son-of-a-bitch had my son in the room watching him engage in sex with another man?"

"Sash, do you know who it was you murdered along with your husband?"

"No. Just some white guy who deserved to die as much as Coleman!"

"Kyle O'Grady!"

"Who?"

"Kyle O'Grady!"

"Thee!"

"Yup. Thee Kyle O'Grady!"

"Uhhh…Thee, as in mayor' s son Kyle?"

"In the flesh."

"Like I said, some white guy named Kyle O'Grady who deserved to die as much as Coleman!"

"Jesus Christ, Sasha, did thinking before shooting ever occur to you? I had to stoop to about the lowest level possible to make this thing disappear. To be honest, if it wasn't for the fact that I have some serious shit on Captain Arnetti, we both might have had to fly the coop!"

I gave Rock one of my startled, 'Who me?' looks and asked him, "How serious?"

"Does it really matter, huh?"

"No. So how did you pull it off, big bro?"

"First thing I had to do was pick my guts up off of your bedroom floor. Two headless horsemen or in this case headless faggsmen was a bit more than my cast iron stomach could handle. Then I got to work. I needed a patsy. One who was either going to live through the setup or die through the setup. I decided on a junkie whose life I decided didn't matter any more. The decisions one has to make when his sister's life is on the line. I went down to 52nd Street and picked up an ex-con/junkie, sometime-informant named Slim Jim. Slim was the skinniest thing on two legs. Skin and bones. I had busted him many times for petty shit like loitering, pissing in public, purse snatching. You know typical bullshit. He was also one of the meanest former killers on the Philly street-gang circuit. Typical scum bag. Slim was in his early thirties but the drugs made him look at least forty-five. Anyway, he wasn't serving the community or doing this world any good so I decided he would die to save yo' ass. Sasha, the decisions I had to make for you. I told Slim I knew of this rich couple that was out of town and I needed his help robbing their home. I promised the fool two -hundred ones! Enough money to get good and high for a couple of hours. When we got inside the master bedroom, Slim, even in his deteriorated mental capacity knew he was done. I guess being 'street wise' never leaves you, even if you are a base head. I will never forget the look of 'Oh Shit' on his face when Slim turned around. It was like he was moving in slow motion. Head. Neck. Shoulder. Arm. Torso. Thigh. Calf. Foot. Slowly. Slowly. Slowly. Knowing that unless he moved quickly his life was going to end. Even though he didn't have a home, or family, or job, or future, he knew he didn't want to die. Fear etched on his brow, he was seeking compassion. Words of mercy on the tip of his tongue. And when he was completely turned around facing me, I placed a bullet in his chest! Sasha, Sasha, Sasha, the totally, completely, entirely, very difficult decisions one has to make when his sister's life is on the line! I never understood why Coleman needed a shotgun. Shit, he didn't hunt or nothing. He just owned a shotgun. I held the gun in Slim's growing-cold, very much dead hand, and fired a shot into the wall. The gunpowder residue would seal his fate. Guilty as charged, killed at the scene by an everyday hard working foot soldier. I called Captain Arnetti and explained that I surprised a 'perp' trying to rob my sister's house and I had to kill him. Cap' said he couldn't understand how and why a junkie would be in Sasha's neighborhood trying to rob her in broad daylight. For the high I suppose, he answered his own question, which he was prone to do. When I explained that Slim Jim had killed Coleman and Kyle O'Grady, Captain Arnetti surely had a heart attack on the spot. It didn't help to know that a cop's sister owned the home where the mayor's son was lying dead."

"The captain came to your house and helped me dress the bodies. We both agreed that nobody else in the city needed to know that Kyle was gay. The ambulance picked the bodies up from the living room of your house. The home of the murders we couldn't hide. But the exact location of the bodies at the time of death would never be known. It's a good thing the medical examiner was Captain Arnetti's brother-in-law. Cap' just told him this was an 'open and shut' case. Do the basics and get the hell out. I am convinced his brother-in-law is a punk. Just shook his head and got to work. We needed all day yesterday to formulate a report that would satisfy the media. Captain Arnetti, who happened to be a good friend to the mayor, tipped Rozen's hat to the fact that his son was an unfortunate victim. That he would also be best advised to announce publicly that his son was murdered in a horrendous fashion while visiting a close friend. Period. His son would be buried with dignity. His family name and his image as mayor wouldn't be damaged."

"Rock. You're the best and I love you with all of my heart and soul. I can't say that I am sorry that I put that miserable dog to sleep, but I am sorry that you had to jeopardize your career for me."

I don't understand why Coleman had Demetrius in

that room with him? Why? Why? Why? What was his motivation? I didn't even know that Coleman was bisexual. I knew that he was goal oriented. A hard working man. Proud. He loved and treated me the way a woman deserved to be loved and treated, like a queen. However, he never could get over the fact that his son was autistic. Coleman knew that Demetrius would never be the man his daddy was and never make him proud.

Maybe that's why he had his son in that room watching him have anal sex with another man. His own insecurity about not being able to father a son that was adequate in his eyes; a son that he would be proud to call his own. So Coleman forced his son to watch him, almost as if to say, 'This is what you drove daddy to son.' I don't know. What I do know is that the bastard's dead. He had it coming."

I spent the next ten minutes crying in my brother's arms. I cried because my son had to witness his father having sex with a man. I cried because my son had to witness his father being killed. I cried because I knew that my brother would do anything for me. I cried because through all of this madness, if I had to, I knew I could kill again! I cried because I knew that if I wanted to, I would kill again. Killing for the first time, I found out wasn't hard. Something was growing inside of me that seduced my desires for righting any wrong...My way!

Any wife would have done what I did. Well, I kept thinking about my parents. A message was sent to me when they were executed by a maniac who still walks free. You're not always going to get caught. Now, I walk the streets. Maybe I have become what I have loathed for so long. It doesn't matter though. Coleman got what he deserved.

I have to admit, I might have reacted a bit harshly when I discovered Coleman getting the 'back packs,' but what was I supposed to do? There was no way in hell I could have dealt with the emotional trauma and humiliation of losing a husband to another man. I never once considered what life would be like without my man. I never considered how life without a father would affect my son. I was sure of only one thing. Coleman destroyed the core of our marriage when he betrayed me. Every positive belief that I ever had in a man was dismantled beyond repair. I had to figure out how to move on with my life. After I left Rock's I knew that I would never again shed a tear for Coleman Timms.

A new environment was the first order of business. The thought of ever sleeping in the room where I killed my husband made me nauseous. I sold the house and moved into a condo in Wynnewood, Pa., another suburb of Philadelphia. I was very happy that Coleman wanted my future secure in case something happened to him. The very, very generous lump sum that the financial consultant, since there are no more insurance salesmen in the world, dropped off would definitely ensure that I wouldn't have to work or want for the rest of my life. I bet Coleman never imagined I would be the one who ended his life.

Because of the conflict in my life I felt it was best that I take Demetrius to stay with my best friend Jeanette.

Jeanette's a successful, self-employed businesswoman. Stocks, insurance, and anything else she can get into to make money. Single, no children, but enough love in her heart to take care of ten children. Or at least one, her godson. He'd be fine, I knew it. We went to college together. Pledged together. She's also the only person I trusted, and who had the time to take care of him. He needed stability in his life, attention. I knew that I couldn't give him the time that he deserved. The time that he needed. It broke my heart, but I took him to Maryland. I could hardly look at him. His chocolate complexion reminded me of Coleman so much. The scar over his left eyebrow was barely visible. When he fell and cut himself on the coffee table I thought I would die. I loved the way the barber cut his hair. Nice and even all around. Long enough to comb. Something Demetrius didn't like to do. He loved to brush his hair. He was going to be tall too and muscular. My handsome little baby. The longest two-hour ride I had ever had in my life. I cried all the way home.

My work became the sole motivating factor in my life. Being the liaison between hell and happiness for women who couldn't turn their lives around was rewarding for me. I couldn't suggest my form of justice to my clients, especially pre-KC, killing Coleman, but now something fermented within my spirit. I felt this unsettling obligation to solve and resolve my patients' problems for them.

The first couple of months, post-KC, I thought it was just my belief that all women should redeem themselves in any manner that suited them. If that meant the bastard had to die, then he had to die. I was putting myself into their problems and thinking I could solve them the Sasha way. My job as psychiatrist/counselor was to lead my clients to a resolution of their problems, not suggest a solution for them. Each day it was becoming harder and harder to squelch the animal that was vehemently fighting to get out of me. Trying to overcome the sense of urgency to right each and every wrong, my way. I felt that each injustice that was done, any that I knew about, must and will be resolved. Capital punishment. The only form of justice that will allow me to have sweet dreams. Sweet dreams.

I think back when I anticipated making love to Coleman for the first time. The nervous anxiety wouldn't let me eat for three days. How bad I wanted him to touch me, everywhere. How I longed to be enveloped in his arms. To lay on his chest and know that I was with a real man. To not have to coach in bed. Looking forward to total and complete ecstasy. Knowing that the first orgasm wouldn't be the last. Coleman didn't disappoint me. Like I never have bad hair days; Coleman never had bad lovemaking days. I almost hated to have good thoughts in my remembrance of him. I couldn't dismiss the animal that seemed to be governing my consciousness. I couldn't fight the desire to react to every unjustifiable action on the part of any sorry ass who transgressed violently on a friend or client of mine.

I actually hoped this killing thing would pass. Then Sanya Harper came for counseling, and told me her story:

"Melvin was so inebriated I should have ushered him into the kitchen and had him light the pilot light on the stove. An inferno of sorry-ass Niggah would have saved me from the worst beating I ever had. Terrified as usual I only planned on asking how his day went and was he ready for dinner. The fear of not knowing if my husband would love me or hate me each evening when he came home from work made every day of my life hell. Melvin also said he would kill me, just like he did his last wife, if I ever tried to leave him. I believed him. I had on my rose colored pants suit when he came home. It was his favorite outfit. I also had the biggest synthetic smile I could muster. 'How was your... was all I could get out before his fist shattered every bone in the left side of my face."

'Bitch! Why in the fuck you always got to be in my mu' fuckin' face. I done tol' you a hunert mu' fuckin' times to stay the fuck out my face...'

"With each curse a size thirteen boot was delivered to my face, head, stomach, back, and breasts. It seemed as though each time he kicked me bones in every part of my body splintered like cheap furniture. The force of every blow went through my body like ten-thousand volts of electricity. Melvin gathered me in his arms so that I was looking him straight into his bloodshot eyes. I was broken, bleeding, and barely cognizant of what had just taken place." He slurred, *'Bitch...Bitch...Mu' fucking' ugly, buck-toof ass bitch...if I didn't love yo' ugly ass, I would keel yo' stuck up ass right now...'*

"He backhanded me so hard I was airborne. I passed

out before I hit the floor. When I came to I knew that I had died for my sins and that being abused was not enough to get me into heaven. Why the good Lord had banished me to hell, I could not figure out. I considered myself a good Christian. I had cried on the altar many times. I begged my God with every fiber of my being to save my soul from sin. When I opened my eyes, Melvin was collapsed in the chair next to the bed, covered with grief. He looked like a Mamma's Boy who just found out his mamma had died. Flowers in hand..." *'Sanya...baby. I, I-I-I-I, thought you were going to die. Baby, I am so sorry. I swear, the Lord strike me down dead if I ever touch you again.'*

"In my mind I repeated what he was saying, word for word. This wasn't the first time I heard this speech, and surely it wouldn't be the last, unless I do something about it. Sasha, surely, I must be in hell."

Sanya's story really got to me. I had to wipe the tears from my face, clear my throat, and compose myself before I could give any type of advantageous, professional advice. It had been barely a year since Coleman's death. But like a pit bull in a rage, I could feel the animal inside of me aching to get out. At that moment I knew that I would right that wrong.

"Sanya...honey, are you willing to give your life for this monster? You have to realize that he is going to kill you. He is not fit to be called a man. An animal so full of hate and rage that he has no regard for your life, for your existence."

"What can I do? He said he would kill me. Melvin is

possessed with the spirit of the devil."

"You have to take control of your life. You have to stop giving thought to what your husband is going to do and think about how you are going to get on with your life. You have to make one positive step towards life without Melvin. Sweetheart... you need to rest."

"Where can I go where Melvin won't find me? I have tried to leave him before. He always finds me and beats the shit out of me."

"Just say the word and I will do everything in my power to help you."

"Sasha... Please help me."

Sanya was a battered and broken-down woman. We both cried in my fifth-floor City Line office. I called Rock and let him know he would have company when he got home from work. I let him know that Sanya just needed a place to stay for a couple of days. When we got to Rock's place Sanya was noticeably hesitant about staying away from her husband, especially without his permission. I took her hand and placed it on the scar tissue on her once attractive face.

"Sanya, you must do this for you. My brother is a police officer who doesn't take any shit off of anybody. Even if Melvin knew you were here, believe me he would not cross my brother. You will be perfectly safe here for as long as you want to stay."

I took Sanya straight to Rock's guest room in the lower level of his duplex. I stayed with her until she went to sleep. As I slipped her house keys out of her purse, I whispered in her ear, "Don't worry honey... everything is going to be all right!"

Sanya was still sleeping forty five minutes later when I returned her keys after I had made a copy for myself. She lived on Whitby Avenue. Southwest Philadelphia. I took the bus to her house that evening and waited for that no good alcoholic son-a-bitch to come strolling in the house. I sorta hoped he wasn't drunk because I wanted him to know exactly how and why he was going to spend his remaining days in hell!

The key turned around eleven-thirty. I could see my pulse vibrating on my wrist. My heart pounded a slow steady thump...thump. It was time to right that wrong! I waited upstairs in front of their bedroom door.

"Sanya! Where you at? Sanya, I'm home. Sanya! Sanya!"

Hallelujah! He was sober. I entered the bedroom quickly, making sure I slammed the door loud enough for Melvin to hear. I could feel each heavy thud of his footsteps reverberating on the floor beneath my feet. When he opened the door he received the shock of his almost ended life. No doubt I was the most beautiful woman he had ever seen. Simple-minded bastard probably thought he was going to get laid.

"Sweeeeeet Jesuuuus! The goooood Lord mus' be answering my prayers. I don't know who the fuck you are or why you're in my bedroom, but I am very glad to see you. You 'bout thee finest lady I done ever seen. My name's Mel, you can call me Sweet Daddy!"

"Hello, Melvin, my name is Sasha. Sasha Timms. I have a very special gift for you. Something a big, strong, vibrant brother like yourself deserves. Something that is going to change your life forever!"

I used a small-caliber pistol to shoot Melvin in the balls. I wanted him to be in excruciating pain. As he dozed in and out of consciousness I used duct tape to secure his wrists, legs and mouth. Lover boy had a silk robe in the bathroom, perfect. I tied his arms around the bedpost with the belt from the robe. I took the liberty to browse through his closet. Ahhh, size 42 belt. One black, one brown. Great. I fastened his big feet to the opposite end of the bed. Nice big, heavy, oak bed. He wasn't going anywhere. A couple of slaps upside his head brought Melvin out of his painful sleep.

"Melvin, you have beat Sanya for the last time."

He gave me this pitiful, sorry, terrified look at the mention of his spouse's name. I didn't want him to be able to move an inch. Now let's see... Lighter fluid? Check! Matches? Check! Bucket of water? Check. Didn't want him to burn too long! Very good!

"Sanya mentioned to me that she would like to see you burn. She might not be here physically, but her soul will know, because her burden will be lifted when I finish killing you."

I am almost sure that Melvin was pleading for clemency when I looked into his eyes. Through the pathway of the eyes you can reach the soul of any man. Because his penis was already in shambles, it wasn't very difficult to keep Melvin's arms pinned, tied tight.

"Melvil, dear, I can promise you this. You will never hit another woman in your life."

I set fire to his wrists and watched it eat away at his flesh until his bones were visible. He passed out several times. Of course, I made sure he came back to. Beads of sweat poured down the sides of his head. By the time I splashed water on his burning hands, Melvin was out for good. I used a butcher knife I found in the kitchen to carve a big smile into his neck. I whispered into Melvin's ear, "Don't worry honey... Everything is all right now."

I called Sanya at Rock's the next day. She said that my brother treated her like a queen.

"I'm sure you can stay with my brother as long as you want."

"I don't want to wear out my welcome, I'm going to my mother's. I'll call Melvin from there, make sure he's calm before I go home. By the way, thanks for everything, Sasha."

I went back to my office and waited for her phone call to tell me about the horrible fashion in which her husband had been murdered. The wrong had been righted. My Way.

Session II

4

Sasha

I know what you're thinking, Evelyn. Okay, maybe I acted a bit harshly. Maybe Melvin didn't deserve to die. My next client reinforced the existence that the animal was steadily growing inside of me. It was going to right wrongs.

I could tell when Malinda Chaney came to my office, she was a woman who needed guidance. When she initially explained to me why she sought my services I started to direct her elsewhere. After all, I generally assist women who are or have been abused. She said that she had been raped. I asked her did she report the assault to the police. Usually you see the police before you seek therapy. There's a man who needs to have his ass incarcerated. She said no, because there was no forced entry.

"Honey, was it that you didn't agree to have sex with this man?"

She said she had been led astray by a person in whom she had given all of her trust. She said that she was suffering from severe emotional trauma because she had been emotionally raped and physically seduced by her pastor! She also said that I had come highly recommended and she was desperate for professional help. She wanted to get on with her life and had nowhere else to turn.

Non-physical abuse wasn't the norm for the cases I treated. But the extenuating circumstances of her strife was certainly worth my attention.

"Malinda, make yourself comfortable. Take your time and tell me everything you can remember. Before, during, and after your rape. Don't leave out any details. If you get too upset to continue we can always pick up next time."

"Sasha, I want to express how happy I am that you are willing to help me. My best friend Sheila West was a client of yours a couple of months ago. She had nothing but high praises in describing you."

"Hold on, Malinda, there's someone at my door. Hey! Scotty, my favorite UPS man. Look here, handsome, I sure hope you brought me something good this time."

"Ms. Timms, you the one ordering all the secret catalog stuff, you'd know better than me if it's good or not. Although I would be more than happy to give an eyewitness opinion of the quality and goodness of whatever you ordered."

"Man, if you don't get your ass out of here I'm gonna call your wife!"

"Have a nice day, Ms. Timms.

"You too, baby! Sorry for the interruption, Malinda. Sometimes it's easier to shop from the office. I can't always get out."

"That's quite al right, Sasha."

I gave her an encouraging smile. "You just start yacking and don't stop 'till you get tired of talking."

"I don't know if you are a religious woman or not, but I certainly am. I got saved when I was seventeen and have been a faithful member of my church ever since. For ten years I have been what you might call a Holy Roller. I didn't have a need or strong desire for a husband because Jesus was all the man I needed. Jesus filled all of the voids in my life. I was single, childless, but happy. I spent most of my free time at church. Any committee that needed help never had to look past Sister Chaney for a willing worker. I was a dutiful servant to the Lord.

"Life for me was wonderful. 'The New Christian Baptist Church' was my home, for nine and a half years anyway. But, my pastor, the Reverend Austin Morgan changed that. Sasha, you know you have heard the word whenever you've heard Reverend Morgan preach. He had to have been hand- picked by God to deliver the word. The respect that his mere presence commanded at the young age of 42 was beautiful. *King* -type respect. Each and every sermon was food for the soul. I brought a cassette tape of one of his sermons just so you could get a better idea of Reverend Morgan at his best."

"Play the tape, honey!"

"Okay, but just a little. He might get you to thinkin' that I am making all of this up because a married father of three, pastor could never do what he is being accused of doing. I give you Reverend Morgan:

"*...Chuuuurch! I saaid that God. Not Just Any ole' God. But My God. Yo' God! So luuuuved the World. That he GAVE- Y'all didn't hear me. (Come on Preacher). I saaid he GAVE. No he didn't charge not one red cent. There wasn't no admission ticket you had to buy. There wudn't no toll you had to PAY! I said he GAVE his only* begotten SON. Y'all didn't hear me. (AMEN, Take your time!) I saaaaid he gave his only begotten SON. Now how many of us so-called Christians would give our ONLY of anything? Can I git an AMEN? (AMEN, AMEN) I saaaaid, how many of us so-called Christians would give our only of anything? Look at how good you all look this mornin.' But I bet a whole lot of us be covetin' what we ooooowwwn. I say, we covet what we ooooooown. When was the last time we took some NEW clothes to the Salvation Army? HUH!? When was the laaaaaast time we gave the fresh, just-cooked dinner to the homeless and saved the leftovers for ourselves? I, yiii, I, say, when was the laaaaast time?. HUH!? I say, when was the last time, we gave our ONLY of anything? Some of us is too caught up in whaaaat we have. (AMEN) We toooo caught up in what we have to give a thought about givin' our only of anything. But GODDDD!!! AHHH say GOD! (YES) He GAVE! (U-HUH!) He GAVE!!! He GAVE! Help me, Lord! (Take yo' time pastor. Preach! Preach!) USE ME LORD!! I say he GAVE HIS ONLY...BEGOTTEN SON!!! That whosoever BELIEVE! I said whosoever BELIEEEEEVE!!! That don't exclude nobody. Dat mean everybody. Not just the White man. HUH! Not just the Black man. Amen! (AMEN) Not just the Chinese, Japanese, Spanish, I-talian, Breed, Roman, Protestant, Caaa-tholic, Jewish, Episcopalian, Baptist.... But! WHOSOEVER!!! I, YIII, I SAY! WHOSOEVER BELIEEEEEEVE IN HIM... should not perish but would have LIFE..."

"What do you think, Sasha?"

"Fire and Brimstone. I'm ready to pay my tithes and offering right now!"

"I was hooked from day one."

"Tell me about the rape." Good preaching always made me feel good on the inside. Reverend Morgan made me feel good. But if he hurt Malinda I didn't want to have these feelings. I guess that's why I wanted to move on to the real issue. I didn't want to become soft for a smooth-talking, hell -raising preacher.

"I am sure you can imagine the level of admiration any woman would have for a man of Reverend Morgan's stature. He was always available after service for a Christian word and a smile. His office door was always open for counseling, prayer, or whatever your soul need-ed. Anyway, one particular Sunday it seemed as though Reverend Morgan's post sermon hug was extra firm and affectionate. I smiled and complimented him on the ser-mon like I always did. I thought my mind was playing tricks on me because this man had watched me mature from teenager to woman. He was a father figure in the purest sense of the word. Why would I think his hug was filled with lust or desires for me? The following Sunday, from the pulpit Reverend Morgan commented on how good everybody looked. Only thing was, his eyes were on me. Since I hadn't been with a man since I was sixteen, I figured my dormant sexual desires were just teasing me.

"The intimate hugs continued. It wasn't until after he raped me that I understood all the signs. The pecks on the cheek seemed to last a little bit longer. The 'good morning' compliments were always directed at me. I have to admit I did have a crush on him, but it was a fatherly, respectable type of crush. If there is such a thing. I mean Sasha, this man is handsome as all get out. He's a tall, very handsome man. When you think of the typical Baptist preacher, what do you see? Belly, belly, belly! Out of breath most of the time; can't hardly see straight from all the sweat drippin'. Towel somewhere close so he can dry off after his message. Reverend Morgan didn't fit the mold; matter of fact God musta' used a new mold for Reverend Morgan. He was not only a pleasure to hear, but also a pleasure to know personally. Reverend Morgan is a great man. The shining example he set for the men in our church and the constant reminders to his parishioners that God would rather us marry, led me to Reverend Morgan for help. I was a young woman, kind of mixed up in the head. For some reason I wanted to be around him. I figured he would lead me in the right direction.

"I didn't know how to go about looking for a husband. At age twenty-seven I knew that time was winding up. If anyone could show me the way, Reverend Morgan could. The first three times we talked I was full of hope and encouragement. We talked about forming a singles ministry so that the single people in church could fellowship and worship. I guess this could be considered a holy dating service. The New Christian Baptist Church is located in an old established neighborhood in Mt. Airy. Most of the members are married. A singles ministry just never seemed necessary before. Sasha, one thing I have to make clear. Having any type of romantic relationship with my pastor was never my intention. Even if it were, I would never expect a married man of God to backslide and violate one of God's commandments."

"Malinda, I have no way of helping anyone who doesn't want to help themselves. If you sat here and lied to me it would only stop us from finding a true resolution to your problem. I am not here to doubt you. Speak from your heart, honey, and tell me everything. Okay!?"

"See, that's exactly what Sheila was telling me. She said Sasha will make you feel like you are talking to your sister. Not to someone who wants a check just because they listened to you rattle on for an hour."

"Thank you for the compliment, Malinda. You would never believe how much it is a pleasure for me to serve my sisters in this capacity. Now, continue."

"Okay, Sister Timms! My fourth session with Reverend Morgan set my salvation and emotions in a total state of confusion. I didn't know my head from my toes. Let me tell you how it happened. We met in the afternoon on a Saturday in his office. The church wasn't empty. We were just in an area of the church that was primarily secluded. *"Sister Chaney! You lookin' good as always. Come in and sit down."*

"He had a tremendously large smile on his face as he hugged me tight and surprisingly planted a juicy but light kiss on my lips. He acted as though this was a normal act. I, on the other hand, was confused. No man this fine had ever kissed me. But, at the same time my Christian Soul told me this couldn't be right. I have to admit, I wasn't mad. Actually I was flattered that he thought enough of me to want to kiss me like that."

"Afternoon, Reverend Morgan. I must say you're looking handsome as usual yourself!"

"Why thank you, Sister Chaney. Please sit yourself down and rest that beautiful body of yours."

"Once again I was hit with a compliment that crossed the line between proper and improper conduct. However, I let the words ease through my ears and float around my body; just enjoying the sole attention that I was receiving from such a respected and handsome man. It was as if the high school quarterback asked me to the prom even though I was considered to be just an average-looking babe by the other boys."

"Sister Chaney, I think it's time that we take a more realistic approach to showing you how to choose a husband."

"What exactly do you mean, Reverend?"

"Sister, in order for me to show you what to look for I have to know what you have to offer. For example, do you think that God would have sent David to slay Goliath if he didn't think David could get the job done?"

"Of course not, pastor."

"Do you think that God would have chosen Moses to lead his people if he didn't know if Moses could actually lead?"

"No, sir."

"I couldn't help but smile at Reverend Morgan when he made a point using Biblical context. It put me right back in the Sunday morning service. First seat, third pew on the right. He knew the Bible and he never hesitated to use it to paint a clearer picture so we could fully understand the word of God."

"Anyway, dear, God has put me here to lead this church to salvation. To show the way to righteousness. God has told me that in order to help you I must first know you. I dare not question the Lord. I simply obey his commands; death comes to anyone who dares defy God."

"Pastor, you know that I am a willing servant to the Lord and would never disappoint or defy my God. I am a bit confused as to what you mean when you say 'know me,'" "I was sure I knew, but if he meant what I thought he meant I wasn't sure it would be the right thing to do. Reverend Morgan rose confidently; moved from his side of the desk to mine. He reached out for my hand. I rose obediently without any effort from him. I think the attention I was getting was keeping my better judgment from taking control."

"Sister Chaney. When was the last time a man told you how beautiful you are?"

"Been a while, Pastor."

"I couldn't help but blush. Here he was the most distinguished man I knew giving me, *plain Jane*, a compliment."

"And when was the last time a man told you he loved you and you truly believed him?"

"Been a very long while, pastor."

"When was the last time you made love?"

"Reverend Morgan, the last time I had sex I was sixteen years old. I got saved when I was seventeen. But you already know that because you opened the

doors to the church to me when I joined. I cannot say that I have ever been made love to. But what do all of these questions have to do with finding a good husband?" Inside I started to think that these questions were a bit unusual. But, I went along for the ride just like a kid on a Sunday drive to Grandma's house.

"Sister, my heart goes out to you. A woman as beautiful as you deserves to have someone in your life to love. Someone to treat you the way a Queen should be treated. I can help you find that someone. But by first 'knowing' you I will be equipped with the knowledge of exactly who Malinda Chaney is."

"Reverend Morgan..."

"Sister, before you speak I have one last question. When was the last time you were kissed like this?"

"Sasha, if it were possible for a sweeter kiss to be placed on my lips it would had to have come from the sweetest angel. I melted like hot butter in Aunt Molly's kitchen. You know the one Aunt down south that don't believe in air conditioning."

"I hear you, girl, keep talking."

"Reverend Morgan proceeded to touch and caress every erotic area of my body. All the while smoothly, slowly removing every stitch of clothing that I had on. I found myself returning the passion, practically tearing his clothes from his body, no longer cognizant of the fact that he was a married father of three, and my pastor. As I became hotter and hotter the thought of saying no was shoved away into my subconscious, just like the clothes we were throwing around the room. I am convinced that

I saw guilt slivering across the carpet and out the door. Reverend Morgan entered me as I laid on his sofa with my legs willingly spread wide open. He made love to me that day. After I had reached my climax three or four times he guided my head to his still erect penis. I, for some unknown reason; I guess we'll call it passion, was more than willing to give him what he wanted and caressed his manhood as best I could. I wanted to please him. He made me feel truly loved for the first time in my life. After I had completed my best imitation of a blow job, I must have been doing something right because his eyes took a good while to roll down from the top of his head, he reentered my still very wet and ready vagina. We came together like old lovers. Reverend Morgan helped me dress myself with the care and attention of a father dressing his own daughter. Made sure my bra strap wasn't twisted. My dress completely buttoned. Slip not showing.

"I asked myself, how could something this good be true? How feeling this wonderful could be anything but the work of the devil. Maybe Reverend Morgan could explain it to me. So I asked him."

"Reverend Morgan, making love to a married minister has to be wrong. I mean didn't we just commit adultery?"

"Sister Chaney. I know it has been a while since you have been with a man, but please don't act so innocent. I felt the vibes you had been giving me in church. I thought for sure that you wanted me, but you were just too afraid to make the first move. I know you don't believe you are the first woman I have made love to in

this church. Like I said earlier, in order to help you or any other lady in this church, I have to know you."

"He kissed me again on the lips, but that time I was not moved. If someone had taken a knife and cut off my ear, the pain would not come close to the knawing, burning sensation that I was having in the pit of my stomach. It suddenly occurred to me that I was just another toy there for his pleasure. I was glad I didn't faint in his office. I smiled as best I could and replied:

"Of course not, Pastor."

"When I got outside on Stenton Avenue, I threw up until I was empty. My body trembled out of control. I thought that I might lose my bowels on the spot. I don't remember getting on or off the bus. I don't remember walking two blocks to my apartment. All I remember is it being Monday afternoon and me answering the telephone. My boss wondering if I had planned on coming to work sometime that day. I was already four hours late. I told him I needed a break from computer programs for a couple of days. I hung up not even caring or considering whether he agreed or if I still even had a job. Sasha, this leader of men tricked me into thinking he could help me find a husband, a husband I was convinced I needed because of his teachings of the Holy scriptures. All he ever wanted was a piece of ass. I just can't view the church in the same fashion as I used to. The position of Pastor just doesn't mean what it did in the past. I was betrayed at the highest level. I was vulnerable and hungry for companionship. Reverend Morgan recognized this and exploited me to fulfill his own sexual appetite. I haven't been to work steady in a month. I have already had one nervous breakdown. Sometimes I feel like life isn't worth living. If there is a God, there is no way he would have allowed this to happen to me. I mean, isn't Reverend Morgan supposed to be representing God himself? I just can't believe that God would do this or even allow this to happen. Sasha, I am at the end, and I am ready to let go. What can I do to get myself together? I want to put my life back together. I want the Good Reverend Austin Morgan to get his just do. Not in hell where he is sure to burn, but right here on earth. I believe that God will deal with Reverend Morgan in his own way. But the world needs to know what type of man is leading and deceiving the New Christian Baptist Church. I just hope that one day he is exposed for what he is. But more importantly, I just need you to help me become a whole woman again. I know that I can never again, not that I would want to, step into New Christian. The sad part is this church has been the biggest part of my life for the last nine years. Now that has all been snatched away from me. It hurts."

"Malinda. You sweet, sweet girl. We're going to take care of your problem. You will be able to cope soon enough. Trust me! Just trust Sasha!"

I found that after Coleman's death I needed an outlet in my life, something that would take my mind elsewhere; something that would take my mind off of Coleman. Aerobics was good for me but it wasn't enough. I decided to become a disciplined student of Tae Kwon Do karate. In the past year I have obtained a high degree of discipline, greater physical strength and superb stamina. Karate did not kill off or control the animal inside of me; it was just an outlet. But I loved it. I encouraged Malinda to try martial arts as an outlet. As my instructor used to say, 'If the body is strong, then the mind is strong, because it takes a strong mind to build a strong body.' Malinda agreed to give karate a try and she promised not to think about, if possible, the New Christian Baptist Church or Reverend Morgan. We also met once a week to talk. Some days we would just go downtown and have lunch. Malinda needed a friend. I did too, for that matter. A friend can be the most valuable commodity. I enjoyed our girlfriend companionship as part of Malinda's recovery process. One small problem though, the animal was pulling on my sleeve. Said it's time to pay Reverend Morgan a visit.

The saying "men are dogs" is probably true. But what's even truer is that all men are suckers for beautiful women. Sometimes I get extra sharp and hit Center City Philly just to see if my theory is true. Naturally, Philly's bow-wows never disappoint me. My mauve suit was the choice for the day. I liked this outfit because the skirt laid perfectly at mid-thigh. My legs were on display the second I walked out of the house. I didn't carry a purse because I wanted to swing both arms just enough so that the sway in my hips would turn every head in my direction. I always believed that a matching hat gives a hint of sophistication. Sophisticated, self-confident, and of course, stunningly beautiful; what can I say, that's me, Sasha Timms!

The Gallery at Eighth and Market was where I chose to confirm my theory of suckerology. I noticed three gentlemen standing at the entrance to the mall. They watched each and every woman walk through the door, never moving a muscle to open the door, as a true gentleman would. I sauntered over and almost couldn't stop myself from laughing at the sight before me.

"Here you go, Miss Lady!"

"Let me help you, darling."

"Baby, if you want, I will just walk behind you and hold open any door you come to!"

"Lawd have mercy on me. Here you go, Miss Ma'am. Woman fine as you, yo' man got to be crazy lettin' you out by yo'self. Um, um, um!"

"Thank you, gentlemen. I'll be fine on my own. And as far as 'my man' is concerned, I killed him because he didn't like the mall!" I put all 32 Pearlies on display and gave the guys a wink.

"Damn, baby, you so cold you make me shiver! I guess you can make it out here without my help!"

I went into the mall unescorted. I love clothes stores with salesmen. My entrance automatically means discount. I can afford to buy whatever I want. It's just the pleasure I get watching these men do whatever they can to please me, like they are going to get a date. All they can do for me is give me a discount. I brought two dresses that were 50% off plus 'Charles' gave me an extra 20% when I told him he was the handsomest man in the mall, maybe all of Philadelphia. He was fine, but also a fool. Next, I made my way to the food court. I had a tossed salad, chicken sandwich and lemonade, free. How? I just asked the manager if he would wipe off my table and sit with me while I ate my lunch. I have never seen a 260-pound man move that fast in my life. I have always been amused at how important store managers in the mall feel when they display their authority by giving a discount or a free meal, then turn around and treat their own employees crappy for drinking too much 'free' soda or eating too many fries. The conversation and company were nice. I do enjoy men but there is always another side, male bullshit and betrayal; it reminded me of Melvin and Reverend Morgan. It seemed to set off a time bomb inside of me, ticking, ticking, ticking...

Having successfully tested my theory and getting two new dresses for church, I was ready to hear the gospel as told by Reverend Austin Morgan. I wanted to appear before him, in need of salvation, in need of love from the church, and in need of a man in my life. I also wanted to appear before him as the most stunningly beautiful woman his sorry eyes had ever seen. He would always remember the first time he saw me. He just didn't know how much he was going to regret ever seeing Sasha Timms. Reverend Morgan was going to see God face to face sooner than he thought. How God was going to judge his arrival was a different issue.

The New Christian Baptist Church was a wonderful sight to behold. The church was set about two-hundred feet from the street. It seemed to be perched on a hill as if the church was keeping a watch out over the neighborhood around it. The landscaping was absolutely perfect.

Small shrubs lined the walkway to the church entrance.
Red, white, and yellow roses surrounded the entire struc-
ture. Along the outside, trees full and equal in height
lined side by side like soldiers, marking the entire param-
eter of the church. A huge sign was set off to the left for
all to see:

**COME AND WORSHIP WITH US
WE'LL GIVE YOU A NEW WALK
WE'LL GIVE YOU A NEW TALK
WE'LL MAKE YOU WHOLE
HE WILL SAVE YOUR SOUL
COME HEAR PASTOR AUSTIN MORGAN!**

The perfect church for the perfect pastor. I wanted to
ask Reverend Morgan if the "He" in his sign was God or
himself? A man like him probably thought he could save
souls all by himself. I bet his parishioners were going to
miss him. I knew that Reverend Morgan wasn't going to
be hard to manipulate. He might be the most esteemed
leader of this great edifice of worship; he might be a loving father and husband; he might, from what Malinda
had told me, even be a truly anointed saint sent by God
to deliver his people from sin, but underneath his armor
of holiness was rust. He was still a man. He was still a man
who could not or would not resist temptations of the
flesh. He was a man who would just as soon look you in
the eye shouting and screaming the gospel of Jesus and
still have the most unpure heart amongst the entire
church. He was a man who loved women. Nothing wrong
with loving women, but if you make a promise to one

woman you ought to at least keep it. Right?

I made sure I was on time for the service because I wanted to get my favorite seat. First seat, third pew on the right! Devotions, testimonials, opening hymns, first offering, hymn, holy ghost intervention, middle offering, (greedy) were all just preludes to the man, Reverend Morgan. I have to admit he was a wonderful sight. An extremely handsome man. Handsome, yes, but scum just the same. As he stood on high and surveyed the church I knew he wasn't prepared to see me in the seat where Malinda caught his eye on numerous Sundays.

"Good Morning, Church!"

"Good Morning, Pastor Morgan!"

It sounded as though everyone in the church responded on cue. They must practice a lot.

"Praise the Lord!"

"PRAISE JESUS!"

"Is He Worthy To Be Praised?"

"MOST WORTHY!"

So much for spontaneous responses. I have never heard three-hundred people all give the same response to a question in my life.

"Everyone is looking very beautiful on this day that God has made."

Then he saw me looking chaste, pure, innocent. What can I say? I am sure his heart skipped a couple of beats before he found the right words. He did the smart thing and found his wife, I suppose, because he reluctantly took his eyes off me and stared in another woman's face. He did a triple take on me, that's how I know his eyes were reluctant to leave. The woman he looked at looked to be playing the role of dutiful wife and first lady. Or she was just someone he felt comfortable looking at because he was sleeping with her and she liked the attention. Maybe she was too in love with him to have shame about their sinful, disgusting, sexual encounters. I know I can jump to conclusions. I don't know who he was looking at, but I know he wished it was me. When he finally found his words he said:

"I must say, God has shined his light extra radiantly this morning. And the entire church is blessed with its presence! AMEN! Lord Have Mercy!"

"AMEN, PASTOR!"

Funny how the male dog operates. A man's stage is where he stands. Downtown, I hear. 'Um, um, um! Lord, have mercy. Miss Lady, you are looking very radiant today!' New Christian: 'Lord, have mercy. God has shined his light extra radiantly this morning.' All dogs might not live in the same yard, but it's more than obvious to me that barking is still barking! Like most Baptist churches that I have been to, Reverend Morgan requested all visitors to stand and introduce themselves. My pleasure. "Good morning. I am Ms. Timms. A good friend recommended that I come and hear the word of God at the New Christian Baptist Church." Then I looked that maggot square in the eyes and said, "...and I am very glad to be here!" Smiled and humbly took my seat, never bothering to see if the adulterous rascal was blushing. An arrogant man like Reverend Morgan would surely think I was spellbound by his presence and just had to make a subtle pass at him. I am not sure if it was before or after the third or fourth offering but I decided to leave just a little early so that Reverend Morgan could have a good look and possibly stumble over some scriptures, lose his train of thought. I also wanted to play with his head a bit, as the girls used to say. I wanted him to wonder all week and maybe the rest of his life if he would ever see me again. I know that I have that type of effect on most of the dogs that are walking around calling themselves men. As I sauntered down the aisle I heard Reverend Morgan going over some crap about properly filling in the offering envelopes for tax purposes; even visitors. I never looked back. I knew that Reverend Austin Morgan had a sweet tooth and the candy was called Sasha Timms!

I didn't want to be distracted with planning the death of Reverend Morgan right away. I wanted him to suffer awhile, thinking about me. So I planned on spending the next three weeks concentrating on positive time with Malinda.

The time invested was well worth it because she looked and said she felt better. Said she felt like her life was turning completely around. Whenever I help someone I feel as if my life is significant and that I am doing something worthwhile.

When I returned to New Christian, Reverend Morgan damn near broke his neck rushing down from the pulpit to shake hands with his members and friends of the church. Namely me. He was just like a modern-day hustler. All of his routines were just part of an act designed to get him a little closer to the woman he had selected to be his next conquest. If you gonna preach, then dammit, stay in the pulpit and preach.

"Brothers and Sistuuhs, I just want you to know today that God truly loves you. I want you to turn to your neighbor and tell um you luuuv' um! We have got to luu-uuvvv one another right here on earth. You know God says, how can you luv Me who you have not seen, yet despise yo' brother, who you see every day? Now, shake yo' neighbor's hand and tell 'em you love um!"

Sly. He had stopped his fine, grinnin' ass directly in front of me. "Ms. Timms, glad to have you with us this fine morning that God has made. Hope to see you again real soon!"

"Glad to be here, Reverend Morgan."

He didn't stay long, but there was definitely a lot of gladness in his handshake. Following the service I made my way to the pulpit to solicit the good Reverend's expertise on Christian dating in the nineties. He suggest-ed that I come by the office on Saturday to formally arrange some counseling sessions. He also let me know that the singles ministry met every Thursday at eight p.m. For all of the sincerity in his voice and the overall believ-ability in his genuine Christian concern for my personal welfare, it was hard to believe that he was nothing more than a lying, deceiving, sack of horse manure. But deep within his eyes I could see his soul. His soul was dying to get next to Sasha Timms. His desire to have me was obvi-ous in the way he watched my mouth move when I talked. It was obvious in the way he shunned his regulars so that he could continue our conversation. It was obvious he wanted me because as eloquent as he was in the pulpit, in person he was stammering and stuttering, at times, over his words. Just searching for the proper thing to say. Trying to keep an air of professionalism, yet throwing in just the smallest hint of his intentions by mentioning how beautiful God has made me. Wasn't I the lucky one to hear this first-hand from the man of God. Reverend Morgan was going to be easy. The hard part was finding the right time and the right place.

One-on-one conversation with Reverend Morgan was what I had looked forward to all that week. Saturday morning, time to set the hook.

"Excuse me, Reverend Morgan. Ms. Timms is here to see you." Eunice, his very old and unattractive secretary, showed me in. Mrs. Morgan must have hand-picked Eunice herself because she didn't trust her husband.

"Morning, Reverend Morgan!"

"Ms. Timms...Eunice, shut the door on your way out, please. Bless you. Ms. Timms! I am glad you made it here today. In today's world, with all of its sin, it is important that Christians realize that being 'on the market' is not the way to go about finding a proper mate. If you find your mate in a den of sin it is very difficult to keep that relationship erect in a Christian type of lifestyle."

"Reverend Morgan, may I sit, please?"

"Surely, I am so sorry. Sometimes I am so anxious to help that I just start rambling on and on before a person has a chance to catch their breath."

"That's quite all right. Reverend Morgan, I do have one question. Since I am not a member of your church, is it okay for me to take your valuable time away from your members who rightfully deserve it?"

"Ms. Timms, God has put me here to help save souls, to turn lives around. It is not my place to say, 'God she's not a member,' and then refuse you help. Anyone who seeks shall receive. I just pray that you will consider making New Christian your church home."

"I really appreciate knowing that, Reverend Morgan. I never want to infringe upon someone else's quality time with their minister." I had to smile at myself because I could see that I was touching his emotions. I knew that quality time with the minister meant bumping bellies in the nude. I enjoyed watching him squirm in his seat. He couldn't sit still. He was about as restless as a teenager on his first date. I almost wanted to look under his desk and see if he had a hard on! He was a man, he couldn't help himself. I kept my composure. I had to. Malinda had been wronged and I had to ensure that justice was served on Reverend Morgan. I couldn't let on that his counsel was not the true reasons for my being in Reverend Morgan's church. I didn't want him to have any doubts about my sincerity for companionship. I wanted him to know that I was anxious for a mate, that I was vulnerable. Almost easy, for the right man that is. Knowing Reverend Morgan, he was going to point me in the right direction.

"Ms. Timms, I have to ask you a few questions, a couple slightly personal, just so I know exactly what you seek and how I can go about showing you how to get what you seek. First, have you ever been married?"

"Yes, once. But my husband was murdered. I really

don't like talking about it though. It brings back so many horrible, horrible memories."

"Murdered? Well I'm very sorry to hear that. It's good to see that you have been able to get on with your life."

"Thank you. It's been hard, but I'm managing."

"Why did you come to the church? To find a husband? Why are you asking me for help? If I might say, a woman as beautiful as you certainly doesn't have to go far to find a husband. Choosing the 'Right' husband might be an issue, but I am sure any man in his right mind wouldn't mind marrying you!"

"I came to the church because I need a man! Not a male, but a real man, a Christian man. Someone who knows how to take care of a woman. Secure. Upright. God-fearing. Someone, if you don't mind my saying, like yourself Reverend Morgan."

"What do you mean?"

"When I first heard you preach I was awestruck. The way your members listened, willingly attentive. I am sure you have been to other churches where the members start getting restless because it's almost one o'clock and the football game is about to start and the preacher is still preaching. It's like they're there but they're not really there. Know what I mean?"

"Yes."

"When you speak, everyone listens. Your oral presentation is always an Oscar-winning performance. Always energetic. You have the respect of the men and women in your church. Where you lead, they follow. No woman could look at you and not know that you are a man, in the purest sense of the word!" I know he agreed with me, only he didn't know that my interpretation and his interpretation of man were different. Mine meant DOG! And yes, all of this buttering up, this ego boosting was getting the dog to drool. I could only imagine the number of women he had seduced since he started leading the church. He was trying to feel me out, but he was losing his grip. Beauty was my biggest advantage. He was a worthless, womanizing, full-of-lust bastard, who couldn't wait to add me to his hit list. However, Sasha was going to give him a shock.

"Reverend Morgan, it is clear to my eyes that you are a leader and a builder of Christian men. I need a man in my life and I think that I am in the right place to at least start looking."

"Ms. Timms, I noticed that you recently started visiting our church. Where did you come from? Where do you live? I mean what brought you to my church?"

"I live in Wynnewood right outside the city, but I work downtown. I first heard you one Sunday morning on the radio. I mentioned to a friend of mine how much I enjoyed your service. She strongly suggested that I come and hear for myself. She also feels like the best place to find a good man is in the church. 'If he's as good as you say, **GO**! You ain't gittin' no younger girl! You need to find you a good Christian husband!' This is all I hear from her. So here I am, Reverend Morgan. Can you help me?"

"Ms. Timms, it will be my pleasure to help you find that which you seek. Why don't you come back next Saturday at two-thirty and I will do what I like to call a complete personality profile? That way I can get to know exactly who you are. Then I can direct Ms. Sasha Timms in the proper direction. Okay with you?"

"That will be fine, Reverend Morgan. May I have your phone number here at the church in case I have to reschedule?"

"Sure. Take my card. Don't hesitate to call me here or at home. My office hours are printed on the card. I will always be accessible for any request that you may have."

Reverend Morgan walked me to the door and gave me one of his fatherly Christian hugs. I knew that he could no longer control his desire to touch me. I hugged him right back. Made sure my breasts rested on his chest long enough to be the subject of his next dream. A touch would be his reference for just how good he knew I would feel in his arms. He had to let me know that he was a strong man through his hug. I was reading him like Dick and Jane. Simple. Time was winding up for Reverend Morgan!

Later that week I checked into the Adam's Mark Hotel on City Line Avenue. Jane Smith. When you're paying in cash the hotel doesn't usually ask for ID or anything. I know I didn't look like a Jane Smith. Maybe my disguise helped. Phillies cap. Hair tucked inside. Randall jersey, blue jeans and Cons. Yeah, I looked like an everyday girl who just wanted to crash for the night. A quiet peaceful night away from the kids. I had to go in low key. Nobody would pay any attention to me going in. Nobody would pay attention to me going out.

On Wednesdays his office hours were four to six. I guess you could say I was confident that he would come. Otherwise, why pay for the room in advance. Like I said, all men are dogs. Austin Morgan is a man, therefore...

"Hello! Reverend Morgan, this is Sasha Timms."

"Hello, Ms. Timms. How are you?"

"Not at all good. I need to talk to you. I need your help."

"What's wrong? Why don't you come down to the church? I'll be here for another hour or so. We can talk."

"Reverend Morgan, I need you to come to me. My spirit is deflated. My heart aches for... Can you come, please? I need your help."

"Where are you?"

"I am at the Adam's Mark Hotel on City Line Avenue. Do you know how to get here?"

"Yes... Are you sure you can't come to the church? I wouldn't want anyone to get the wrong idea about my being there."

"Why would anyone think that?"

"Being a man of the cloth, people are always watching. You know the devil uses any avenue he can find to try and bring down one of God's disciples. Speculation. Hearsay. Endless and sometimes harmful gossip are situations I have to deal with daily. Putting myself in a compromising position would just be irresponsible. That's why generally I prefer to counsel one on one at the church. How could I explain my being in a hotel room with a beautiful woman and convince people that we were just having a conversation? That you needed my help during a crisis. I would definitely have a hard time explaining it to my wife."

I bet the whole time he was feeding me his line of holy bullshit he was getting excited. His johnson was probably smacking him in the face for taking so long on the phone instead of making a beeline to the hotel.

"Reverend Morgan, I am in room 1210. Just come right up and nobody will know that you are coming to see me. I will be patiently waiting for you."

I hung up without waiting for a reply. From Mt. Airy at the end of rush-hour traffic, it would take about twenty-five minutes to get to the hotel. I could wait all night for Reverend Morgan to get here. I bet he couldn't wait five more minutes for me.

Whenever a man thinks with the wrong head he is a sucker for a setup. He couldn't see a trap if it was printed across the sky. Lust cancels out fidelity. Beauty, like mine, makes a man forget that he even has a wife. Reverend Morgan would have run around the world barefoot if he knew it meant he could be with me. He was going to get his wish, in a weird round about sort of way. Yes, he was going to be with me, but not sexually like he thought. He was going to leave this world and I was going to be with him when it happened.

I left the door slightly open. He knocked. I heard his little willie saying, 'Get yo' ass in there fool, babydoll left the door open so she knows we coming in!' I left my silk teddy on the bed with a note:

Austin, the bath is ready. Jump in and get

ready for me. I can promise you, I will not disappoint you. I am better than the dream that you had last night.

Sasha
P.S.. I couldn't wait any longer to be with you!!!

Now a rational, thinking man might say, 'This is too good to be true. Why would a woman, make that extremely beautiful woman, a woman I barely know, want to have sex with me? After all we just met.' But rational was not a word that described Reverend Morgan. If he were a suspicious man he might have noticed me watching from my position in the closet. I wanted to witness his every move. I wanted to see infidelity grab him by the testicles and thrust him into a pool of eternal damnation. Although he had yet to see me, Reverend Morgan wasted no time disrobing. He had on a Fila sweatsuit and a Kangol cool cap. I guess he didn't want to be noticed either. I wish I could have told him ahead of time that they might know him going in, but coming out it's hard to recognize a dead man when he's zipped up in the black bag.

I left a trail of roses to the huge sunken bathtub. I placed a red heart shaped pillow at the head. It was floating perfectly in a sea of bubbles. At the foot of the tub was a boombox that I picked up from a flea market in New Jersey. I had a slow jams tape that I had made playing. I wanted the entire scene to be just right. My scent was in the air and he knew it. That's why Reverend Austin Morgan, butt naked, did not hesitate to jump in the tub. He never called for me. He just laid back and waited. Confident, I suppose. I guess he knew he had me bagged and there was no reason to rush. Eyes closed, singing along with Luther.

"Austin?"

I let his name roll off my tongue seductive like. I had on a low cut silk robe. When he saw me I wanted him to be on top of the world. I wanted him to believe he was about to strike gold.

"Sasha! You don't mind if I call you by your first name do you?"

I was thinking, he does have a wonderful smile. Too bad this would be his last time showing it.

"Not at all. You don't know how glad I am that you could come to me."

"The pleasure is all mine. I hope you don't plan on standing there. I can't wait much longer to feel your beautiful body next to mine. And how did you know I dreamed about you? From the moment I first laid eyes on you, I couldn't stop thinking about you, Sasha. I was shocked that you called."

I really despised holding a conversation with a snake, but I had to respond.

"Austin, I know you dreamed about me because you are a man. How could a man like you not think about a woman like me? You say you were shocked that I called? It's funny you should mention the word shocked. I told Malinda Chaney that one day you would get the shock of a lifetime."

Even though the big head knew what was coming, the little head kept him in the tub waiting to get laid.

Before he could react, I dropped the boombox into the warm water. Austin did the boog-a-loo until his soul left his body and made its way to hell! I got dressed, picked up my note, dusted and left. Funny he would mention the word **Shocked**!!!

5

Sasha

"Did you want to say something, Evelyn? You've been so quiet."

"No. it sounds like you really need to, ah, talk. I wouldn't want to interrupt your flow. I'm sure it only gets better. I might hate myself for saying this, but, please continue."

When the animal was sedate, I was able to go back to my everyday as if nothing ever happened. Murder was becoming easy for me. I didn't know if that was good or bad. That's just how it was. One lady wanted to talk about her insecurity around others because she weighed too much. One hundred and ten pounds! Husband says she's fat. Please! Carmen, another client, thinks her boyfriend is using her for sex. 'How do you know?' I asked. 'Because he only comes over at one in the morning, and all we do is have sex.' 'Don't answer the door, honey. Don't worry this session is on me, good-bye!' I only wanted the meaty cases.

I had decided to go home for some rest. Peace. Me alone with my thoughts. So I thought. As usual, soon as I got out of the shower, dried off and put my feet up to watch Oprah, the phone rang. I let the answering machine pick up. 'Hellooooo, sorry Sasha can't answer, leave your vitals at the beep... I recognized the voice right away and almost spilled my drink trying to get to the phone. It was Jeanette. My heart stopped for a second. If something had happened to Demetrius I would just die.

"Sasha?"

I didn't like the sound of her voice, but I refused to draw conclusions. I would remain optimistic.

"Jeanette, good to hear from you. What's up? How is my little darling?"

"Honey, I just wanted to hear your voice, that's all. I always feel better when I talk to you."

"Are you feeling bad?"

"No. I just miss talking to you on a regular basis. You know lately you haven't been calling to check on Demmy like you usually do."

"I know. It's just been hell up here. Seems like every other day I am rippin' and rollin'. Know what I mean?" What I really meant was every other day someone had earned the right to die. Jeanette sounded funny. I knew something was wrong. She was just warming me up for the kill. I just hoped the news she was going to drop wasn't too heavy.

"Sasha, Demmy is doing fine. I know you're sitting there saying, Jeanette done called me in the middle of the day, something must be wrong with my baby. Trust me, girl, he is fine. Growing like a weed and looking more and more like his father every day."

"Please don't remind me. Thinking about how good that handsome, dead, husband of mine looked makes me miss my son ten times as much. What I really want to know is how is my favorite Soror?"

"Good as gold!"

"Really?"

"Yes, really. Sasha, I am fine. I want to know how Ms. Busy-Self-Employed-Black-Woman-of-America is doing since she has no time to call her son." Jeanette's voice was doing more crackling than the cereal. She was on the verge of crying She is a good crier. I just wished she would talk instead of forcing me to draw the news, or whatever it was she had to tell me out of her.

"Jeanette Jones!"

"Yes dear."

"How long have we been friends?"

"Shit, I tell you that and I will start remembering that I am over thirty. Last guy who tried to pick me up believed me when I told him I was still 28."

"How long?"

"Long time!"

"Very long time."

"True."

"Girlfriend, you have about thirty seconds to tell me what's up and then I am on 95 South to come and choke it out of you. Jeanette I know you about as well as I know the nipples on my own tits! Now what the hell is the matter?"

"Sasha?"

"Talk!"

"I am embarrassed to say."

"You're pregnant!"

"No."

"What?"

"What? Kill the suspense already. I get any closer to the edge of my seat and my ass hits the floor."

"Familiar with the term date rape!"

"What the hell happened... don't... look, don't start crying... Jesus, stop sobbing and calm down.... Just tell... Matter of fact, don't even talk. I'll see you in two and a half hours. Don't leave the house. Get some sleep or do whatever you do to take your mind off things. Wash the dishes! Just don't leave the house. Sasha will be there shortly!"

"I love you Sasha."

"Me too!"

I called my answering machine at work and changed the message. There was no doubt that I would need a few days off to spend with Jeanette. *'Hello, this is Dr. Timms, I will not be in the office until Monday. Please leave your name and a brief message. If it is an emergency please dial eight, seven, nine, seven, two, zero, zero, Dr. Lisa Marie, will be able to help you.'* I grabbed an outfit for the trip. I'll take Jeanette shopping. I can also shop for a couple of outfits while I'm in Maryland. I set the cruise control at 71. It seemed like I had just left home five minutes ago when I was turning into Jeanette's driveway.

She has a beautiful home in Columbia. For a single, hard-working, self-employed sister, she is doing quite well. I am proud of her. Matter of fact, I am extremely proud of her. Jeanette has built her business on years of hard work. She didn't have the advantage of a dead husband's insurance money to assist her in attaining financial stability. But she is there and I am delighted that my sister has made it in this cruel and harsh world.

I laid on the horn until Jeanette came out. Shit, I didn't care if this was a quiet community. She needed me and I wanted her to feel good about seeing me. A loud horn, friendly face, and your best friend is usually a good pickup. She seemed the same. Pleasant, kind face, the demeanor of an angel. Her hug warmed my heart. Holding J helped to lift my spirits, but I knew she would drop the bomb on me any second. I just hoped I could handle it. If I had to make amends for her situation, I could never let on to Jeanette that I had anything to do with it. When she put her head on my chest and started sobbing, I knew it was deep. I never envisioned being 125 miles from home, standing on the front porch of my girlfriend's house, holding her in my arms and trying to reassure her that everything would be all right. I could only imagine what the neighbors were thinking.

I stroked Jeanette's beautiful, black hair. "Jeanette, let it all out. Baby, you cry 'till you don't have one tear left in those beautiful eyes. You hear me?"

"Sasha, it is so good to see you. You're the best friend I ever had. Ever. I am so glad you're here. Let's go inside. Demetrius is upstairs taking a nap. Wake him up. He will be thrilled to death that you're here."

"Are you settled enough to make me some herbal tea, little lady?"

"For you, anything. I'm really glad to see you, Sasha.

We have a whole lot to talk about."

As I tripped up the stairs I tried not to let my imagination run. Sometimes it is just so hard for me to be optimistic. I can't help but to think the worse about every bad situation that I get involved in, ever since that X'd husband of mine disappointed me. As hard as I try to not think about killing- the drizzle of trouble- it always seems to turn into a thunderstorm! Ah, surprise, surprise, surprise. Light, shining brightly in my face in the form of my son. I tried to hug Demetrius tightly, but he pushed me away. I couldn't hold back the tears. I bet he wondered why his mother was always crying.

"How is my handsome young man doing today?"

"Hi, Mamma."

"Guess what Demetrius? Mamma is going to spend the entire week with you and Aunt Jeanette. Isn't that great?"

"Yes."

"How about a song?"

"Okay."

Autistic. Developmentally Delayed. Learning Disabled. Special. All words that put a handicap on the handicap. Trapped in his own world. As far as I am concerned, my son understands me.

"You are my sunshine... my only sunshine...

"Love you."

"I love you, baby. Mamma is going downstairs to talk to Aunt Jeanette. You go back to sleep. See you when you get up, okay!?"

"Okay."

Seeing my son caused memories to erupt that I wish would stay dormant forever. I see Coleman. I see Coleman in his smile, Coleman in his eyes, Coleman in his build. I see my son, in his own world, taking in the entire scene.

I took my time going down the stairs that led to the living room that led to the dining room that led to the kitchen that led to the whole story that Jeanette was going to tell me.

"Ms. Jones, have you, gotten yourself together yet?"

"Ain't nothin' wrong with me to be gettin' myself together for, Ms. Thang!"

"Well, since nothing is wrong with you, I think I will say good-bye and carry my tail back to Philly. Is that okay with you?"

"Bye!"

We laughed, but I could see she was about to break down.

"Dammit, Jeanette! What the hell is going on? You better talk to me right now or I am going to start throwing shit until I get a response."

"Jesus Christ, Sasha, calm down. Sit your hips down. Humph! As big as they are they could use a chair, your legs have got to be tired. Girl, it's just so hard for me to talk about it."

"It!"

"Yeah, it!"

"It what!"

"Nothing."

"You know all that good china you bought while we

were in school, well I am about to start the first Columbia China Frisbee throwing contest. Talk!"

"You take two lumps or three? Cream?"

"You're going to get three lumps in a minute!"

"Sasha?"

"Yes."

"Are you listening?"

"Of course."

"I am so embarrassed by this whole situation. It's difficult to talk about."

"Jeanette, if we were any tighter we would be Siamese Twins. For all that we have shared together, there is nothing you can tell me that we couldn't handle together. Now tell me I am lying."

"You speaks the truth, as always. Okay. All right. Now pay close attention because I am only going to tell this story once in my lifetime.

"I started taking an aerobics class about two months ago at the recreation center. It was a coed class. Fine with me and some fine men too. I like to show off my body when I work out anyway. Now I know you remember how we said we would never date white men, well anyway, there was this very handsome Caucasian gentleman. At least he started out as a gentleman until the bastard..."

"I like how you put that, 'Caucasian gentleman,' 'like that is going to change the fact that you dated a white man. And don't tell me he is the one that turned you into this basket case. Is he the one who raped you? You would think after 400 years of forcing themselves on us, the sisters could get a break, or even the common courtesy of asking for our lovin' which they can't get enough of, instead of taking it like they always have."

"Damn, I get your point. Think you can let me finish? Thank you!"

"The floor is yours." I couldn't believe my ears. Jeanette had actually consented to dating a white man. We always talked about how we would never allow ourselves to be violated by a white man. But who was I to judge? I had spent almost two years of my life, killing. Not exactly the type of lifestyle that could degrade interracial relationships. Jeanette was attractive. Why a white guy? She didn't seem to be totally devastated, but I knew she was hurting, bad.

"So, our class was full, about twenty students. This one particular guy, Dave, thee um, Caucasian gentleman, at first I thought he was fine. I mean for a white guy he had it goin' on. Anyway, Dave was always jumping right behind me in class. Grinning non-stop. Now I said to myself, with all of his kind of women in the class checking him out why was he paying so much attention to me? Outgoing sister that I am, I had no problem conversing with Dave before or after class. Our conversation was always pleasant:

"Jeanette, I see you made it to class. Now I will have a smile on my face for the rest of the day. You guaranteed that when you brought your sweet swinging hips in here today."

"Dave, I asked you more than once to not get fresh with me. At least not before class!"

"I couldn't keep myself from blushing. There I was

acting like a sixteen-year-old who ain't never been on a date or talked to a man before."

"Ms. J, I ain't being fresh. You are beautiful and that's a fact. I can't help but to call them as I see them and I see there is plenty of you to go around."

"Dave, you ought to stop! Shut your fresh mouth, class is about to start. And don't spend the whole class looking at my ass."

"What can I say girl, I was getting hooked. Lately for whatever reason, the brothers hadn't been paying me any mind. Now, I know that we always talked about this being a bullshit excuse, but living out here I really believe that when a brother sees me pull up in my Convertible Saab, my sharp outfits, looking like a sophisticated, educated, employed bag of money, they get intimidated. Especially if they know that they make less and cannot offer me anything more than I can buy for myself."

"J, everything you say can be considered true or bull-shit, but that still ain't no excuse for selling out. Why didn't you just go to Harlem and find you an employed doctor to marry?"

"Whenever you decide to stop cracking jokes, I will continue with my story."

"Okay. I'll try, but, were you desperate or what?"

"You're getting your ass kicked when I'm done. Now stop joking because you're cheering me up and I won't want to tell you anything that is going to spoil a good mood. I have so few of them these days.

"By the forth or fifth week of class, Dave had already asked me out about a dozen times. I mean he was sweatin' me hard:"

"Jeanette, I know you have told me a hundred times that you won't have dinner with me because you don't date white guys, but I was wondering, if you weren't busy tonight or tomorrow or just before I shrivel up, grow old and die, would you consider having dinner with me?"

"Wednesday my godson has his enrichment group meeting from 6:30 to 9:30. Pick me up at my house at 7:00. Don't be late. Bye!"

"Wait, I need your address!"

"If you want to go out with me as bad as you say you do, you'll find me!"

"I left him standing there with that same stupid grin he gives me in class. I was feeling all giddy inside. It was just nice to have a date for the first time in months. I have sorta been in a drought. Black, white, Native American. It didn't matter. A man had asked me out and I was going. Shit, lonely as I've been JJ Walker could have asked me out and I probably would have gone."

"Girl, now we know that there ain't that much lonely in the world!"

"You know that's right! Anyway:"

"Dave, now just how did your little investigative mind figure out where I lived?"

"You know that blond that works at the front desk? I told her that she had the prettiest blue eyes that I have ever seen and the loveliest, blondest, blonde hair of any woman in Columbia. Then I slipped in that you were a co-worker and I had to get some important infor-

mation to you for a business meeting the next morning. I also mentioned how pretty her smile was and that your line was busy and if I had your address then I could take the info to you personally. Oh, and maybe one day I might have to deliver something to her in person. What can I say, sometimes these looks get me whatever I want."

"I bet they do. Let me grab my purse."

"Sasha, this man was a charmer as well as a looker! I never would have suspected that he was really a monster.

"We went to Baltimore to the Inner Harbor to eat, walked around for a bit and then he rushed me home so I could get my car to go and pick up Demmy. I thanked him for a lovely evening and told him I would see him in class the next day. Next thing I know he puts on the puppy dog eyes and begs me to let him come in for a few minutes. I relented:"

"Allright, David, but not for long, I have to pick up Demetrius at 9:30 and I can't be late."

"Great, I will respect your wishes."

"The perfect gentleman? I could have never been so wrong."

"Jeanette, have I ever told you just how beautiful you are?"

"Yes you have as a matter of fact. Let me think, yes, at least twice a week, Tuesday and Thursday to be more specific, for the last five weeks. Why do you ask?"

"Cause I wanted you to know that I think you are a beautiful woman."

"Thank you David. You're a decent looking man

yourself. Tell me something: why did you want to go out with me?"

"Because none of them make me feel the way you make me feel. Jeanette, you walk by with that high-class swagger. You carry yourself as if you know first-hand that your great, great, great whatever, grandmother was an African Queen."

"Well Dave, she was!"

"I get a rush, and I am not going to say to where, when I see you move. Every curve of your body moving in fluid motion to the music just makes me want to hold you close."

"Next thing I know, he pulls me to him. Close. Real Close. His breath was like a cool summer breeze against my face. His touch was gentle. I felt comfortable in his arms. Only problem was I hadn't planned on moving this fast. This was my first date with a white man. Matter of fact, it was my first date with any man in a long time. I had promised myself that I would take it slow ever since that last disaster, Lacy. Hard as I tried, I just couldn't fight the feelings I was having. Instead of pushing him away I placed my hands on his chest. I had been aching to feel that rock hard chest almost since the first time he spoke to me. Sasha, his kiss was the sweetest these lips have ever tasted. Next thing you know I am floating away. I was in this man's arms and loving it. We hugged and touched and kissed for what seemed like an eternity. Even though the stoplight was blazing red, I continued to allow my passion to come out and enjoy the time. His hands were soft and gentle. Just making pit stops everywhere.

"You know how some guys are, get their hands on a titty and act like they trying to squeeze all of the juice out of an orange. Squeezing like they milking a damn cow or something. Naw, I ain't ragging on the brothers, but that's all I been with lately. Shit let them feel a nipple and they yankin' and pullin' like they are trying to pull it clean off. You know I am right. Shit, don't act like you didn't date before you married Coleman. Not Dave though. He was a gentle and smooth tit caresser. "How he got my shirt and bra off so fast is another issue. I was out of my head, I suppose. Now the average horny devil will treat a nice ass like a big balloon that they're trying to pop in their hands. Squeeze, squeeze, squish, squish. Not David. The smooth bastard! His touch was so light and soothing that I could feel the hairs on my butt standing at attention. Before you know it we're a few small garments shy of standing in my living room butt-naked. By now the stop-light is a three alarm signal. My mind is cursing me out. 'Jeanette, what the hell do you think you are doing? You have got to stop and use your brain. You don't know this man. There is no reason to rush into a physical relationship. There is plenty of time for sex. Have a few more dates, get to know Mr. Smoothie a little better before you give it up. Dammit girl calm the fuck down! **PUT YOUR CLOTHES BACK ON!** Jeanette! Jeanette! Do you hear me...' Bang, I snap out of it! I know a man in heat has to be cooled off real carefully. Otherwise it's like throwing water on a grease fire. **NO GOOD!** I glanced at the clock on the mantle":

"David. David! Honey, we have to stop this. I have

to pick up my godson in ten minutes. I lost track of the time. Sorry. Don't worry, we'll get together again next week. Maybe even start the date where we left off. Okay?"

"I figure I let him taste my lips one more time. I gave him the best kiss I had, stroked his chest hairs as sensually as I could. Then asked him to get dressed. Well, I guess I threw water in the frying pan because he gave me a glare so icy it could have frozen Brazil":

"Now you just let me ask you one question. Do you really expect me to just put my clothes back on and leave here without letting the air out of my balloon? Huh? Is that what you expect?"

"David ,I don't mean to disappoint you but I have to go. Besides, I really didn't mean to move this fast. Let's take a couple of steps backward and get to know each other a little better. How 'bout it? Is that cool?"

"Not cool at all!"

"David was furious and I was in trouble. I was damn near naked. All I had on was my panties and my socks. The socks sure weren't going to slow ole' David down. He pulled my panties down around my ankles before I could blink an eye. Then he did one of them karate moves you always trying to teach me. He kinda put his arm across me and stuck his leg behind mine and flipped me down toward the floor on my back. I hit my head on the floor and was slightly dazed. I was also very scared and furious at this time":

"You son-of-a-bitch, what the hell is the matter with you!?"

"I tried to hide my fear behind toughness, but he had his hand around my throat. I begged him not to do it:"

"Jeanette ,you are the sexiest woman I have ever seen and I am going to have you whether you like it or not. Now open your fucking legs bitch before I kill your ass!"

"Sasha, I struggled. I kneed him in the stomach. I scratched and clawed until everything went black. For all of my fighting I could not free his hand from my throat. He damn near choked the life out of me. I didn't lose complete consciousness, but I wish I had. Next thing I know David is pounding away inside of me. I couldn't hold back the tears. I never envisioned anything like this ever happening to me. He only relaxed his grip around my throat enough for me to breathe. I didn't have any strength left to fight. I wished I had a gun. It seemed like an hour passed before he finished. I have never felt so dirty, and cheap, and used, and so...dirty. I hate myself for not being strong enough to keep this from happening to me. David finally rolled off of me, got dressed and uttered, **"Don't even think about telling the police. Who in Columbia would believe a black woman over a successful white businessman, such as myself?"**

"Then he strolled out the door! Can you believe that shit? The audacity of that man. Shit, I had never even considered going out with a white man before in my entire life. My subconscious got me over to the center to pick up Demmy. When we got back I thanked God for giving me the strength to pick him up. It would have been a disaster if I wasn't there when his class was over.

Lord knows Demmy doesn't need any more emotional trauma in his life.

"I feel like this whole situation is my fault. I never should have let a man I barely know into my house. I should have never insisted that he find out where I live. You know what really busts me up? Society says when a woman is raped by somebody she knows that it's date rape. Helluva date, huh? The police wouldn't offer any help. Sasha, what can be done? What can I do?"

"Jeanette, first thing you have to do is stop blaming yourself. No is no! There are no exceptions. That's the end of that guilt trip, do you understand me? Unless you give permission there is not a man in this world who is entitled to take what you ain't giving! Second, that bastard is going to get what is coming to him. I can't say how or when, but you know how the preacher in Sunday school used to say, 'What goes around... Huh! Children, you reap what you sow!' David sowed a bad seed. He will get his due. Trust Me!"

My heart ached for Jeanette. It felt like the animal was in my toes and slowly working its way up through my body. The rage. I knew the kind of hurt that my best friend was feeling was going to cause me to respond if I never responded to anything again in my life. Something inside of me said I had no choice but to respond.

After what seemed like hours of crying in each others' arms, Jeanette finally got herself calm enough to talk.

"Sasha, I'm glad you're here."

"Where else would I be? Where else?"

I had to control myself. No big displays of rage or anger. I didn't want Jeanette to think that I was going to, in any way, try to fix this for her. I wanted her to think my anger was just hot air that most people give off when something bad happens. Everybody who talks the 'bad-ass Niggah talk' isn't always ready to back it up. When it comes time to do some real swinging, most of us just run and hide. Me, I am about the business of action!

I had a week. What me, angry? Mad? Probably could have fried an egg on top of my head. Enough time to take care of business. Enough time to right a wrong- My way, because when Dave raped Jeanette he might as well have raped me. Time was winding up for Dave and he didn't even know it.

If Jeanette knew my thoughts she would have sent my ass back to Philadelphia in a jet. I made every effort not to let my emotions take control. My insides were going haywire trying to figure out a way to rectify this matter in the proper fashion. You know, the Sasha Way! All I could do was comfort her as best I could. Rage is a difficult emotion to control. The rage I had for David was almost as bad as when I X'd my husband. But just as calmly as I walked that hallway and got the gun, I was going to exhibit the same manner of coolness when it came time to kill David. Time. Time. Time. All I needed was a little bit of time. But I had to come fort my sister first. Calm her down. Reassure her that she would be all right. Sometimes a hug is the best therapy one can give. Just holding someone you love and squeezing them tight. You don't even have to talk about the way you feel; how much you care. Their burdens, their hurt, their pain can flow out of their body and into your loving arms. A hug can help ease the pain, make it better. Hugging is excellent therapy for the aching soul. I hugged Jeanette with all the love I had inside of me. We have true sisterly love for each other. I was going to get her through this.

"Tell you what J, you take yourself upstairs and get a nice warm bath. I am going to fix you a dinner fit for the most beautiful black woman that Columbia, Maryland has ever had. Deal?"

"Deal. Sasha?"

"Yes."

"I..."

"I know. Now take your ass upstairs before we flood the kitchen again. You know how I hate mopping!"

"You are the only true friend that I have ever had in my life. You know that, don't you?"

"Likewise! Now get up those steps."

I went to the village center and rented **Fried Green Tomatoes**. I figured a quiet evening and some laughs would cheer up any woman. Demetrius, Sasha, and Jeanette, cooling out, checking out a flick.

Tuesday morning. Beautiful May day. Columbia, Maryland. The things we take for granted—green grass, blue skies, birds chirping. Because we see them every day we forget to stop and enjoy, pausing long enough to let the beauty seep into our being. For the first time in a very long time I got my son ready for school. Made sure he brushed his teeth. Checked behind his ears. Clean underwear? Favorite breakfast, pancakes and sausage. Orange juice, freshly squeezed. It has been so long since I have done the little things that mean a lot to someone else. I have been so wrapped up in Sasha that I have forgotten how important it is to have your own mother help you tie your shoes in the morning. To brush your hair and lotion your face, the soothing, comforting hands of your mother. I didn't have a mother most of my life, but Demmy has a mother. I would not initiate a plan for eliminating David. Demetrius would play hookey from school for the first time in his life. I knew that I couldn't bring my son back into my daily life until I got myself under control. I had to be able to give him the time he needed and deserved. Even though I don't have to work, helping others with their problems is really my outlet. I am a beautiful, wealthy, intelligent, educated black woman who was hurting on the inside and I needed my son in my life. I knew it was impossible right then, though.

I was thinking this must be how alcoholics and drug addicts feel knowing they have let their loved ones down. But they get the rehab they need so that they can re-enter their families lives as a whole person, independent of detrimental persuasions. Killing was my rehabilitation. I had to admit, I enjoyed my rehab. However, I hoped, to be cured one day. My son and I went sightseeing. Washington, D.C. took my mind to a happier place.

6

Rock

"Send that brother of yours in here. Maybe he can fill in some of the blanks for me."

"Okay. Cecil! Wake up! Dr. Doolittle wants to talk to you."

"Huh? Oh. Right. Dr. Davis. Whatcha wanna know?"

"Honestly? Never mind. While Sasha was planning on disposing of David in Maryland, what were you doing?"

Shit, two things were starting to bug me right from the jump. First, I hated my first name and the Captain only called me that when he had some heavy shit on his mind. The way he screamed you would think my desk was on the other side of the office, not right outside his door. Second, it was only 8 o'clock in the morning. Anytime Captain Arnetti summoned his best cop, that early, sleep was going to be at a minimum for a while. Overtime galore. But, I loved to sleep more than I liked working overtime. Now that I think about it, I loved sleeping more than I liked working, period.

"CECIL! CECIL! DAMMIT! SERGEANT CECIL ROCK, GET YOUR ASS IN HERE RIGHT NOW!"

"Yes, sir!'

"Cecil, you been keeping up with the front pages?"

"No, sir. I go straight to the sports and then on to the comics. I only read the important sections of the paper. Why do you ask?"

"Well, mister funny pages, whether you are aware of it or not, there have been a couple of very unusual murders in the city recently. Neither one of them took place in our jurisdiction, but for some reason the Mayor has decided that we need a special task force in the city to solve these crimes. You do remember our distinguished Mayor, don't you?"

"Uhm, Rozen something or other? O'Grady? That's his name?"

"You know, Rock, the day you stop being a smart ass will probably coincide with the day you become an excellent police officer."

"I will take your advice under advisement, Captain, but for now I will just settle for being a very, very, good police officer. Sir."

One thing I had to admit, I respected Captain Arnetti. He was an outstanding officer when he was in the field. And he never traded in his self respect or dignity just to receive another stripe on his shirt. Blue collar cop. Took me on like his pupil. Showed me the ropes. Everything I know and do is because of him. Even though we come from different sides of town; shit I wouldn't get caught dead in his part of South Philly at night, we seemed to get along okay. Mutual respect.

"You were saying about his Honor!"

"Yes, the city government and police department

citywide are getting a great deal of pressure to bring some killers to justice. Only problem..."

"Manpower, budget, no excessive overtime, etc., etc., etc., same bullshit we hear every time the locals go crazy over some crime."

"Correct. I have to pat myself on the back for grooming such a fine young officer of the law. As I was saying, the Mayor and I are in the process of formulating a special task force to solve unusual homicides within the city. It will collaborate with other precincts to solve these crimes-"

"When you say unusual, what exactly do you mean?"

"Don't interrupt me, Sergeant. I am getting to the good part. The Mayor and I have decided that as opposed to having a big, as in five or six man team, logging in hours and hours of overtime, we decided to appoint one very special officer to handle the operation independently."

"Sounds to me like somebody's head is going to be on the chopping block. I mean anybody who has the entire city looking over their shoulder is going to be a target for the head-hunting media if they don't get fast results. So why did you want to talk to me? You want my advice on who to setup? I'll tell you. Anderson would be an excellent choice since he's the department's biggest asshole. What about Jackson? Shit, his dumb ass wouldn't even mind the heat. Being so gung-ho and all. He'd probably enjoy it. Hey, how about-"

"Sergeant. Cecil Rock!"

"Hell no! Why me?"

"You're the best."

"Try again."

"The Mayor recommended you."

"Door number three!"

"Cecil, I ain't gonna' bullshit you. I suggested to the Mayor that we use you."

"Thank you, sir! Any particular reason why you suggested me? I mean just a minute ago we both agreed that I haven't even reached my potential as a police officer. Plus, I haven't even made detective yet."

"Oh, congratulations on your promotion to detective, Detective Rock. The Mayor agreed with my recommendation. He has officially made you a detective. I told you the task force will specialize in solving unusual homicides. We're talking the far out, what-the-hell-happened-here type of murders. So, I gets to thinking, who do I know in this department that has experience dealing with outrageous crimes? I do a little mental research. What does my ingenious brain spit out..."

"Believe me, I don't want to know. By the way, did you get my two-weeks notice I put in, uh, just about two weeks ago? I had an uncle die and leave me a million dollars. I would have retired on the spot but I was wrapping up my case with the junior high kids who were cheating on their tests. Sorry, but you'll have to get someone else for the Mayor and the entire city of Philadelphia to barbecue this summer. You know that Spanish guy they just promoted over in North Philly would be a great choice. He was on all the front pages of the comics last week. Did you happen to read about him?"

"...It spits out the home of Sasha and Coleman Timms. Two dead bodies. Coincidentally, Sasha is the sister of Sgt. Rock. Weird, weird shit. I helped you make sure the fire never got lit behind that mess. I guess the little switcheroo we pulled with the drunk driver was a good enough reason to help you and your sister."

Switcheroo. I was thinking, ain't that a bitch! Boy, that was a time I could never forget. The Captain was referring to that night six years ago. I had just started working without a partner for the first time in my career. I was cruising along Cobbs Creek Parkway when I pulled up to the accident. It was late, about three in the morning. I had been sucking in the night air and cursing the Captain all week for putting me on the graveyard shift my first week solo. Philly can be a nightmare in terms of dealing with crime, but budget cuts meant the end of most two-man teams. I ain't no punk, but I just wasn't mentally prepared to be out there alone all night.

The Captain gave me a line about how nights would make a real cop out of me. Make a man out of me. 'You survive this, Rock, and we'll allow you to stick around for a couple of years.' Hating life. Wish I had gone to grad school like Mom wanted. Kicking myself in the ass for not trying out for the Sixers. I guess it would have helped if I could play.

I crossed Walnut Street and what did I see? A head-on collision. A red Bronco had turned a little Honda Civic into what looked like a block of recycled cans. Jesus was the only one who could have saved anybody in the Civic. From what I could see the two people inside didn't get that visit. I knew the owner of the Bronco as soon as I saw it. Joey Arnetti. Biggest lush the city had ever seen. No coincidence. He was the Captain's little brother. That's the only reason why his drunk ass still had a license. Seemed like every other week Stiles, my old partner, and I were dragging his ass down to the station. Captain would curse him out, then beg him to get some help. Joey, when he came to, would always make promises he would keep for about as long as it took to get to the next bar.

I should have just lit a match and put Joey out of his misery. Seemed like I could smell the alcohol before I got within five feet of his truck. This was his biggest fuck up to date, two dead. Police captain's drunk ass brother responsible. This was not going to be good press for the department, especially after the way the 'Move' situation was handled. That's when three city blocks burned to the ground. A lot of people blamed the Mayor at that time. I called Captain Arnetti and assured him that he should get here immediately.

"Captain, this is Rock. Joey done fucked up but good. Sir, if I were you, I would have been here five minutes ago."

Captain said he'd be there in seven. I believed him. I set up some flares and promised myself that I would shoot anybody that got within a hundred feet of the accident scene. I didn't anticipate any visitors since it was 3 a.m. The captain looked like his mother had been shot when he got there. Desperate. Eyes all glassy. Sweating.

"Cecil? What we got?"

"Your brother, Joey. Well, from what I can see, he just guaranteed some business for the local mortician!"

"Cecil, this is what we're going to do…"

Captain goes into this quick speech about how the negative publicity would hurt the department; plus, the duress his family would have to endure. Then, he orders me to find another drunk to pull from behind the wheel of Joey's Bronco. He also assured me that even if he had to handcuff his brother to the bed, he was going to 'detox' and was going to be cured of his disease. 'I promise,' he said.

"Sir, he's your blood. You don't have to promise me shit. I was just thinking that why not let his ass 'detox' at Rikers!"

"Move your ass, Rock! We need to do this like now. Stiles or Johnson could cruise by here anytime."

I always remembered the last thing Captain Arnetti said to me that night:

"Rock in this line of work, sometimes you gonna run up against a situation that spells nothing but trouble. The only way out is the bond of brotherhood you have developed with your fellow officers. You came through for me. From this day on we are joined at the hip. I owe you. My brother owes you. Have a report for me in the morning. Vehicular Homicide and Grand Theft Auto!'

"Yes, sir!"

I didn't know about all this joined at the hip bullshit, but that piece of shit we set up was about as worthless as Joey. The captain looked a little miffed at first when he saw that I had brought back a 40 year old white guy. Mackey was a low life who left his wife and kids for the bottle years ago. If he spent the rest of his life in jail he would be living better than he was living, but the Captain should have known when he sent me that there was no way I was going to set up a brother for Joey. I say if somebody has to take the fall for Joey's mess then it ought to be one of his own. Once he snapped back to reality and realized that Joey's ass was still going to be off the line, it didn't matter who I brought back to him.

"So, like I was saying Rock. We need some experience out there to help us and you are our man."

"The thrill and honor that I feel right now has left me almost speechless."

"You know, Rock, there are certain perks for the person assigned to the case. The biggest one being autonomy. The Mayor says anything you need, except excessive manpower, you got. You get to travel all over the city. You can..."

"Please sir, spare me the details. I just feel so special. I'm extremely flattered at the thought of you even considering me for the job. I don't deserve such an honor. Captain if you were pressured because of affirmative action to give me this position I will gladly back you publicly as the fairest, unprejudiced man I know. If you decided to pick a white officer for the job it wouldn't bother me a bit. I can step down before I am sacrificed, I mean before I start and you won't ever hear another word about it from me."

"Detective, here are the first two cases you will be

working on."

"Great. If it's okay with you, I am going to go home and start my homework."

"Like I said before, Rock, total autonomy. It's your show. I will talk to you in the morning."

"Thanks, Captain."

"Cecil?"

"Sir!"

"R-E-S-U-L-T-S! Fast!"

"Aye- Aye Cap'um!"

I felt the need to burn some serious calories. I was about ready to have an anxiety attack. Usually when I get hyped up it's off to the local bakery. But since I was trying to lose this gut, I decided to run instead of binging on sweets. East River Drive. One of the prettier locations in the city. Green everywhere. Trees, grass, oh yea, brown water, and beautiful women. That always helps my running. The city wouldn't be the city without the dirtiest river in America. Still a nice refreshing place to be one with my thoughts. After about two miles of arduous running, I found a nice cool spot under a tree. Aaah, a nice breeze. Relaxation. MAN! Dozed off. It was almost 2:30 when I snapped to attention. Well nothing like a good nap before I commence my duties as weird murders solver.

I stopped by Larry's and got a chef's salad for an early dinner. Even though I hadn't been to work for a full day, it just seemed like I had one of the busiest days of my life. I was glad to be home. Sasha left a message for me on the answering machine. *'Hey, big bro, I went to Columbia for a short vaca,' talk to you on Sunday or Monday.'* I hadn't heard from my sister in a couple of days. I always told Sasha I would spend less time worrying about her if she just let me know her whereabouts. So to pacify me, she checks in.

REVEREND AUSTIN MORGAN, death by electrocution in a big ol' lovers tub. **MELVIN HARPER**, hands burned to the bone; death as a result of lacerated throat. I can certainly confirm one thing, the Captain wasn't bullshitting when he said he had some weird cases for me to solve. Where do I begin? No clues, no witnesses, no motives. Not yet anyway! They were probably not related. Every question led to another question. I just have to get me a big-ass shovel and start digging. Tonight I am going to crash. First thing in the morning I go and find some of Melvin's drinking buddies. Shit, I might even run into a few of his enemies. After the way he died, he obviously pissed somebody off, real bad.

Session III

7

Sasha

"Rock, why don't you go and grab us some lunch? On you."

"Sure thing. But, that pretty smile can't possibly get you your way all of the time. Does it?"

"Soup and sandwiches will do just fine. Bye. Sasha..."

Demetrius and I had a great time in the nation's capital. But, funtime and mother-son bonding was over for the moment. The animal was having hunger pangs! The only right thing to do was feed it. Jeanette was too distraught to take aerobics class, at least not at the Athletic Sports Club. I told her that I just had to see if David was still taking class after what he had done. Jeanette gave me a description of him. I wanted to be absolutely sure I had the right guy before I acted. He wouldn't be too hard to find. Drop dead handsome, on the outside anyway, muscular, and on and on... And a tattoo of a peacock on his left shoulder. A dead giveaway.

I have to admit I wasn't totally surprised to see David, grinning, behind another sister in class. She was an attractive woman. Once David got a glimpse of Sasha, everybody in the class was going to look like leftover dinner. Aerobic protocol asks that you don't enter the class once it has started. I needed a grand entrance. Stunningly beautiful, fashionably late, an attention-getter.

When I strutted in, apologizing to the instructor, all eyes were on me. Male and female. Hot pink body suit, black thong, pink anklet socks, white sneakers, pink head and wrist bands. Sharp! Fine! That's me, what can I say!?

"Excuse me, handsome, can I jump in next to you please?"

I threw out the bait to David; I knew he would bite like a hungry dog.

"Please. I would be honored. A woman as beautiful as you deserves the best spot in the room. And that's next to me!"

David spent the entire class checking me out and whispering to me.

"I know I just met you, but would you consider having dinner with me? Or could I at least buy you a drink after class? Uh, what's your name? I'm David."

I stopped to adjust my thong, then put my hand on his chest and said, "Saasshaa."

Now I am not a flirt and I especially don't like to lead men on, well maybe I do a little. I had only one major problem with this particular fish I was trying to reel in. Time. And not a whole lot of it. I needed to dispose of David in a timely fashion and get my ass back to Philly. I played coy...

"I don't know, Davey. You are quite a sight to see, but cream ain't never gone good with brown sugar."

"Well, Ms. Sugar, let me buy you a cup of joe and we can see how some of my cream tastes in your coffee. How 'bout it?"

"I will think about it. In the meantime, you just be ready for a better looking workout on Thursday than the one you saw today."

I gave him a wink and all Pearlies. I turned and left before he could utter a word. I wanted my words to soak into his brain until the next class. By Thursday, David would be fattened enough for the kill. Pity such a charmer had to die.

"Jeanette, can you believe that maggot is still taking class and flirting like nothing ever happened?"

"Honey, I am not surprised. Being an affluent male in Columbia, Maryland seems to come with special privileges. They seem to make and break all the rules as they see fit. Shit. Would you believe that my aerobics class used to be for women only? After about three months, David and a couple of his friends protested a segregated aerobics class. They were bitchin' about how the best time for them to come was on Tuesdays and Thursdays at the same time our class starts. Plus, 'What harm is there in having a coed class? It's not like the world is segregated!' Next thing you know, bam, co-ed class. Now you tell me that ain't a damn shame."

"Why don't you just go to another class at a different club?"

"Yeah, so I am supposed to rearrange my whole workout schedule because of a few spoiled men. Hell no. So, you saw David tonight?"

"Sure I saw him. He sure is handsome, but what do I really see when I look at him? Rapist! His looks still don't eliminate the fact that that bastard raped you, Jeanette.

That is something that you need not forget. Ever!"

"Sasha, you don't ever have to worry about me forgetting. I hope that one day David gets his just due. I can't wait for the *comes-around*! When that day comes I might be able to start forgetting what happened and move on with my life. But until then, I just have to deal with it."

"Good!"

"What the hell do you mean, Good!"

"It's good that the memory stays with you. There won't be a second in your life where you have even the smallest desire to forgive him for what he did to you. That's good my sister. Very good."

The most important part of the friendship that Jeanette and I shared was our ability to be completely open and honest with each other. Since Coleman's death I had not been able to maintain the open communication. But, maybe one day, I will be able to confide in my best friend. Lord knows I need to talk to someone about my activities, but who? Picture me in confession. First, I'm not even Catholic. Then, I try to convince the Father of my shame and guilt for my actions.

'Father, forgive me for I have sinned.'

'Yes, my child, go on.'

'Father, in the past two years I have murdered my husband and his boyfriend; I have murdered another man of the cloth; I have murdered a man who beat his wife; and I plan on killing the guy who raped my best friend.'

'Do you feel guilty for your sins?'

'But of course, father.'

'Well, give me twelve hail Mary's…'

I don't think so! He would probably have a gang of altar boys upside my head quicker than I could say Amen. Thank God for you, Evelyn.

I needed to go to the mall and buy me a heart-stopping, head-turning outfit for the next class. I wanted David to have a very uncomfortable class. I wanted every thought of his to be on me. I wanted him tripping over his feet because he couldn't keep his eyes off of me. I wanted this punk at my mercy. If I said roll over, Fido was going to be on the ground before I snapped my fingers. I was getting excited. Not sexually, but excited about the kill. I was hurt when I killed Coleman, but he deserved to die. I mean Coleman betrayed me in a fashion that I couldn't live with. He hurt me beyond a bearable realm of hurt. He crushed every ounce of trust. He… I could go on for days!

I had matured as a cold-blooded killer. I looked forward to the next kill more than any previously. Probably because that man—this lowlife—violated the best friend I have. Then he showed no remorse by continuing to participate and practice activities that led up to his crime. I was confident that his thoughts were on me. I would make sure that Jeanette would be his last victim.

8

Rock

I hadn't seen Sanya since Sasha brought her to my house. She lived in a section of the city I rarely visited, Southwest Philly. Crime, drugs, crackheads. Everywhere. A person doesn't have to be a product of their environment if they don't want to be, but in Southwest it seemed as though a large majority of the young people simply go with the flow. Teenage hookers on corners. Twelve year old boys selling drugs. Kids even younger working as lookouts. Shit, most of them dressed better than I did. Grown men at their daily job, on the corner drinking booze. And too too many teenage mothers. I welcome the day when there is a positive change in Southwest Philadelphia.

Sanya lived in a typical row home, which needed a new paint job. Far too much trash in front of her house to walk by every day and pretend like it wasn't there. The lines in her face indicated that life for her still wasn't easy. Her beauty marks were the scars left from her husband's abuse. The smile on her face meant that she was glad to see me. What can I say? I guess I left her with a good impression of me.

"Sergeant Rock! Well, what brings you to my neighborhood?"

"Hello, Sanya. Oh, I hadn't seen you in a while and just wanted to see how you were doing. Can I come in before I get shot?"

"Come on in, you liar. I know damn well you didn't leave quiet, cozy Wynnefield to risk your life on this side of town just to say hi. Niggah, what you want with me?"

Talk about blunt. I guess Sanya had been through enough bullshit in her life to know it when she smelled it. If she didn't carry so much baggage with her I might have considered going out with her. She had a great body and was smart. But she had troubles and I didn't need anybody in my life that I had to baby-sit. Besides, it was hard enough just keeping up with that damn sister of mine.

"Allright, Sanya. And it's Detective Rock now."

"Excuse me, Detective."

"Sanya, I need to talk to you about Melvin. Can you help me out?"

"What do you want to know? The best thing I can say about him is that he's dead."

"Did you find him dead in the house?"

"Yeah, remember, I was at your house for a night, then I went to my mother's for a couple of days. I hadn't talked to him. When I called I didn't get an answer. I figured he was out looking for me. I knew he would be pissed as hell when he found me. I didn't have the heart to go home and get my ass kicked again. I didn't want to impose on you any longer either, even though I must admit I was very comfortable there with you Rock. I think you are the first true gentleman that I have ever met in my life."

"Thanks for the compliment Sanya, I try."

"You're welcome. Anyway, I was afraid of what would happen when I saw Melvin again. I figured if I talked to him first I could get a feel for how mad he was. Plus, I was hoping to catch him sober before I came home. You know, when Melvin was sober, he was the kindest, sweetest, gentlest man. I guess that's why I fell in love and married him. After three days of calling from my mother's, and not getting an answer, I went home. I thought he might be passed out, drunk. The smell hit me as soon as I opened the door. I never smelled no rotted dead body, but the smell that hit me brought tears to my eyes. The sight of Melvin dead, with his hands burned to the bone was an even bigger shock. I mean one side of me was happy because I knew the beatings were over. Still, he was my husband. My first love. I loved him. The way he treated me, though, I knew I would be better off and I would live a lot longer without him pounding on me."

"You have any idea who did this to him?"

"Nope. Don't care either. Why, you got any ideas? By the way, what are you doing here anyway? This is a long way from your work area."

"You can thank the Mayor the next time you run into him. Sanya, can you give me the names of some of his friends, and some of his favorite bars. Maybe I can track down a bad debt or something."

"Sure, Rock. Anything else?"

"Well, how are you doing? Are you still seeing my sister?"

"Naw, I haven't seen Sasha in a while. She was a big help. She helped me find alternatives for dealing with life without Melvin Harper. Mainly she let me come and stay with you. Right after that, Melvin was killed. But I am doing allright. Like mamma used to say, 'You can do bad by yo' self!' Lord knows Melvin made sure nothing good ever came to my life."

Sanya gave me enough names to find out who Melvin was. She also suggested that I check every bar within a ten mile radius. Melvin was well known on this side of town for his marriage to the bottle.

For the next two days I visited every bar in Southwest Philadelphia. Sure, everybody knew Melvin. Besides being an alcoholic and *batterer* he really wasn't a bad guy. He didn't owe anybody money and he wasn't known to be a betting man. He didn't run with women. At least he didn't bring them into the bars that he drank in. He was a hard-working man who drank too much. I had nothing solid. Captain Arnetti wasn't going to be pleased. My first attempt at solving one of these murders wasn't going too good. I knew I just had to keep looking. Something would turn up or my name was going to be Dogmeat. Shit, that's what it became when Captain assigned me to this mess!

9

Sasha

I love shopping in Columbia Mall. The people are so nice. Just plain, ole, friendly, white people. Not like that damn gallery up there in Philly, where it seems like every hoodlum alive is waiting to offer me a dinner date and a night that I will never forget. I needed an outfit that would make Dave curse his mamma before he allowed me to get out of his sight. I picked out a leopard-skin, one-piece bodysuit. Thigh- length, of course. A pair of gold anklets and some brand new cross trainers. Whenever I look my best, I feel my best. I wanted this man to want me bad. A drooling, salivating fool is what I was after. A man blinded. I could go on for days, Evelyn. Dave would be so focused on me, he would never know my black ass would be the last one he would see.

I took my time and cruised up and down the mall. Just taking in all of the sights. Delivery men all over the place. FedEx, RPS, UPS, Airborne. Damn! I pity anybody who delivers boxes for a living. Hustle, hustle, hustle. As I was gallivanting through the mall I noticed that my shadow seemed to double. Every turn, every stop, every store, seemed like I had company. The brothers in Philly were bold. No hesitation. 'Hey, baby I love you, will you marry me? Well, can we at least have sex? Please? Shit, just once, huh? How bout it?' But here they were a little subtler. This very handsome young man seemed to be just one little step behind me. I went to the ladies room and then headed to the food court. I worked up a little appetite with all of that walking. Ahhh, a nice chef salad and a diet soda. Finally, I ditched him.

"Uh, uhm. Uh... excuse me. Hello. Sorry, I hate to bother you."

"Well, I hate to be rude, but don't bother me. Good-bye!"

"It's just that I wouldn't feel like my day would be complete if I didn't ask you just one question."

Here we go again, I thought. Philly, Columbia, it doesn't matter. I thought I had left all of the dogs at home. Don't get me wrong. This brother was very handsome, but I had other things on my mind and I didn't feel like being bothered. Know what I mean? Said to myself, be nice but cold, maybe he will leave quick.

"You might have noticed that I am trying to eat my lunch. Ask your one question!"

"Well, uh, has anybody taken the time today to tell you how beautiful you are!?"

Stop the train! A genuine compliment. I hadn't had one of those since... Since Coleman died. I wished I had a deep dark complexion like Jeanette. That's the only way I could have kept Prince Charming from seeing that he made me blush. I had to get myself together, quick. A coughing episode might help.

"Uuhummm, huuumm, huum. Excuse me, I think I got a piece of lettuce stuck in my throat. Could you repeat your question? I didn't hear what you said."

"You are very beautiful. It's as if God threw down a rainbow from the sky; you were the pot of Gold at the end! Would you mind if I join you for lunch?"

Ninety-nine point nine percent of my brain told me to say no. But the part of the brain that controls the vocal cords said, "No. I don't mind at all."

"My name is Earlston. Earlston Belefont. What's your name? Or can I just call you Sunshine?"

"Sasha. Sasha, will be just fine. By the way, why were you following me?"

"Me, following you. You know, I thought maybe you were one of those palm readers or clairvoyants or something! It seemed like every time you walked into a store, at that very moment I realized that I was going to have to go into that same store. I say to myself, incredible! How could such a lovely and heavenly sight end up in the same stores as me for an entire hour?"

I couldn't help but smile. Earlston was a charmer with a sense of humor.

"Sure, sure. Seriously. Why were you following me?"

I had to admit, he had peaked my interest. Men have always thrown themselves at me. But Earlston, he sort of floated to me in a cool, smooth manner, and I liked it. I hadn't given much thought to entertaining another man, post killing Coleman. I couldn't help it, I was feeling a little giddy.

"Honestly. You are the most adoring sight my eyes have ever beheld. I thanked God for my eyes when you first walked by. I thanked him for my legs so that I could follow you."

The arrogant chump had the nerve to wink at me.

"I thanked Him for my heart. The courage to even approach a woman like you. Finally, I thanked God for my voice so that I could talk to you. Let you know, even if I never see you again, that you, Ms. Sasha Sunshine, are one of the rare and perfect creations that walk the earth."

Parkaaaaaaay! Damn! Now this brother was smooth. Just spreading his words all over me, real easy, real nice. He was trying to get inside of my heart in ten minutes. Oh, it was working. Coleman was a charmer, the most charming and adorable man I had ever met. I guess that's why I married him. That one little flaw of his was the only reason I did what I did.

"Earlston. Thank you. That's the sweetest thing anybody has said to me in a very long time. Thanks for keeping me company while I choked on my salad. I have to go, good-bye!"

"Sasha, when is the next time you plan on lighting up the mall? Another day of your sunshine would last me at least ten years- ten minutes?"

"Hard to say, Mr. Belefont. Maybe Friday. Peace!" I tried to leave him with my sexy cool hip-swaggering walk, but it wasn't working. He had me so juiced up I almost turned over trying to get out of that mall. When I looked back he was still watching, with a smirk on his face, knowing that he touched me where I haven't been touched in a long time. I just wasn't ready for that. Shit! Ready for what. I didn't even know the man. I just sat and talked to him for fifteen or twenty or was it thirty minutes. Whatever! Humpf! Reparations was the only thing

I needed to be focusing on. I had to be focused or I could make a costly mistake.

Earlston Belefont. If I didn't have on heels I figured he was about an inch taller than me. Medium brown complexion. Not too hairy. Matter of fact, he looked like he was trying real hard to grow a goatee. Mustache wasn't too thick. Lean build. His silk shirt that fit him perfectly accentuated his muscular chest. Perfect crease down the center of his pants, shoes shined. Very nice dresser. Kiss my ass, he also looked old enough to be my younger... younger brother. Couldn't have been a day over twenty-eight, I thought. Handsome. And he respected me every second that he was with me. Something rare, a gentleman. My trip to the mall went just a little better after I met Earlston Belefont. What a weird ass name. Black folks always trying to have royal sounding names. Beautiful young man though. Unique. I had a feeling on the inside that I hadn't felt in a long time. I felt like somebody who didn't have to, cared about me. It was nice.

Back to reality. I had a killing to do!

I stopped at the drug store to get a special item just for David. Something that would give him the boost he needed to get on with his afterlife. The school bus was dropping Demmy off right as I pulled up.

"Hey, handsome! Let's take a walk around the block." Maybe, I was thinking, if I walked long enough I would forget about killing David. I could get back to enjoying life with my son. Get back to normal. Impossible! My life would never be normal. I might get rid of this animal one day, but never be normal.

I still had a few hours to kill. Huh, to kill. So, I allowed myself a pleasure I rarely experience these days. I spent quality time with my son. He is innocent to this wicked world we live in. The sooner I can give him all of me, the sooner I will be at peace. Soon. Soon. Soon.

I hated lying, especially to Jeanette. But I needed to be alone that night, so I told Jeanette that I met the perfect gentleman in the mall, and that we were going to have a drink. I gave her a hundred-dollar bill and told her to spend some money on herself and my son.

"Look girl, shopping always makes me feel better."

"All right, Sasha, if you insist. However, let's not make this a habit. You came here to spend time with Demetrius and me. I think I am a little jealous. You have a nice time, though. And please be careful. I couldn't handle it if anything were to happen to you."

"Don't worry, sister, I keeps my blade with me!"

The three of us had a group hug and a laugh before they left. Jeanette and Demmy were giggling all the way to the car. Me? My whole demeanor changed. The animal had made its way to the surface. I got business... serious business to attend to.

I made sure I parked in a dark section of the Athletic Sports Club as far away from the front door as possible. The only time people park here is during peak workout hours and there is nowhere else to park. I backed into my parking space. I knew when I left I didn't want to spend a lot of time getting out of the lot. Change up and conquer! Hell of an agenda!

I swear, David must have lived in that spot. Without fail he was in the back, eyes glued to the door. Wonder who he was looking for?

"Hello, David. How ya' doing?"

"Fine, Sasha. It sure is good to see you. If you don't mind my saying, your gear is fabulous. It just seems to bring out all that you have to offer. You look——"

"Jesus Christ, David. Can you wipe the saliva off of your chin while you talk to me? So I don't feel like I'm a T-bone steak that you are waiting to devour. Huh? Is that asking too much of you?"

"I'm sorry, Sasha. You're just the personification of Goddess. I can't help but drool a little when I look at you."

"Well, maybe you should work out on the other side of the room today. I want you to be able to concentrate. Wouldn't want you to sprain an eyeball watching me!"

"Don't-"

"Ah-aaah, aaaah, don't say a word. Class is starting. I need to focus."

Yeah, you guessed it. I flashed my pearlies and got to steppin'. High-impact aerobics. Love it. Kill a worthless piece if shit. Love it even more!

Class was great. Not once did I make eye contact with David. Didn't have to. I knew his eyes were glued on me the entire time. Looked like some of the girls were a tad bit jealous. I don't know why though. I wasn't about to fight any woman over a white man. If they only knew why I entertained him, they would have formed a line to get a piece of him. I could hear the whispers though. 'Look at her. She thinks she's so fine. Look at that hair.' 'Weave!' 'And where did she get that getup, must think she gonna get photographed for Wild Kingdom or National Geographic or something. And too much makeup...' I only had on lipstick. Seemed like they would just admit it to themselves. I was everything they wanted to be and they hated it. So, I bounced a little more, kicked a little higher, and looked a lot better. Sasha at her best. David was all over me after class. Oh, not physically, well physically in the sense that he was invading my personal space. Still begging, more than you could imagine.

"Look, Sasha, how about a drink or dinner or something? After all that energy you put into that workout you had to have built up an appetite. Or maybe you're a bit thirsty. I know I am. How 'bout it? Please?"

I sure didn't want everybody to know that I would be the last person that David would see. I just toweled, pretending to ignore him as he talked. I made sure enough people heard my next statement though—

"Like I said before David, thanks but no thanks. Not tonight anyway."

Like I figured, David followed me out the door; luckily the hallway was empty.

"I will drive. Meet me at the far end of the parking lot in twenty minutes. Towncar. Try to control your excitement, handsome!"

"Fine, bye Sasha. Maybe next week?"

He said his lines out loud. He handled that quite

well. David was a pretty smooth character. But I guess anybody who goes around raping women and keeps on getting up like nothing happened has to be pretty cool. That made me angry. I hated the sight of him more than any man I have every seen. I hated his arrogance; his ability to live the life that he lived and not give a fuck about the life, or lives he destroyed. If I didn't cooperate he would have probably tried to add me to his list. He was showering and probably thinking he was about to strike gold. Only thing that punk was going to strike. **OUT!!!**

I sat in my car and waited. Listened to some slow jams. Kept the engine running. Went over some moves in my head. Step by step. Perfect practice makes perfect performance. How many times have I heard that? Years of martial arts training. Execute. Speed plus power, plus timing, plus accuracy will secure the results sought. Move fast. Pow! Bam! Bop! Game over! I got out when I saw David.

David came galloping out of the club looking happier than a little kid with an ice cream sundae. Looking around. Covert. Making sure he wasn't being followed. After all, he was keen enough to pick up on the fact that I didn't want anyone to know we were meeting after class. A real eye spy! Sneaky bastard. Guess he figured if he got rough with me he would have the perfect alibi, since everyone in the class heard me tell him I wasn't going to see him that night.

I loved the sound of my engine running. For such a big car, the Lincoln just purred. Sitting and waiting. Ready to roar. I did a visual scan of the parking lot.

Nobody was in sight. It was going to be a good night. I had changed into a pair of dark blue stretch pants, an exercise bra and a 'crop top,' 'cut real high. Just below the breast. I loved this kind of shirt for two reasons. First, every time you half-way raise your arms, the dogs will be trying to catch a glimpse of your titties. Second and more important, freedom of movement. Unrestricting.

I stood sideways beside the car. Profile. Let David know what he was getting. Damn. David looked happy as shit. I guess he liked the pose. Eager. Couldn't wait to get next to Sasha. When he got close enough I reached out my hand as if I wanted him to take hold of it. I damn near vomited at the thought of him touching me. Before he could touch me I raised my right leg and lightning fast, delivered the perfect side-kick to David's kneecap. I heard that dull, sickening pop that just makes you cringe. The shock in David's eyes didn't compare to the pain he was feeling with a broken leg. Perfectly practiced in my mind. Perfectly executed on David. His attempt at groaning in pain was intercepted by a palm heel strike to his nose. I could hear my instructor: *'When you deliver the palm heel strike to the face, drive the nose up into the brain. The eyes water. Temporary disorientation takes place. Hit 'em hard enough and you can kill 'em. Speed, plus technique, plus power will guarantee results that will stop your opponent.'*

As David continued his downward descent to the asphalt I grabbed the bottle of clear glue that I had open on the hood of my car. I filled his broken nose with enough to stop any air from coming in. Quick as a fox, I taped his mouth. I duct-taped his hands behind his back and taped his feet tight together. Then I dragged his sorry ass behind a Dumpster. His face was flaming red. His eyes were bulging. Sweat was pouring from his face. He was struggling with all that he had to breathe. But he couldn't. He was struggling. He was suffering. He was rapidly losing any air he had left. He was going to die. Usually the brain can survive a little while without oxygen.

I said to him, "Hey, David. I want you to hear this before you die. You raped my best friend, Jeanette Jones! Big mistake. *Not cool at all!* Now you're going to die! See Ya"!

10

Rock

I had started with nothing and I ended with nothing. Shit, total autonomy. I said aloud to myself as I drove towards Mt. Airy. I deserved a company car. Independent murder mystery solver, or was that mysterious murders solver? Didn't matter no way. I didn't have to follow no rule but my own. I didn't have to solve one before I started another. Since I was such a great detective in the... I remembered I needed to talk to Arnetti about my promotion to Ace Detective and about my pay increase. So if my autonomous ass wanted to talk to Mrs. Morgan, wife of the late playboy Reverend Austin Morgan, then that's what I was going to do.

Reverend Morgan's jacket didn't say too much. However, judging by his surroundings at his death, either he was waiting for his wife or he was a playboy. I take the latter. He wasn't in his 'hood' and judging by the honeymoon suite, don't think he was waiting for his wife. Now, I said to myself, "Self, ole' Austin surely been running around with women somewhere. Maybe even his own church members. Now who would know? Probably everybody. But who would talk to me? Probably nobody. They wouldn't want to trample on the grave of their beloved leader. Let the man rest with his honor and dignity. Keep his pride intact. The family name would not be desecrated."

Mrs. Morgan, on the other hand, I knew she probably wouldn't want to talk at first. But the curiosity that she would have to be feeling about her husband's death would overwhelm her. If nothing else I figured she could point me in the direction of some of his other women. The wife always knows. She could get me started on the right track, unless she didn't have an excellent alibi, which she did. Report says she was visiting her mother in New Jersey at the time of the killing. This case smelled like the jealous other woman or hysterical-husband-breaks-in-on-lovers type of case anyway. The wife always knows.

I jumped on Lincoln Drive, then headed up to Stenton Avenue. I drove past Reverend Morgan's church on the way to his house. I bet his cut could pay two or three house notes judging by the size of the place. The Morgan home was right off Stenton not too far from the church. It was such a beautiful home. It looked like the people took care of their leader, their knight in Christian armor. Their chosen man of God, who was sent to deliver all who wanted to be saved from a fate of eternal damnation. But he lived a life of deceit and betrayal. I looked at his home and wondered how much is too much. The brother lived well-quite well, thanks to his congregation. No wants, no worries. Pastoring was his job. His livelihood. Shiiiiit, I was thinking, maybe one day, I solve enough of these hi-profile cases, I can buy me one of these two car garages, long ass driveway, pool in the back, big ass houses like the late Reverend Morgan. His people took damn good care of him. I didn't understand and I couldn't explain his actions, but apparently what he wanted out of his life was more important than what he had in his life. You might say I was jumping to conclusions, but I got a good feeling on this one, and it started with Mrs. Jewel Morgan.

Oh, yes, he even had a sweet-sounding door chime, too. It went on forever. Sounded expensive. I wanted it all!

"Uh, H-h-hello! Mrs. Morgan. Hi. My name is Ser- - uh Detective Cecil Rock. I work for the City of Philadelphia's special task force on homicides. Is it okay if I ask you a few questions about your late husband?"

"I don't mean to be rude, Detective, but I have already answered three-thousand questions, at least, about my late husband. Is it possible you police people could just leave me alone and let me get on with my life? I got children to raise!"

"No, Ma'am. It's not asking too much at all. But... I mean... Don't get me wrong, but uhh, wouldn't you at least like to know who killed your husband? Aren't you just a little curious?"

Mrs. Morgan appeared to be a gentle, kind of timid woman. The good little woman. Stayed 'in her place.' Didn't interfere in her husband's business, and did what she was told. She seemed obedient, and didn't ask questions. Enslaved! Not at all an Essence Sister. Maybe, I thought, I could slip through the back door. Play on the fact that she was the perfect wife and still her husband didn't do right by her.

"Ma'am, judging by the fashion in which your husband died, I can understand why you might not want to find the killer. After all, you don't appear to be the type of woman who took part in matters of importance. I mean, I know you stood behind your husband, I mean beside your husband throughout your marriage. You just stayed out of the way, right? Any decision that ever had to be made, Reverend Morgan made it, alone. Right!"

Thanks to my superior instincts, I braced myself, instead of blocking or ducking Mrs. Morgan's right hand as it came crashing across my face. I wanted her to hit me. Boy, to be such a petite woman, she smacked the shit out of me. Babydoll had my eyes watering. Good. Just what I wanted. Some true emotions. I had struck a nerve but good. Now, knowing Christian women the way I thought I did, after she finished cussing the shit out of me, guilt would take over. She would realize that I was right. Truth hurts. Then she'll open her door and her mouth! Give me some good info! Got my fingers crossed.

"How dare you! You asshole! *'Scuse me Lord!'* Come to my house! Insult me! Disrespect me. My husband. You pig asshole! *'Forgive me Jesus'.* '"she smacked me again, only that time I wasn't braced for it. Hurt like hell. I remained cool. "You disrespected my husband. After he is dead! You bastard! *'Forgive me Lord.'* Now you listen here, mister, um-uhh, pig officer Rock, or whatever your name is, my husband was good to me and my children. Very good. And he loved me. Why he ran with other wom... Why he ran with oth... other w..."

Tears! Just what I need. I might have struck too deep. I was the biggest sucker in the world when a woman started crying on me. Sasha been using them damn tears on me her whole life. I gave her my famous big brother hug to calm them down.

"Mrs. Morgan. I am sorry. Really. I didn't mean to insult you. Please forgive me. It's just, well, it's just that I have been assigned to this case. You do understand that I have to find out who killed your husband. That's my job and it sucks. Sorry, it isn't a nice job sometimes, the things I have to do and say. But. Well, I ain't gonna bother you anymore. Could you just get me an ice pack for my face and I'll leave you alone? Okay?"

"An ice pack? Detective Rock, I am terribly sorry for hitting you. I am so sor..."

"Look, it's all right. The swelling should go down in a couple of days. I'll just tell my boss two football players jumped me."

"Let me see your face."

"No, really, I am fine."

"Please, let me take a look. Matter of fact, come on in and sit down. I'll get you a cool rag to put on it. Some of my homemade sweet potato pie should help too. You sit tight. I'll be right back."

Sometimes I marvel at my rear assault tactics. Who knows, I might have made a great marine. Drill Sergeant Cecil Rock! Naaaaa!

I swear, if I didn't know better I would have thought Betty or Mrs. Smith was in that kitchen and made that sweet potato pie. Best I ever had! She offered me more, but I had to be careful. I had too much work to do to be falling in love!

"Sure, I would like to have another piece. To be honest, I could eat the rest if you're trying to get rid of it. But really though, one piece is enough. Thank you. I try to keep my calorie count under 5000! If I can."

Bingo! A smile and just a little chuckle. She warmed up.

"You're welcome, Detective."

"Please, call me Rock."

"Only if you call me Jewel."

"Yes, Ma'am, uh Jewel. Ma'am."

"Rock, let's start over. I really do want to find out what exactly happened to my husband. You know, it's hard sometimes to look in the mirror. Sometimes you just don't like what you see."

I jumped up and ran out the front door. She looked a bit surprised. *Bing*. Love that door chime. She opened the door with a wide grin on her face.

"Hello, Mrs. Morgan. I'm Detective Cecil Rock. I represent the city blah, blah, blah...Homicides. May I take a moment of your time to ask you a few questions about your late husband, uh, Reverend Austin Morgan?" My second entrance gave me the opportunity to really appreciate just how beautiful a widow Reverend Morgan left behind. Petite build, but shapely. Medium brown skin. Hazel eyes. The do was sharp. Nails were done. For a woman who had to have been closing in on forty, she was well kept. Very well kept. I might have picked up on all of her good qualities if I wasn't busy trying to bully my way into her house. My job was always more important than checking out a sister, though. Sometimes. And God, did she have a smile on her. The teeth weren't perfect, but that crooked kind of cute that just makes a smile look all the better. Perfect imperfection. Reverend had him an all-right sister. Man was weak! Mrs. Morgan was flattered that I was taking the time to re-introduce myself to her. She was more than willing to play out the scene.

"Hello, Detective. Please come in and have a seat. Can I offer you a piece of my homemade sweet potato pie?"

"Definitely!" Whew! She wheeled and headed for the kitchen. She glanced over her shoulder at me, all smiles.

"I'll be right back, sit tight."

"Yes, Ma'am."

"Here you are Rock. One more slice of homemade sweet potato pie. I added a little a la mode for you too, to ask your forgiveness for hitting you."

"Which time? The first or second?"

"The second. The first one you deserved. Wouldn't you agree?"

"Yeah. I was kinda being an asshole. Excuse my French. No. How would you put it," I threw my hands over my head like an enthused holy roller, 'Fo'give me, Lawd!'

She smacked me on my leg and told me to shut the hell up. Mamma always said communication was the key. Talk to people. Get to know them. She was always saying something about the souls of black folks! How we got good, loving hearts. We are a people who naturally love and care about one another. It's just the time and the world that we live in. The white man's world makes black folks treat each other the way that we do. Mamma was a smart woman. I miss her. I felt like I was getting to know Jewel. Pretty name.

"You know you wolfed down that second piece of pie like a run-away slave. Just how hard are you countin' dem calories, boy!?"

And a sense of humor. I had a much better feel for this case than I had for Melvin's. Shit, I don't even want to think about Melvin's case:

It reminded me of that feeling you get when you're lost on some dark ass road trying to get to Aunt Velma's house. Just driving, driving, driving. Lost. Don't know where the hell you at or where the hell you going. Just lost. Driving. Just one long dark-ass road. Dark as shit. Can't see a damn thing. No street signs, no signs of life. Nothing. Then, BAM! Dead end! Guess I'll turn around and start over. That's how I felt when I thought about figuring out who killed Melvin. Not a good feeling. But this one with Mrs. Morgan, I had good vibes.

"Jewel, this is the best sweet potato pie I ever had in my life. You sure put a lot of love in your baking. Must have spent hours with Grandma in the kitchen growing up, huh? Deeeeee-licious!"

"You are quite welcome, Rock. Now that we finished playing charades, what is it you would like to know about my husband?"

"Well, could you tell me a little about him? Negative and positive."

"Explain, negative and positive."

"Jewel, from what I have read, your husband had a

huge congregation, who took good care of you guys. But, judging by the way he was killed- well... Kind of looked like he was with another woman. Since your alibi says you were in Jersey at the time of his death, well, it isn't hard to see that he wasn't waiting for you."

"Who am I kidding, Rock? My husband was a damn dog. Every week I had to sit in the front pew for everyone to see. The first lady. His figure piece on display. I had to pretend like I didn't notice his flirtatious ways. It was very demeaning; insulting to me. Always smiling, hugging and kissing every skirt that wasn't with a man. He made me sick to my stomach, but he had this way of reassuring me. He would tell me that he was a leader and that he had to be able to demonstrate his holy-love for all members of the church, make everybody feel at home. Loved! I knew it was a bunch of holy bullshit! *Forgive me, Lord.* Put some pie in your mouth or close it! He took care of me and our children. Treated me like a queen. His first lady. You know, it all kinda doesn't matter now. He used me. He cheated on me, and it finally caught up with him. Rock, my husband is dead. You have to know that I loved him. I hated the negative. Loved the positive. I guess I let the good outweigh the bad, by turning the other cheek. Forgive and forget. I do know for a fact that he had sex with several women in that church. I wonder how a woman can call herself saved and turn around and sleep with her married pastor. Kind of makes her look sorry as hell, too. Know what I mean?"

"I know exactly what you mean, Jewel. I ain't gonna blame or condemn you for putting up with your husband.

Marriage can provide both partners with security. Even if it might be a tad bit dirty, you ain't gonna be cold. You just might not feel as comfortable as you would with a pure, clean blanket around you."

"Rock, if you were this gentle and kind when you first got here I wouldn't have had to smack you. You know that don't you?"

"Sure. But if I was this nice, you would have politely asked me to leave and slammed the door in my face.

"You could be right."

"Jewel?"

"Yes."

"I want you to understand. If I felt like I could have gotten any cooperation from the members of your husband's church, I would have started my investigation there. But I just figured that a loyal congregation wasn't going to spit on the grave of their fallen leader. Corrupt or not. Judging by this house, the folks over at New Christian Baptist Church loved them some Reverend Austin Morgan. Can I get a witness!?"

"Yes, sir! Amen!"

I was so glad I made things right with Mrs. Morgan. I knew I would have to be a little rough to get any info out of her. But after getting to know her just a little, I realized that I had been a shit-head to treat such a sweet lady so bad. She was good people and she didn't deserve a husband like the one she had. She deserved a helluva lot better.

I asked her, "Can you give me the names of any of the

women you think or know that your husband was seeing? I figured if anybody had a motive, maybe one of them did. You know like, maybe your husband promised to leave you for them and he didn't. You know that happens a lot in domestic situations and it gets real ugly. People die. Cold."

"Let me think. Uhh, there was a girl named, uh, Donna. Donna... Donna Williams, about twenty-six. And another girl named Zema. I don't know her last name. And of course, my 'daughter' Malinda Chaney. I call her my daughter because I have known her for years. I watched her grow up. She grew up to be a fine young woman. It broke my heart when she slept with my husband. I didn't think she could do that to me. I knew she slept with him because Austin was in her face every Sunday for weeks. Then, POW, she disappears and doesn't come back. I figured Austin slept with her and didn't promise her a thing. That makes a woman bitter when she thinks she is going to get the goods and ends up with diddly! Pisses them off bad. I have to admit, they were all young, beautiful women, but cold-blooded killers? I just don't see it, in any of them. I wish you luck, Rock. I don't think any of these women killed my husband."

"Thanks for all of your help, and the pie. But Jewel, never underestimate what a woman will do when she has been wronged by her man, or the man who she thinks is her man. A whole new kind of person can come out."

"Whatever you say. If you need any more help, give me a call."

"Thank you. I appreciate that. Oh, and thanks for the

pie."

"You already thanked me once!"

"I know. Did I tell you that sweet potato pie was my favorite?"

"Wait a minute. I'll get you another piece, no ice cream though, you need to keep a close count on those calories!"

I had concluded that Reverend Austin Morgan was a fool. He had a real Jewel in his possession and didn't even realize it. If he did, there was no way he would have dogged her out the way he did. Almost made me feel like he deserved what he got. I don't know. Who's to say who deserves what?

11

Sasha

Time to go home? Should I hook up with Earlston or should I just head on home... I couldn't decide.

...Damn, if those weren't the softest, gentlest, tenderest hands I had ever felt in my entire life. Earlston was giving me a massage. We were both undressed. I was on my stomach and he was straddled across my back. The warm oil that he was rubbing on me smelled like a rose garden. Softly, gently, he rubbed and tenderized my muscles. I was more relaxed than I had been in the last two years. Melting away. It felt so, so good. He ran his hand from my shoulders to the small of my back. Next he touched my butt very sensitively. Never have I enjoyed being touched this way. Earlston used his tongue to torture and tantalize the hairs on my neck. They all stood at attention waiting for their turn to be tasted. Very delicately licking and kissing me all over. I trembled, then he sat at my ankles. He commented on how beautiful and firm my legs were. His touch became firmer as he gave a more intense massage of my legs. Heaven. High! Relaxation had taken on a new form. I was at ease in the hands of another man for the first time.

I couldn't control myself any longer. I didn't want to control myself. I wanted to be free. Free myself. Live. I had to have him. I needed to be loved. I deserved to be loved. My life had undergone drastic changes. He made me know what I had been missing for all of those months. Love. Earlston was going to love me and I was going to give him the best lovin' he ever had. I flipped over so that we were facing each other. Earlston stared into my eyes. I thought he was trying to look straight into my soul, to see inside of me. I stared back. Full of passion and desire. His hands were at work again, lightly caressing my breasts, grazing my nipples in such a way that they stood at attention, waiting, wanting, to be kissed, or sucked or licked. Naturally, he didn't disappoint them, or me. His full, black, African lips kissed and kissed and kissed. From nipple to breast to stomach. Back to my breast, my nipples, my arms, my stomach. For all that talking he was doing in the mall the brother was quiet now, on a mission to please Sasha. Next his lips got familiar with my thighs. I was on fire. My mind was a bowl of oatmeal. I couldn't think. Never have I wanted a man inside of me so bad. I was ready to be loved. I was going to love right back. Earlston anticipated my readiness. Gently he spread my legs even wider apart. As one golden hand rested on my thigh, the other was getting to know my vagina, rubbing my clitoris. I tensed all the muscles of my body at once. Another gentle flick and I was convulsing again. I was so wet. He was merciless as he rubbed my vulva, back and forth. This was definitely the Earlston Belefont Show. Never hard or forceful. Just gentle. As my eyes rolled to the back of my head, Earlston's fingers became his tongue. All I could do was hang on for the ride of my life. He had a very talented tongue, I was soon to find out. My hands played in his hair. My thighs formed a vice-grip around his head so that he couldn't get away before he finished! Earlston ate. Damn well, I might add.

It was time. Earlston would be deep inside of me. He rose with the grace of a king and the smile of a very happy man. Proud of his deed and happy that I was enjoying myself. I spread my legs, grabbed him around his hips and pulled him toward me. Our tongues met. Lips meeting. Passion. Love. Slowly, steadily he came to me. Rock solid. Rock hard man. Big. Ready. I closed my eyes in anticipation....

"MAM! MAM! HELLO! ANYBODY HOME! THE TOLL IS TWO DOLLARS, NOT ONE!" Interstate 95. Not in the arms of my gentle man. I had daydreamed all the way to the Delaware toll booth. Still, the thoughts were nice. I decided to go straight to my brother's house and crash until he got home from work.

12

Rock

Keen. Cunning. Extra high IQ. Excellent tools to possess as a detective. Tools I am proud to say I possess. How else would I get results? I found out that Donna Williams had moved to California two years ago. Her mother told me. Zema left the city over a year ago to finish college. I talked to her dad. Malinda was home. Maybe I could make some headway with her.

"Hi. Ms. Chaney. I am Ser... Detective Rock. Is it okay if I talk to you for a few minutes?"

"Hello... sure. We can sit out here on the steps. What's this about?"

Malinda was the type of woman who you would probably pass by without a second glance. Average, nothing-extra-special type of woman. Her short cropped hair and innocent face gave off an air of purity. I got two glances though. She was allright. Great smile. I bet underneath the Gap jeans and oversized T-shirt was a woman who was special. I could see why Reverend Morgan had the hots for her.

"Uh, Ms. Chaney, I wanted to talk to you about your late Pastor, um, Reverend Morgan. Okay?"

"Sure. What do you want to know? No, let me guess, since they found him dead in the hotel, you want to know what? Did I do it? Or were we seeing each other?"

"Something along those lines."

What luck. An ace detective's blessing. A woman who didn't mind talking. She reminded me of my favorite fish, Mackerel. Don't even need no bait, just set the hook and chomp, chomp, no make that yak, yak, yak. All the information I needed and more. And no back door tactics required, which also saved my pretty face!

"Which question do you want an answer to, Detective, uh Stone was it?"

"Rock. Rock is fine Ma'am."

"Detective Rock!"

"Were you two having an affair?"

"Had an affair. I slept with him, just once, but he devastated me. I know I was wrong. I should have never put myself in that position. I knew he held a level of respect in the church that would never be compromised, even for a woman. But I can't honestly say that I am glad Reverend Morgan is dead. I knew Reverend Morgan for a long time. He raised me in his church. Baptized me. Raised me like I was his own daughter. But the way he treated women, or at least me, he kind of had it coming."

"You say he devastated you. How so?"

"He used me. I trusted him. He was supposed to be helping me find the right husband: an honest, hardworking, Christian man. Somebody decent, like himself. That's the kind of help I expected. Instead he took advantage of me. He should have at least been strong enough for the both of us. I mean, I hadn't been with a man in so long. I was needy. I wanted someone in my life. When you go to your minister, baring your heart, he is there to mend it, not use it. Man, woman or child should be able to confide in their spiritual leader without being taken advantage of. God put this man in a position to help those in need. I have to admit, I had a crush on him. What woman wouldn't? He was intellectual, eloquent, articulate, and handsome. More than qualified to be the leader of our church. I admired his strength and the respect he commanded when he spoke to us on Sundays. I just figured he could recommend someone like himself. But, God is my witness, when I went to his office that Saturday morning, I had no intention of making love, no make that having sex, because if he loved me he sure wouldn't have treated me the way he did. Instead of leading, he took. He took my trust, my faith, and my belief in the spiritual leadership of the church. Instead of helping me, he destroyed my soul. He used me for— That ain't right Rock!"

"Trust no man! The times my mamma told me that. Make your own way son. Don't depend on anybody to get what you want out of this world. Those words never seemed truer."

"You had a smart mother."

"Malinda, if you don't mind my saying, you seem pretty spunky now. How are things? You seem to have put the situation behind you, at least on the surface."

"I had an excellent shrink."

"Mind if I ask his name? I might need one, some day being in my line of work."

"Her name! Sasha. Sasha Timms! But she doesn't see men. She specializes in women. Sorry sport! Maybe she has a brother in the field."

Helluva bombshell. I was sure that Malinda heard my heart thumping through my shirt. Suddenly, I needed some fresh air. Jamaica fresh. Clean water, cool breeze. Needed to get out of the city quick, before I suffocated. I thanked Malinda and hit the road, fast. She seemed a little startled, but didn't question my leaving so abruptly. Good. I didn't want to believe that my sister was behind these two murders. Sanya had mentioned that her husband ended up dead, right after Sasha brought her to my house.

I screeched my Red Convertible Mustang 5 point Oh... Yeah, yeah, yeah, reality check. I screeched my Blue Honda Civic to a stop in front of Sanya's house. She jumped up hollering and cussing about my wild ass driving and something about the kids playing in the street. Before she could finish I had her arm and was dragging her into her house. I had to remember that I couldn't manhandle a former battered woman. Next time she might shoot me as opposed to smacking the shit out of me. Twice in one day!

"Mother fucka' you better get your damn hands off of me. What the hell is the matter with you!?"

"Shit, sorry, sorry Sanya, I didn't mean to startle you. Damn, you sure pack a helluva right hand."

"Sorry, Rock. It's just that you scared the shit out of me; you know grabbing me the way you did. Melvin used to come home in the same reckless fashion and beat the crap out of me. For the first time in my life I was ready to fight back. Ain't that a trip. Maybe if I smacked that big

Niggah the first time he grabbed me, he never would have beat— naw my ass would have been dead. Anyway, what do you want?"

"Just wanted to ask you a couple of questions about the day you came over to my house."

"Sure."

"Uhm, uh, when Sasha brought you by, did she stay with you?"

"Yeah, I mean, yes, she was there. Well, actually I kind of passed out in your basement. But when I woke up, she was right there. She said she had been working out on your Stairmaster for the last forty minutes."

"Guess you were pretty tired, huh?"

"Yes. I deserved and needed that rest."

"Thanks, Sanya, sorry about the scare."

"You come blazing down my street, reckless as hell and that's all you want?"

"Well... honestly, I was gonna ask you if you'd have dinner with me in a couple of weeks, you know after I clean up this murder mess? And uh, that's usually how I drive."

"You a little on the violent side. Give me a call when you ready, I'll let you know then, okay, Detective?"

"That's a bet. Don't forget me now. Peace!"

"Take care!"

Sanya was a sweet lady. As I was questioning her it dawned on me that I couldn't give her the impression that Sasha was a suspect. If Sasha was behind this nonsense then I wanted us to deal with this, not have the pressure of a widow wanting some answers. Sasha and I really needed to talk. She should have been on her way from Maryland. If I only had a jump shot and some foot speed. Vertical, just a little. NBA all the way. Wouldn't have to be putting up with this kind of shit for a living!

Red Lincoln Town Car in my driveway. Either Ed McMahon stopped by while I was at work or Sasha was in my crib.

13

Sasha

Uhmm! I loved pizza. Oh, the smell just teased me. I looked and there was my big brother waving a pizza under my nose. I had fallen asleep on the sofa. Nothing like a good talk show to put me to sleep.

"Hey, Rock, what's up?"

"You what's up. Figured you would be hungry after your drive from Maryland."

"Sure you did. That's why that pie is loaded with sausage and pepperoni. You know I don't eat that mess. Plus, you didn't know I would be here."

"Yeah, you're right. But when I saw your car in the driveway, I ordered you a salad from the spot around the corner. Chef salad for Ms. Fine Figure!"

"Thanks, Rock. Let me go freshen up before we eat. Be back down in a few."

"Okay. Don't leave no lipstick on my towels, got a little honey comin' over tomorrow and I don't want her to think I got some babe livin' here with me!"

"Whatever you say, Big Daddy!"

14

Rock

Sasha looked well. Normal. She didn't seem to be carrying the burden of somebody who had been killing people. It was time to bust that grub! Check out the news:

...And in other news across the nation. A brutal and baffling murder in the peaceful, planned, community of Columbia, Maryland. The body of David Arnold, of nearby Ellicott City, was found behind a Dumpster, in the parking lot of the Athletic Sports Club. His legs and mouth were bound with heavy industrial tape. Police say they have no motives, no witness, or clues at this time. In other news, the Washington Bullets defeated...

You know, I really wasn't up for television the way, I thought I was. Wasn't really hungry either. Pizza gives me heartburn, cause I sure was starting to get heartburn. Felt like I needed some more of that Jamaica fresh air, too! I put my pizza in the fridge. Paid the delivery guy for Sasha's salad when he arrived. Then I waited. Waited for my sister to bring her narrow ass downstairs and answer some questions. She had just left Maryland. Columbia, Maryland. Same place her son lives. Where Jeanette lives. Same place where David Arnold was mysteriously murdered. Yeah, Sasha and I need to talk. Like Grandma used to say, 'She had some serious 'splainin to do!'

Finally, she came downstairs. Looking at my sister reminded me of all the hell she put me through when we were growing up. Seemed like every day I was chasing some fool away from the doorstep. All up in my baby sister's face telling lies and making promises he knew he couldn't keep. Just wanted some Sasha so he could go bragging about how he screwed the finest babe in the neighborhood. Well, I wasn't having it. So I stayed busy. Sasha would just sit there all innocent looking. Enjoying the attention. Marveling at her big brother's concern for her well being.

I remember that one chump, Chuck. Lived 'down the bottom.' Unless you was driving, fast, you didn't go in his neighborhood. Chuck was a big, black, bold brother. Figured just because he was from a tough part of the city, that gave him the right to grab Sasha's breasts in school. Word got out quick after that. If you messed with Sasha Rock you was gonna get your ass kicked but good by her big brother Cecil. I beat Chuck's ass. His boys respected me because I was protecting my family. I loved my sister to death. She's just been putting me through hell our entire lives. Well, it was time for the shit to stop. I had a bad feeling that Sasha was out of control again. Thanks to Captain Arnetti and our distinguished Mayor, I was the fall guy.

"Cecil! You ought to be ashamed of yourself. I know you didn't eat that entire pizza that fast. Man, you gonna have heartburn for—"

"Damn, Sasha, stop flappin' your jaws so much. I put it in the fridge!"

"Did my food get here yet? I'm starvin!?"

"Yeah, it's here, you owe me $4.50. Plus tip."

"Thanks honey, cut you a check later."

"So, how was your trip? How's Demetrius?"

"He's doing great. You should see how big he's getting. And just as handsome as the day is long!"

"Ms. Jones?"

"Well, she's doing okay, all things considered."

"What things? Is she all right?"

"Rock, Jeanette was raped. Some jerk who she met at the club where she took aerobics. Isn't that terrible? So how come you aren't eating? You usually put away at least five or six slices before you remember that you are trying to trim down?"

"Well, I had chucked down one slice and was working on another when I heard a shocking story on the boob tube. Seems like some guy was murdered in Columbia, you know where Jeanette lives? Found him behind some health club. Guess the same place where Jeanette worked out. A, uh, David Arnold!"

Son-of-a-bitch! Yeah, she did it. Cause she just stared at me with that ice cold glare she has. Eating her salad. Eyes that told me, 'Yes, I did it, but he had it coming.'

Session IV

15

Sasha

I knew Rock was pissed as hell. Probably borderline furious. But I didn't know what he expected me to do. Shit, I ain't no damn police officer. I can't go around arresting people. I make sure that the crimes punishable by death, are punished by death! The Mayor ought to give me a medal for saving the taxpayers thousands of dollars. No court costs, jail costs, or rehabilitation costs. Like prison helps, most come out worse than when they went in. I do it my way, the Sasha way, and there's one less monster for the world to worry about!

"Rock, I know what you're thinking. But what was I supposed to do? That, that mother fuc— that maniac raped my best friend!"

"Can that shit, Sasha. Just tell me what the fuck is on your mind. First Coleman, which I understand, but please, tell me you haven't been killing like as sort of a hobby or something. Can you tell me that?"

"Rock..."

"Sasha, whatever you do, and I know you won't, well I used to think that you wouldn't, but don't you lie to me!"

"I don't have any reason to lie to you, Rock. What do you want to know?"

"Can you hear!?"

"Yes, I can hear. I was gonna ask if you could lower your voice an octave or would you rather just go on the porch so the neighbors don't have to strain their ears to hear you?"

"Baby girl, now is not the time for your wise ass mouth. There's so much shit in the fan that it's not even turning. You get what I'm saying? Huh?"

"Cool. And my eardrums thank you too!"

"Sasha, you think you're slick as hell. Trying to appeal to my humorous side, as though talking about killing for a hobby is an everyday conversation. My job mandates results. I can't cover for you forever. My career is in jeopardy, my livelihood. I need answers to questions that I don't want to ask. Shit, I really don't want the answers to the questions either. Cause each answer, knowing you, is gonna sink my ass, make that our asses, further and further into a gigantic ass hole. I asked you have you been killing people as sort of a hobby or something. What the hell is going on in your life?"

"Killing as a hobby? I never looked at it that way before. But yes, I guess you could say that."

"David Arnold?"

"Yes. He raped Jeanette. What was I supposed to do? She knew the guy; was intimate to a degree with him. But she still said no, so it's rape. He would have walked and all she would have had to show for it was the embarrassment of a trial."

"And you, the judge and jury, have figured this out all by yourself?"

"Cecil, now look—"

"Reverend Austin Morgan? Melvin Harper?"

"Jesus Christ, Cecil. What the hell you been doing, spying on me? Have you been following me? How did you find out about them?"

"Oh, since I haven't talked to you in a week, I haven't had the opportunity to share the good news with you. I got a promotion. Detective. Head of a special homicide task force. Any idea what my area of specialty is?"

"Clueless!"

"Investigating unusual, sorry, make that highly unusual murders! Now ain't that a kick in the ass!?"

"Unusual?"

"Electrocution in a bathtub!"

"Highly unusual?"

"Hands burned, throat slashed!"

"Murders..."

"Columbia, of all fuckin' places, Maryland!"

"You're yelling again!"

"Sasha! Girl, you know I love you, but you are out of control. You done gone too far. You need help. Major fucking help!"

I didn't know exactly where Rock was going with our little talk. Or where he expected me to get this help. Like who could I talk to about my problem. 'Well, you see Doctor, I can't control my urge to kill people whenever I deem it necessary. Do you think you can help me? Oh and by the by, I would appreciate it if you didn't involve the police. Yeah, right!' He didn't understand what it was like

to have something burning out of control inside of you.
When it surfaces it's not me. It's what's inside of me that
makes me do what I do. There's no way he could understand. Coleman started this shit. I wished he were alive
today, so I could smack the shit out of him and kick him
in the balls for causing all of this pandemonium in my
life.

"Okay, Mr. Self-righteous, Mr. Cover Fucking-up!
What kind of help do you suggest I get?"

"Oh, so now we's a damn critic too, on top of a murderer. Huh? Yeah, I might make some shit easier to smell,
but I did get your ass out of a big fucking jam!"

"Look, Cecil, let's try and calm down and talk sensi-
bly. Okay?"

"Sure, Sasha, but first you got to tell me how in the
hell do you make calm sense out of three, no make that
five dead people? Wait, just five right?"

"DAMMIT, CECIL!! All five deserved to die. And
that's a fact. Yes, and to answer your next question. I
appointed myself the damn **JUDGE AND JURY!!!**
Period! Big Bro,' you just don't understand…"

"Sasha…"

"Just let me talk for a second, okay? Thank you. I got
something inside of me that just burns like a raging—All
out of control, but at the same time in control. You know
how them fires hit in California. Just burning up shit
everywhere. And Action News talking about how the
fires are out of control. How the firemen can't contain
the fires. But you ever sit back and look at that fire? Huh?
Next time you see a fire, look at it real close. Then ask it

if it knows what it's doing. Where it's going. Cecil, you ask that fire if it's out of control, do you know what you're doing? Do you know where you're going? See what answer you get. That fire's gonna tell you, I know what I am doing and I know where I am going. Big Bro, I have something in common with the fire, but I know what I'm doing is wrong. Me and the fire know exactly where we're going and know exactly what we are doing. Consuming!

16

Rock & Sasha

I looked hard at this woman in front of me. That flowing, full black hair, just like moms. That Rock shaped head, and I know this is my flesh and blood, my sweet little sister. But deep inside her soul is a woman that I don't know. I'm afraid to find out who she really is. Afraid to get answers that I have to deal with. Answers that I can't just accept and live with. There's a big problem when you start covering shit up, because sooner or later it's gonna start reeking real bad.

"Sasha, everything has come full circle. My boss and the Mayor have put me in charge of solving these murders. My job is on the line along with my ass. I got to get results. The farthest thing from my mind was finding out that you were the cause of all of this mess. Now you got to promise me you are gonna chill, I mean, deep freeze. Understood?"

"Rock, the only thing I understand is, there is only one person who runs my life and tells me what to do. And that's me, Sasha Timms! You understand?"

"The last thing I would ever want to do is arrest you, but if that is what it will take to stop the killing machine, then that's what I will do. I've got to deal with this the best way I can. But if bodies keep turning up it's gonna be mighty difficult to keep coming up with no results. Now

I mean it, you got to promise me you gonna cease your shit and let me figure something out. Look Sasha, you and I both know that corruption, deceit, some pretty underhanded, sleazy shit goes on in the department, but we can't just keeping shoving shit under the rug. Stuff just doesn't disappear. Sometimes certain things are highlighted for the entire city to see. So every citizen with a TV or a newspaper can ask the big question. What's being done about this? Are we going to be safe? Right now they have Cecil Rock poised for a public hanging. I can't keep coming up craps and expecting everyone to be satisfied that I lost their money for them. Somebody wants to get paid and right now it's the Mayor and my Captain. You following what I'm saying?"

I reached over behind the sofa and picked up Cecil's .38 from the holster. I looked at his gun long and hard. A single second is the difference between life and death. Justice and injustice. Freedom and captivity. War and peace. Right and wrong! I could go on for days! Life and death?

"Big Bro- Man- I got a burning deep within me. I just can't turn it off. It's just always there!"

"So now you holdin' my gun and telling me that if I stand in your way you gonna move me no matter what?"

Seemed to me like I was in a daze. Sitting there holding Cecil's gun. I heard him talking, I just couldn't focus enough on his words for my brain to make sense out of them.

"If somebody doesn't have what it takes to rectify a situation, a horrible situation, I can't sleep knowing.

Knowing that the villain is walking this earth, knowing they done messed over somebody, and acting like their own shit don't even stink. No sir. I'm gonna do something about it, I have to!"

"Flesh and blood. We're all the family we got. And you telling me that you would shoot me if I stood in your way?"

"Rock! Don't be an asshole. I know you always take out your clip when you're home. I was just reflecting on how quickly a bullet can change the course of your life. But you can be assured, you are not gonna stand in my way."

I was starting to tremble. I wish my brother could understand. I longed for a loving, brotherly hug. I hated to cry. I wanted Cecil to know that I was strong; that I could deal with my situation; that I could bear the weight of being the problem solver! I wanted to let him know that I was trying to get myself together. I was going to get myself together. I needed time. I just didn't know how much. But all the emotion inside of me seemed to be coming out. I could no longer control them. I realized that my brother and son are all I have in this world. I just couldn't control the animal.

"Sasha, now ain't the time for them damn tears. Crying sure as hell ain't gonna solve your problems. We have to deal with you."

"Rock- - -c-c-can y-y-you just h-h-huggg me- - -p-p-please?"

"Come on."

"Thank you. Rock, I got this thing in me. This hate. It's like, uh, you know since Coleman did what he did, it's like the fire's been on. This rage... this deep imbedded hate of men!"

Finally! Self realization. Self actualization. The junkie has to say to himself, 'My name is John, and I am a junkie.' And that drunkard has to say, 'Hi, my name is Robert, and I am an alcoholic.' And my sister has to say, 'My name is Sasha. And I hate any man who screws over a woman!' Now that she knows where the cancer is coming from, maybe she can aim the radiation in the right place.

"Sasha.. you've got to promise me you are going to chill out. Maybe you can take some time off of work. It's not like you're hurting for cash. If nobody is bringing you problems, there won't be anything for you to fix. Sasha, you have to realize that this shit has got to stop. I want you to listen, if you can't... if you won't stop killing...then I will lock your ass up. Do you understand!?"

"Rock, all I can do is promise that I will try. I can close the office for a few weeks. But what are you going to do? You got some kind of plan figured out?"

"Plan! Saving your ass again or lockin— Look as far as solving this here, I ain't got the slightest fuc— I don't have a clue. If I can work toward a solution if there are no more corpses slapping me in the face every time one of your patients complains about her man, then maybe I can get an answer."

Talk about a sarcastic SOB. Women are always the victims. First, the man does whatever he wants, then the system says whatever it wants. And it never fails that the woman is made to look and feel like she had it coming. Sasha ain't having it! I got my stuff and headed for the door. I was ready for my king sized bed. Didn't have nobody to keep me warm, but nothing beats home.

"Cecil, I promise that I will do my best. That's the best I can do!"

"Thanks, Sasha. I just need time to work something out. Just give me more time and less—as in no dead-bodies. You go home and hibernate! Yeah, go home and get some rest. Go on vacation. Do something besides work. Question? How in the fuck did you plan on getting away with this madness?"

I turned and looked my brother straight in the eye and answered his question the best way I knew how, my way! His mouth dropped open when he heard my answer. ***"Ask the fire!!!"*** I love Rock. I am afraid of what would happen if he stood in my way. I wonder if his gun was loaded, and he threatened me would I have used it. Could I kill my own brother? Is the hate and the rage so deep that I would spill my own blood? I don't want to know the answer and I hope I won't ever have to find out.

17

Sasha

I figured a trip to center city, Philly style, would give me a chance to think about my future. I really love coming to the city in the middle of the day for two reasons. One, the majority of the people are shuffling to and from work, so everybody pretty much is minding their own business. Second, what you see is enough to make you remember that your troubles might not be as bad as you think.

The homeless have a home, Broad Street! Picking in trash cans, begging for change. The modern vagabond is amazing. Standing in the middle of the street, face so black with dirt that you can't tell if he's black or white. Hair all greasy and full of bugs. Doesn't matter what the temperature is, trench coat and boots! Holey blue jeans, always too big. A dress shirt and a T-shirt. Fingerless gloves... And the sign. **"HOMELESS! WILL WORK FOR FOOD!"** My heart goes out to anybody who is having a hard time making it in this jungle.

"Hey, big fella! You want beef or turkey?"

"Lawd done sent me an angel! Pastrami with Swiss, beautiful!"

"Be right back!"

Sure, it's easy to bring a hungry somebody some food. But it sure is nice once in a while to pick what you want off the menu. Big fella thanked me and I was on my way! Two teenage boys arm in arm, one black, one white. 'Come on honey, let's go get some ice cream.' Happy as hell and not a care in the world. Just seemed a little too young to have already figured out that they were gay.

Long straight hair, down to her butt. Black sheer cape. Black shirt. Black leggings. Black knee-high boots. Black laces, of course. Black lipstick, black eyeliner, and black mascara. Earrings in eyebrows, nose, lip, bellybutton, and ears, at least ten in each ear, including that little tiny piece of ear that sticks out from the side of your face, ouch! Here I am thinking I am treading the revolutionary treadmill by getting two earrings in each ear. I felt like a dinosaur! I wondered where that hot little mamma was off to. I wondered what her mother said when she left the house. I started to follow her but figured I might end up at a Rocky Horror Picture Show or something. Wondered what her boss thinks? Plus, I didn't want to miss anymore real live Philly people sightings.

Couples everywhere. Black and black. Black and white. White and Chinese. Big and small. Fat and skinny. Old and young. Old, and a little too damn young. Men and men. Women and women. I could go on for days. Nobody cares. Everybody's just out doing their own thing. Funny though. They all seemed to have something that I longed for. Love. Philly people don't care who is watching them. Don't even care what they look like. As long as they are with the one they love they are happy. Great place to visit.

Empty trash cans. All the trash is in the street and on

the sidewalk. Taxis driving like, taxis. Septa buses, too big and too noisy to be in center city. Hot dog stands on almost every corner. Soft pretzels, water ice, cheese steaks, cheese fries, greasy, greasy goowy thin sliced pizza, Italian style. Good stuff. It'll kill ya, but you can get your grub on, big time. Street vendors selling authentic, imitation merchandise at cheap prices. I could hardly pass up the deal the gentleman was offering me on a beautiful gold chain. I guess, because in place of the lobster clamp was a safety pin; he probably was planning on snatching it back as soon as I turned around.

All the suits. Big Wigs. Important folk. In a rush. Places to go, people to see. Big time and big money. I saw a group of high-profile executives having a power lunch. They all spent $2.95 on a hot sausage, chips and soda from Manny who's been on the same corner for the last fifteen years. How could anybody love all of this? Philadelphia? How could you not?

I saw this woman. Very beautiful. Hum, sharp outfit. Casual but classy. Matching shoes and bag. The do was kickin' girlfriend! Sharp. I looked harder. I didn't mean to be rude, but I was staring. There seemed to be pain in her face. Like she was hurting. Like something was missing in her life. Her eyes, lonely, hollow. Except for the tears that were welling in them. Her soul seemed empty. Sad. She took a step back the same time that I did. Jesus, people put mirrors anywhere these days.

I walked from City Hall to the Art Museum. Rock was kind of upset with me. That's understandable though. He just didn't realize what I was going through. I can't explain what I feel. If you don't feel what I feel then you could never understand why I do what I do. Empathy! A man should be just that, a man. Not some low-down, miserable, piss-poor, wife-beating, woman-raping, sister-killing, alcohol-abusing, drug-using, worthless, poor excuse to even have the title of, a man. A man should be just that, a man. Take care of his family and do right by them. Love his woman. Especially the black woman. We've been catching hell since we got here. If nothing else, we deserved to be loved just for what we have been through. Hell, what we are going through even today. Raising our children most of the time without the benefit of a father or a decent father figure. Sexually harassed on almost every job we do. From Kizzy to Anita, men have been doing us wrong. I am not taking it anymore. If and when I do decide to stop, it won't be because a man, not even my own brother, told me to!

I ran to the top of the Art Museum steps and pumped my fists in the air. Just like Rocky. Great scene. Great movie. Got more than a few stares and giggles. The Art Museum is never deserted, except when it's closed. I felt liberated and free to do as I pleased. I didn't necessarily want to kill. I like to kill, but that doesn't mean I want to. If those that do wrong don't cross my path it would make fighting this animal inside of me a lot easier.

I had made my way back down the steps of the museum. I couldn't let the Jack and Jill man get by without getting a strawberry shortcake. I sat right on the edge of the big fountain and let the breeze blow sprinkles of water into my hair and face. No better way to cool off and stay dressed at the same time. Yes, I was thinking, I might be able to control myself with a little time off from work.

Off to my left a teenage mother with two kids was arguing with the daddy.

"Raheeeeeeeem! You ain't right and you know it. You promised me you was gonna give me some money today!"

"Look Shante,' I told you once, soon as I handles my bi-ness, I would give you some ends. That's the end of it, okay!?"

"Okay my ass. The kids are hungry. I am, too. What are we supposed to do till you handle yo' business Mister Bigshot?"

"I really don't give a damn what you do, just stay the hell out of my face till tomorrow. I should have some extra cash then. Besides, one of them bastards ain't mine anyway. Shit, if Chandra wasn't so black and so fine, like me, I wouldn't think she was mine either!"

"Raheem, you can kiss my black ass. I know your partner, Skippy is home. Bet if I give him a little piece, he'll give me some money so me and yo' kids can eat!"

POW!!! Big bad Raheem slapped the shit out of Shante,' "Don't you ever dis' me, especially in front of nobody." Then he turned and jumped on his BMX and pedaled off, to handle his bi-ness! They didn't look much older than sixteen. I took over some hot dogs and soda. Gave Shante' fifty dollars, some professional advice about not begging or being involved with a sorry ass Niggah, and headed home. If brothers this young are mistreating their women...

"Jeanette! Hey girl, it's me. I just wanted to let you know that I made it home in one piece."

"Damn Sasha, what time did you get in? You should have called me hours ago. I was kinda worried about you."

"Oh, sorry about that. I stopped by my brother's house first. You know he worries about me worse than momma ever did. We had a nice long talk. Caught up on a few things. Nothing heavy. How you feeling Grandma, you okay? How's my man?"

"There you go again with your rapid fire questions. Can I answer one before you ask the next twenty? Or should I just mail in my responses?"

"Keep getting smart, see if somebody don't burn your weave off your head!"

"Demmy is fine. I could tell he was a little depressed after you left. When he doesn't see your face his appetite leaves for a while right along with you. Otherwise he's fine. Don't worry, he'll be back to normal by tomorrow. Guess what?"

"I give up."

"Well, you know David? The guy that, uhm, raped me, well, well, they found his body behind a Dumpster at the club yesterday. Bound and gagged dead. Now ain't that a kick in the tits!?"

"Sure is. Let me ask you a question on the serious though J. How does that make you feel knowing that the man who violated you is dead? Knowing that he will never again in his life harm another woman. Huh? How do you really feel?"

"Sash, it's kinda hard to feel anything. You know

what I mean? I mean, on the one hand I wanted nothing more on this earth than to see that ass suffer, bleed and die! On the other hand though, well, it's like..."

"Damn, Jeanette, you getting soft on me or what? How could you feel anything for this man after what he did to you? Huh? How could you feel anything? I just don't understand what the hell you feel for him. Can you explain that?"

"Hey sis,' you seem to be taking his death and my feelings kind of hard!"

"Jeanette you know, and God is my witness, that you are the best friend that I ever had. When that man raped you he raped me, too. All the hurt and pain and anguish that you felt, make that feel to this very day, is a part of me. I hurt right along with you. Can I get an amen?"

"Yes, I love you too, Sasha! It's just that despite everything that went down, David... well, Dav... well, he was still a human being. I just can't imagine somebody killing him like that."

"Like what?"

"Well, from what the police are saying, his leg and nose were broken and he was taped up like a mummy. They say he suffocated. When you die like that, you die fighting to live."

"And just think girlfriend, you're still living and suffering with your nightmare every day! How 'bout that?"

"Sasha? Let me ask you a question. What do you feel about David's death?"

"I feel like, he got what he deserved. Sure, his death may be a tragedy to his family, if he had any that loved him, but I can't say that he didn't have it coming. I just hope that you aren't upset with me because I don't feel how you feel. But one thing I can say, when I first came to you, I could feel devastation. David didn't know anything about that. All he knew was that he had you, and life as he knew it was going to continue on like nothing ever happened. David was a life without a soul. He didn't have a care for his victims, so why should I have a care for him?"

"You know, Sasha, everything you said is absolutely right, but do you have to be so damn cold!?"

"North Pole, sweetheart. Look, I will talk to you next week. Okay? Love you! Kiss my man for me."

"Love you back! Hussy! Bye!"

"Bye!"

Jeanette has a big heart. That's all I can say. For as much as I had a need to talk to her about my little problem, I knew that I couldn't because it would just crush her. She's the type of woman who would stay in an abusive relationship for the sake of the kids. I just couldn't understand how she could have any feelings left for that man. But what better woman is there on this earth than one with a pure heart? Forgiving. Understanding. Just won't hold onto a grudge for more than five minutes and she refuses to hate. Maybe that's why I killed David and she didn't. It's not in her blood. Killing...that is!

18

Rock

Sasha had really messed my head up. I was pacing and talking to myself. Ask the fire? Humpf! Now ain't that some shit. Who the hell do Sasha think she is? Like she in the mob or some shit. Or hell, maybe she think she Dirty Harry, no Harriette or some shit. Just, bang, bang, go around killing folks and don't give no damn about it neither. Woman makes my head hurt and my English go bad. Damn! Does she think she's living in her own world making her own rules? It's like every time I read the newspaper and see a crime, especially murder, I think my baby sis did it. My dreams... are like...Sashamares....

...Hey Rock! Look! I killed somebody else! Whatcha gonna do? Huh? I tell you what... Here! Here's another body for you. And look this one's got no head! Ha! Ha! HAAAAAAA!! You gonna turn me in? Huh? Are ya!? Do you love me, Big Brother? Do ya? Do ya? Do ya. Rockooooooooo? Do...You... Love.....Me....? Huh? Do Yaaaaaaaaa...

My dreams were all nightmares. She was just haunting and taunting me. What was I to do? I had a long day. If I could just doze back off to sleep and not dream. Maybe tomorrow will be a better day! If I only had a jumpshot. I went to sleep thinking—

19

Sasha

"Sasha?"

"Yes, Evelyn."

"Please come in here and explain to me why you are causing your brother to have nightmares."

"Nightmares? Cecil's full of shit and he knows it."

"You know, you are two very different kind of people."

"You're in tune to one another in a way that's pretty special. And your brother is hilarious."

"Corny!"

"That's beside the point. So tell me what your plans were. Did you take that vacation like your brother suggested?"

"Yea, I went to visit the Nation's Capital!"

Oh well, another day at the office or another day on vacation. That was the dilemma in my life. Sure, I want my brother to be happy. And I was certainly not trying to make his life difficult. Well, not any more difficult than he could handle. But, Rock is a strong brother. He'll be fine. My problems were far deeper than his. If he only knew. If he could only understand. I decided to go spend a few weeks on some island. Alone. I was trying to contact Wonder Woman. Figured I could hang out on some Amazon island and not have to even worry about seeing a man screw over a woman. However, that's just like treating a brain tumor with aspirin. Sure, the headache might go away for a little while, but the problem is still going to be there until it's dealt with. I was minding my own business, just finished tying up some loose ends at the office, on my way to the travel agent and what did I see? Sasha was backed into a corner once again.

I saw this woman on the corner. Damn! Skinny as a pipe cleaner. She was picking out of a trash can. Then she turned around and ran up to some guy, flashed her titties, begging for money. She was dirty as hell. Damn, it was sad. She happened to notice me looking at her. Through her dirt and grime and life of hard living she recognized me!

"Sasha Rock! Damn, girl, you sure did grow up pretty!"

"Do I know you Miss?"

"You always was stuck up, too. I don't know why I ever picked you for a friend in the first place. Miss Lucky Charms!"

There was only one person on this entire earth that called me Miss Lucky Charms. That was Vanessa Brown. But, Vanessa weighed about 175 pounds in high school. Graduation was the last I ever saw of her. She went North to college and I went South. We kept in touch for a few years but never managed to get back together. She was one of my best friends though. She called me Miss Lucky Charms because she said I had the best charms in all the right places. That's why the boys were always after me. What the hell happened?

"Vanessa?"

"Yup, it's me. How you been?"

I wasn't in the mood for food anymore, so Vanessa and I walked the length of the strip mall. Did a little bit of window shopping, some reminiscing. I did a whole lot of listening. She told me a very sad story.

"Me? Oh, I'm doing. What happened to you? I mean I hate to be so frank, but, my God, I mean you are sick skinny, not diet skinny. What happened to all of that baby fat?"

"You remember that fine ass brother we used to call, Buck Wild?"

"How could I forget Nathan? He chased after the both of us all four years of high school. He was always trying to rope one of us. What about him?"

I was in the process of, at least making an effort to chill out for a while, but she tore my heart wide open.

"Nathan and I hooked up after college. Matter of fact, he was still chasing me all through college. Can you believe he followed me all the way to Buffalo, New York? I finally gave in. He seemed to have gotten his head together; seemed like he had good intentions for me. I could have never been so wrong. We never actually married, just lived together. Nathan had a good job at first. Before I know it, we out partying all night and day, every day. He got me hooked on drugs. Look at these tracks! Beat the shit out of me if I wouldn't fuck his friends for money. He sold everything, including me for drugs. Now he's this big-time pimp in D.C. He kept me on the streets, sometimes fifteen hours a day. I was so hooked on that shit, I just had to go back to him every night. He took my money and I got high. You ever seen any of them folks downtown giving away free needles to junkies to help stop the spread of AIDS? If I was in any frame of mind to use any of my God-given common sense, I would have listened. Instead, I cursed it back to wherever it came from. Now I got AIDS, and I am dying. My last night of tricking I took my two hundred-and-fifty dollars, got on a bus and came home. Not that I had a home to come to. My Mamma don't want me. You know she's big time in the school system now. Having a junkie-hooker daughter around would only ruin her status in her make-believe important society. I just mill around the city. Suck a few dicks or fuck when I can find somebody desperate enough to even want to lay with my dirty ass, and I wait for this disease to finish eating me up. Miss Lucky Charms, I bet I can fit all your fancy ass clothes now!"

Wow. I might be borderline psycho, but that's nothing compared to what Vanessa had been dealing with for the last however many years. How can a man say he loves his woman, get her hooked on drugs, prostitute her, beat her, dehumanize her, and then still say that he loves her? Nathan 'Buck Wild' Simmons was a piece of shit. He didn't even know the animal and he had already pissed it off. So I asked myself, what should I do? You know the answer!

"Vanessa, I know you're dying. But honey, you are going to leave this world with your dignity intact. I am going to put you in a place where the people will take good care of you. When you leave this earth you won't leave hungry and you won't be doing something that I know you don't want to be doing, like blow jobs. Would you like that?"

"Sasha, you always been the sweetest girl I know. Thank you."

"When I was watching you, I could tell that you weren't really crazy. Why you out here talking to yourself and carrying on so?"

"If I act like I got some sense then nobody gonna feel sorry for me and give me anything. My next meal is coming from God only knows where. I'm just seen as a crazy, skinny-ass junkie who is definitely malnourished. A pathetic sight."

"Tell me one thing? Where can I find Buck Wild?"

After the doctor examined and tested Vanessa he said she probably had two to four months to live. With the proper diet and medication, she might live six. But she would die in good hands. I paid for seven months in advance. Big Sis wasn't gonna die like no trash in the streets. I couldn't say the same for Buck Wild.

I couldn't be concerned about my brother. He had a job to do and so did I. I took the Amtrak to Union Station in Washington, D.C. Vanessa had given me Nathan's address. She said he didn't have any bodyguards hanging around him. He really didn't need any. He was the biggest lineman on the football team in high school. Vanessa also said he had built the reputation of being the best Player to work for in the District. Sometimes women would knock on his door begging for a job because their last pimp dogged them.

I stood across the street in the dark. Waiting and watching for Nathan to come home. Around three in the morning a black Jaguar pulled in front of his house. Nathan, big black angry-looking brother, got out of the car alone and strolled into the house. Within ten minutes at least five women, hookers, came and left almost immediately. They must have been dropping off their money. Didn't look like they was done hookin' for the night either. I guess he made them make a drop, get a fix and hit the streets 'till the sun came up. What an enterprising brother Nathan turned out to be.

Maybe one more day and then I would take care of business. I could go and sightsee and then pay him a visit early the next morning. Nope. He had lived long enough.

I knocked on his door around 7 o'clock. I knew he would be groggy and not have all of his senses. Khaki shirt and pants gave the early riser the impression that some form of utility person was at their door.

"Meter reading, sir. Good morning. Just have to read the meter. Be out of here in no time."

"Huh? Oh, sure, come on in."

Nathan was still a big boy. He stretched his arms overhead and let out a hearty yawn. He looked as though he had just had the best night's sleep of his life.

By the time he said 'come on in' I had already brushed past him and was searching for the basement door.

"Basement?"

"First door on your left."

I descended the stairs quickly, pulling out my favorite toy when I reached the bottom. I called out to the low life.

"Excuse me, sir. Can you show me where the light switch is?"

Bang! Bang! You're dead. I just shot Nathan in the head twice as soon as he reached the bottom step. Silencer! No noise. One less pimp for the world to worry about! I had noticed this great little eatery at Union Station on my way in. I decided to stop and get some breakfast.

I went to see how Demetrius and Jeanette were doing before going back home. Hopped on a train from Union Station to Baltimore. Jeanette and Demetrius came and picked me up from the BWI Amtrak station. She was surprised that I was back in town so quickly. I told her that I just wasn't ready to go back to work. I wanted to spend a little more time with her and Demmy. Hell, I had money, and I didn't have to punch any clock except my own. Jeanette put on some Luther and I leaned back. Her comfy leather seats were perfect. I cradled my baby in my arms and drifted off to sleep.

If I didn't have Demetrius I didn't know what I would do. He was the center of my joy. He completed the circle in my life. You can take away a husband, a lover, even a friend, but there is no tie that bonds like your own flesh. Demmy's my man. I love him. I hoped he realized that. One day, I believe he will let me all the way inside of his world. I bet it's a fascinating place.

I must have been exhausted, because it was near twelve when I popped up. Sitting up all night waiting to kill a pimp will drain you. Demetrius was playing with his Genesis. If he isn't like that 'Fat-head' uncle of his, then I don't know who is. I showered and grabbed an apple. No sooner than Jeanette heard me milling around upstairs, she shouted,

"Hey, Girlfriend, I'm out for the day, see you and Demmy tonight!"

"Huh! Jean..."

The door slammed and she was gone. She thought her ass was slick. She knew that if she was here I would-n't spend time with Demmy like I should. Maybe guilt keeps pushing me away. But there's no doubting the importance that he has in my life. I decided that we'd head out to the mall.

I hate to admit it but I was kind of hoping that I would run into Mr. Belefont. I didn't need to be sweatin' no man, but he had definitely piqued my interest. Handsome man. I needed to be held; to be loved. I was-n't quite sure if I was ready for loving another man at that point, but my soul was empty. He was the perfect gentle-man. I could go on for days, wishing for a man like Earlston. What kind of name is Earlston anyway?

Before we got two good steps into the mall Demetrius made a mad dash for Brookstone. I had to break out in a fast jog just to keep up with him. He was jumping from gadget to gadget.

"Come on! Let's play!"

"Slow down, boy, you movin' too fast!"

"Let's play ping!"

"Ping pong."

"Ping pong!" he chirped in. He can learn.

"Allright, but I'm gonna win!"

"Betcha don't!"

"We'll see— "

We got to yelling and screaming and laughing so much that the manager finally had enough of us and kicked us out. Demetrius ran around the corner to the Disney Store. I couldn't understand why the manager of that store was upset with us. I was sure Demmy wasn't the first child to dive headfirst into the pile of stuffed animals that they had in the back of the store. And just because he played tumbling dominoes with a whole row of video tapes was no reason to threaten to call security. I tried to explain as best I could to my son that some people aren't as patient as others.

So my son was a little on the hyper side of things, especially when the mall and toys were involved. He's all mine, though, and I love him. After getting kicked out of all of the children stores in the mall, I convinced him that the food court would probably be our best option. Pizza always soothed the savage beast, and any twelve year old who had spent the last two hours getting on the last nerve of every manager of every children's store in the mall. He agreed.

"Lotta cheese."

"You mean extra cheese?"

"Uh-huh, lotta cheese."

"Yes." I couldn't help but correct him. Deep inside of my handsome, mentally challenged son there is a normal little boy who has the capacity to listen, to learn. I think I can reach him sometimes. The things he says. Sometimes I believe I can touch that little boy.

"Yes, mamma!"

He started chomping down that pizza like it was the last meal he would ever have. Too many calories for me. I had to stay looking my best. Plus, I actually liked chef's salads.

The voice that was talking over my shoulder could only bring a smile to my face. I had to remain cool though and in charge, by doing things *My Way!*

"Hello, Mizz Sasha Sunshine. The radiance of your beauty is a glow that I instantaneously recognized. Unconsciously I was drawn to this table where you now graciously eat a meal, in the company of..."

"Demetrius. Timms. My son. How are you, Earlston?"

Lord have mercy, if that man didn't have a smooth command of the language. Just a soft, smooth brother. The average brother would have promised me anything my heart desired: clothes, jewelry, and all the loving— their ultimate goal—my little heart could take. Not Earlston. Just chillin'. Telling it like it is. Observing and letting me know what he thought about me. It's one thing to be self assured and self confident, but he verified it for me, free of charge. It felt good.

"Hello Demetrius, nice to meet you."

"Hi."

"Sasha— it's very good to see you."

"I must admit, I hoped I would see you today, too, Earlston.

"Is that so?"

"Don't get excited. Why don't you join us?"

"Are you sure?"

"Yes, I'm sure. Instead of standing there with your hands in your pockets and that silly grin on your face, why don't you sit and join us for lunch?"

"To say that your presence alone makes what would have been an empty day full, wouldn't be too flattering. Would it?"

"No— Not at all. What you said was—"

I hated this— Blushing. I didn't want him to think that he was getting to me, but he was. Belefont was smooth. His light was shining pretty bright. "Thank you for the compliment. And I have to admit, you carry it well yourself, brother. You got it going on!"

I said to myself, 'Jesus Christ, Sasha, you need to shove a big piece of turkey in your mouth so you can shut up.' Earlston just let my words roll down his sleeve like he didn't hear. He mumbled something about thanks and was immediately focused on fighting Demmy for the last piece of pizza. Demmy enjoyed every minute of it. Aside from his uncle, he really didn't have any men in his life who wanted to spend time with him.

I sat there looking at Demetrius and Earlston, pushing and pulling at each other; laughing and giggling. This man barely knew us. In fact he didn't know me at all. But he showered me with the kindest words I have ever heard. He played with my son as though they had been friends for years.

God makes beautiful men, too. I saw it with my own eyes. I couldn't let him get too close though. I was not ready. The way this animal reacted inside of me... There's just no way I could get close to him. Not right now anyway.

"Demetrius, are you just about finished playing with your pizza?"

"Yup."

"Yes!"

"Yes, mamma."

"Good, because we have to go. Aunt Jeanette is expecting us. And I'm sure Mr. Belefont has more important things to do."

"Believe me, Sasha, there's no place I'd rather be than here."

"Well, that's sweet, but we still have to go."

"When can I see you again?"

"Soon. You always seem to seek me out when I come to the mall."

"To be honest, I own the men's clothing store, Well Dressed Male, right over there."

"I see everything-coming and everything-going."

"You slick little devil. I'll see you soon!"

I couldn't hide the big smile on my face. Neither could Earlston. At least I didn't trip over my heels this time when I walked out.

I couldn't explain the way I was feeling. Kind of giddy inside, butterflies jumping all around in my belly, hands sweaty. Felt like somebody had a needle in my knees and every time I got my balance they twisted it around a little, just to make me buckle. Why I kept checking in the mirror to see how my hair looked, I don't know because my hair was sharp. It stayed sharp. Always! It was almost as if I was insecure all of a sudden. Making sure that I was looking my best, as though I was trying to impress someone. Shit, sounded to me like I was falling...hell no...naw. Ain't no way. Well maybe just a little. He's young enough to be my little brother, but handsome. I hadn't felt this way in years. Long time. Matter of fact, not since the first time I met Coleman. Earlston Belefont. I could go on for days. Maybe he could help me get this animal under control. Maybe he was just sucking up to get next to me. No way. Perfect Gentleman. A date? I'll think about it. It was time to get my hips back to Philadelphia.

20

Rock

I never really appreciated the cellular phone that Sasha gave me for my birthday. Shit, she sure as hell didn't pay the bill. But, I needed to put my man on this, quick. And I didn't want anybody listening. Carlous always hung out in the basement of the department, doing God only knows what. I called him on my way to the station.

"Carlous! Como esta! Yeah, it's Rock."

"Que' pasa!'

"Dump the trash in Captain's office. Captain and I gotta talk, heavy. Comprende!"

"No problemo. And fuck you and your Espanol. Just cause my mamma call me Carlous don't mean I'm Spanish. Been telling you that shit for years. Punk!"

"My Nigguh! Thanks. Give me a buzz later!"

"Peace!"

Carlous and I grew up together. He was the janitor at the police station. His niche was bugs. Not the kind that crawled around in corners, but the kind that you stuck inside telephones or underneath table tops. I figured now was as good a time to test his skills. Thought I might need them soon. Brother swore he was the master of covert operations. I waited until he left the Captain's office before I went in. On his way out he rubbed the side of his nose like Redford did in 'The Sting.' Never making eye contact. He cracked me the hell up.

"Uhh, uhhum! 'Scuse me. Captain, sir, uh we need to talk. Can I…"

"Rock, stop all that damn stuttering and get your ass in here!"

"Yes, sir!"

"You know why I put you in charge of this task force? Don't you Rock?"

"Ye,s sir. Results?"

"That's right, results, smart ass. Do you understand what your job is here? My ass is about to get chewed. I sure hope you realize that. The Mayor expects results. I tell the Mayor, 'Don't worry, sir, I have one of my best men on the case. He will get us results in no time.' But do I have anything to tell our Mayor?"

"Well, why would you go and do a fool ass thing like that, sir?'

"Because Detective, the Mayor wants some closure. Period. He doesn't care who, why, and how. Just bring the perps to justice. That keeps the media happy and it avails the citizens of our great city the opportunity to go to bed knowing there is one less maniac on the street for them to worry about. Every day Rozen is screaming in my ear that he's reading the morning newspaper and can't find anything about any murders being solved by the city's 'two-legged' task force."

"I know, but—"

"Now I ain't up for no excuses. What do you have for me?"

"Uh— results, maybe."

"What do you mean maybe?"

"Well, I'll be glad to explain, if you give me a chance, sir."

"If you persist with your wise-cracking comments, you are going to be an eye witness to pissed off! Is that understood, detective?"

"Yes, sir!"

"Now you came busting in my office, what the hell do you want?"

I got up to close the door. What the Captain and I had to talk about needed to stay in that room. My eyes hurt. My heart hurt. Matter of fact, I think my balls were aching, too! Everything that was good and decent and right in my life had dissipated, and been replaced with corruption, deceit and dishonesty. Everything that was not good. I joined the police academy in the first place because I had a desire to do good. To protect and serve, to bring a little sunshine to a city that had some very dark days. Crime and Philadelphia go together just like the Philly and the Cheesesteak. I just wanted to make a difference, not to be some hotshot, or superhero, just an ordinary Cat going out and doing his job to the best of his ability.

I had to ask myself, should I trust Captain Arnetti? Could I? After all, he raised me in the police force. Protected me. Showed me how to be a good cop. So what was the alternative? Turn my back on my sister? The only family we have is each other. But Jesus Christ, 'Ask the fire!' and those damn nightmares. Sis had lost it and I didn't know how to stop her. One thing I knew though, she was on a collision course with destruction. She couldn't continue to do the things that she was doing and expect to live. She would make a mistake. It was bound to happen someday. That big black wife beating Niggah that she is trying to stab is gonna get hold of her and choke the life out of her. She couldn't keep committing the 'perfect' murders and getting away with it. One song kept ringing in my head though. 'The ass you save will be your own.' Yours and your sister's! But I needed help with this. There weren't too many people I trusted, but the Captain had been there for me. I hoped he wouldn't let me down.

Honesty? Integrity? Forthrightness? There was a time in my life when I can say I possessed such fine qualities. I was an outstanding and respected member of the police community. While I might still be viewed as such, my soul knew otherwise. Something had to be done. I held onto that doorknob that was connected to the door, that was connected to the wall, that was connected to three more walls, a ceiling and a floor, three pictures, ugly plant in the corner, five softball trophies, desk, three chairs—one comfortable, behind the desk, where else—pencils, paper, paper clips, stapler, files, more files, file cabinet, junk: that made up Captain Arnetti's office. I felt like I was about to jump off of a bridge. I held that doorknob real tight. I knew when I let go that things were going to be different. I knew that when I let go that I would be commencing a new chapter in my police career. My life. I held on tight to the brass, not wanting to let go. But I knew that I had to, for my own peace. I had to let go for what was right. I had to let go for my sister! As each finger peeled away, it seemed as though some type of force was propelling my hand. Forcing me to let go of my past. Telling me to start over; start being a good police officer again.

I stared into Captain Arnetti's eyes. For the first time I noticed that his left eye was green and his right was green with brown edges. And I never noticed that little black mole between his eyes; the wrinkles that crease the edges of his eyes and mouth; how tight his jaw was. He was sitting erect in his Captain's chair ready to bark out the next orders. Yeah, I took a good long look at my Captain. Our lives were about to change. He knew it and I knew it. It was time to let Arnetti know exactly what was on my mind.

"Captain, like I said before you started yelling, we have to talk."

"Damn, Rock, for once in your life you look serious. I almost like it. What's up?"

"Well, sir, about these two murders you put me on, you see..."

Captain got all excited and I hadn't even gotten two sentences out of my mouth. He jumped out of his seat, and jumped to conclusions at the same time, grinning like somebody who just won a car on the *Price is Right*.

"Tell me you solved them. You Son of a Bitch! I knew there was a damn good fool ass reason why I put you on this project. That's right, me. Shit, I'll be the next commissioner for sure. And don't worry, Rock. Where I go, you go. I'm taking you to the top right along with me, I—

"

"Captain! Captain! Jesus Christ, sir. Would you please allow me to at least finish what I have to say? Sir!"

"What? You didn't solve them? Huh? I don't have time for any of your bullshit, Rock."

"Sir! Like I was saying. About these two murders. Do you know what a paradox is, sir?"

"Yeah, like you got two fucked-up situations to handle and you can't handle either one without making the other worse."

"Well, Webster's would say that it is something along the lines of a seemingly contradictory statement that may nonetheless be true! Sir, right now I am facing a paradox! And a very fucked-up one."

"How so, Rock?"

"Right at this moment, I can't go into full detail. Bear with me, please?"

"Fine, Rock. I'll play along— for now."

"Okay, sir. Suppose that your ace detective has a damn good idea about who committed these murders, but he doesn't know what to do about bringing the murderer to justice."

"Detective Rock? Are you an officer of the law?"

"Yes, sir!"

"Then maybe you could explain to me why you would have a problem arresting a person who appears to be a ruthless killer."

"Like I said, sir, I can't go into full detail right at this minute."

"Enough of your bullshit, Rock. Who the fuck are you

protecting? I told you before, the Mayor has been on my ass ever since I put you in charge of this Task Force. Exactly when do you plan on delivering? Do you know who the murderer is?"

"Look, Captain, I'm doing my best. This thing is starting to get messy. I came to you thinking you would understand."

"Rock, I understand how you feel. After all the tragedy that has surrounded your life."

"Sir?!"

"Your parents were murdered in cold blood. You find two dead bodies in your sister's house. You might be feeling a little vulnerable right now. Maybe you aren't the man for this project like I thought you would be. Personally I thought you were a lot stronger, had some balls. Sometimes we have to make tough choices in our job. Sometimes people get hurt. Some suffer. Some die. It's part of the job. You know it as well as I do."

So the bastard wanted to get personal. Why did he have to bring my family into this? Even if Sasha was the cause of all of my anxiety, he shouldn't have brought it up before I did. Bastard!

"Captain? Remember how all you could think about was getting your brother, Joey, some help—"

Damn, the way the Captain moved so quickly from behind his desk, I thought maybe he wanted to box or something. I thought I was gonna have to kick his old Italian ass. He was a big boy though, I might have needed my gun. I didn't know why he was all excited. He knew his brother was a lush. Besides, he started the family shit.

"Hey, what the fuck does Joey have to do with all of this? I'll tell you what. Nothing! He's been in detox, he's gotten himself together. And I know for a fact that he isn't running around killing anybody. Don't bring my family into this conversation. Tell me, who are you trying to protect?"

Between the Sashamares and all of the Captain's yelling and screaming, I felt like my head was going to bust.

"Captain, all I want is to get some help for this person. She doesn't deserve to be locked away with a bunch of criminals."

"She? You're protecting a woman. Why did you get so sensitive when I brought up your family? And why did you bring up my brot— Kiss my white ass! I knew you were hiding something back then. I just didn't know what. I didn't want to know either. Let me guess. Sasha walks in on the two lovers, freaks, and blows their brains out. Something like that.

"I plead the fifth."

Captain's eyes had become bright blue.

"So, tell me, Cecil, what does Sasha murdering her husband and Kyle have to do with the other two murders?"

"Captain, right now, I have no comment. I gotta go, Sir!"

He just stood there. Staring at me. Didn't mutter a word when I turned and reached for that doorknob. I guessed the Mayor really had been coming down on his ass. Everybody wants answers; problems solved, murderers brought to justice. But Sasha's my flesh and blood. I just didn't think she needed to be growing old in a jail cell. Naw, to hell with that. But the killing machine definitely needed to be put out of business. How to put her out of business was the real problem, though.

"Look, Captain. Man, I'll keep you posted. Okay?"

"You do that, Rock. You do that."

I always admired the Captain. My Captain. That day though, I didn't know. He just seemed a little edgy. Irritated. I don't know. I decided to go home early. Try to figure something out. Bust a grub. Get me a fat cheesesteak from Larry's and call it a day. To hell with a diet.

As I was leaving the precinct, Philly's most distinguished leader was heading my way. Tall, athletically built Irishman, hairline was gradually making its way to the back of his neck; as usual, Armani suit. Gator's keeping his dogs warm. Confident gait. Important, at least he thought so. In charge? Definitely. Two 'yes' men escorted him. Oh; maybe they're called bodyguards, and of course, his personal assistant Linda, fine. Blonde hair, blue eyes. She wanted me. I'm sure his wife wasn't around when he hired her. He didn't look really happy that day either. Harried. In a rush. The last person I wanted to run into.

"Mayor O'Grady. I haven't seen you in West Philadelphia since the election."

"Detective. How are you today?"

"Trying to make it, sir. Trying to make it."

"Captain Arnetti tells me you are a fine officer of the law. A brilliant young detective are the words I believe he used. Is that right?"

"Well, sir, modesty—"

"Then why haven't you solved any of these murders yet!"

Son of a bitch. Not only did he dis' me in front of his crew of ass-kissers, but he turned and stormed into the precinct before I could rattle off a good lie. Just left me standing there with my mouth open. Yup, that's our Mayor. The right man for the right city. At least that's how he billed himself. The cornerstone in a place that millions called home. Asshole!

It sure didn't take the Captain long to panic; we only talked twenty minutes ago. Since I had announced that I had to go, there was no way I could attend a meeting I wasn't invited to. I had a good idea what the Captain and the Mayor were going to talk about. Where their conversation was going to lead to was the real issue. I would find out later when I talk to Double-Oh Carlous.

It was time to hit my favorite spot and wait for the good news. Something about me and West River Drive. Whenever I needed to sort things out that is where I ended up. I love the boat houses, the way they got all them Christmas lights around them all year round. That dirty ass Schuylkill River. So fuckin' dirty that you'll die of pollution before you get a chance to drown. Somehow the fish survive. And that ten-foot waterfall. No Niagara, but it's cool in its own Philly type of way. Green grass, trees everywhere, and not a weekend goes by when somebody ain't 'queing. Just lay your head back in the grass and open your nostrils. Let the aroma of that barbecue hit you just right. Sometimes it smelled so good you actually thought you could taste it. Man, mamma could make some barbecue.

I remember when a high school buddy's engine locked up and he slammed into a tree. Died doing what he loved. Driving. Driving fast. His death broke my heart. I couldn't even go to the funeral. I didn't want to see him in that casket. I remember one of our classmates, Karen, said he was burned so bad. She said it wasn't him in that casket. I wanted to remember him full of life, with that big smile on his eighteen-year-old face. Died right here on the Drive.

When Moms and Pops got shot down... Man seemed like I spent a month out here just walking around in circles. Looking for something, anything to fill the empty. Nothing could fill the space left by losing both parents at the same time. I love the Drive, its memories, the tranquillity. Gotta think.

I had shit coming at me from all angles, everywhere I turned. Captain and the Mayor on my ass. Sasha. Damn. Baby sis' was gonna drive me to the nut house. Oh, yeah, the crazy house was due for a new resident from the Rock family. Was it gonna be Cecil or Sasha? I had dead bodies piling up.

Now I know I had been involved in some crooked shit in my lifetime, I mean some real raunchy shit. Shakin' down prostitutes for my cut. Coppin' a free meal at the best restaurants in the city, even when I wasn't hungry, just to let chez whitey know that I could do what the fuck I wanted, when I wanted and there wasn't shit he could do about it. I guess I really didn't have room to talk when it came to Sasha. When I think about it, in a crazy, fucked up-way, she was more right than I was. I shake down a chump just for the hell of it. Just to be fuckin' wit' somebody. Make sure I gave as many white boys speeding tickets as I could. Cause I hated white officers who pulled me and my boys over back when we was kids. At least Sasha had a reason for doing what she did. Plus, she believed she was right. Maybe I am the one with the problem. Maybe if I had some integrity about myself I would be in the position to rightfully demand that Sasha get herself together. Hell, I didn't know.

I was looking in the water thinking, wow, how in the hell do those fish survive in that nasty-ass water? Kind of reminded me of me. Through all the dirt and trash and filth that I live in, somehow, I make it to the top to get some air. Yeah. Just a gasp of that Philadelphia Fresh Air. Baby sis was gonna have to do some time. That's just how it was. There was no way she could continue killing people at will and not end up dead herself. Soon she would end up killing me or somebody I know. I was gonna have to stop her. That's how it was going to be. Gotta think. Need to think. Solve problems. But first...I'ma bust this grub!

"Mayor. Good to see you. Come right in!"

"Arnetti. You said it's urgent that we talk, so let's talk."

"Trust me, it's urgent. Rozen, there is not one word of this conversation that you are going to want your people to hear. Why don't you ask Linda and your bodyguards to grab something to eat in the snack room?"

"Okay. Linda, why don't you and the fellas go have some lunch. I shouldn't be that long. So Arnie, you have some leads. Anything. Has your one-man task force accomplished anything? We've got two dead bodies, and no account for either one. Right?"

"Look, Rozen, Rock is a good officer, for a Negro. I mean give him some time. He'll turn something up soon. I'm sure of it."

"If he hasn't found anything, then why the hell did you insist that I come over here right away? Dammit, you know these type of problems aren't going to go away. I am not going to jeopardize my political career because of the incompetence of your department. One of us isn't going to be in office next term if the public doesn't get some answers. Don't think for one minute that I am going to take the fall for you or anyone else. You got that? I put you in this seat. I can sure as hell take you out!"

"Mayor, I guess there's no easy way to tell you this. Well, Detective Rock did make some headway in his investigation. Kind of added some things up. He's a good detective."

"The point. What's the point!? You're starting to irritate me, Arnie."

"It has to do with Kyle."

"What about?"

"Well, it seems when Detective Rock found your son, he was—

"Was what? He was murdered by some thief, right? At

least that's what you told me!"

"Yes, it was a thief, far as I know. One small detail. Kyle was upstairs fucking Coleman Timms up the ass when he was killed."

"That's bullshit, no way my boy was a fag. And fucking a nigger on top of that. What the hell you trying to pull, Arnetti?"

"Calm down. This is the reason why I had to sweep this shit by you in the first place. I know this is a hard ass thing to hear. Let me explain."

"Talk fast!"

"Rozen. You have to work with me on this one. I don't have to tell you, we can't let this get out."

"You're right. Now what happened to my boy?"

"Detective Rock did not give me a whole lot of details. He's protecting somebody..."

"Christ sakes, Coleman Timms. That was his...uh.. wasn't that his sister's house where they found Kyle?"

"Yes, it was."

"Let me guess, that fucking Nigger's sister killed my boy. Is that what you're trying to tell me? Is it?"

"I'm only telling you what you're allowing me to tell you. Let me finish. Can't say that I blame you for being upset, but this situation is highly flammable! As I was saying, Detective Rock found the bodies first. He called me to the house. He had killed the alleged perpetrator, Slim Jim, by the time I got there. I decided that it would be best that your son not be found in the master bedroom with his dick up the nig's rear end. I would have been hard-pressed to get my brother-in-law, the coroner, to keep that to himself. Shit, I probably would have had to kill him. Rock has reason to believe that maybe, and this is a big maybe, his sister is behind the killing. Not positive. Just maybe."

"Use your brains, Arnetti. Who else does he have to protect? You know how it is nowadays with Blacks. African-American this, stick-together that. Uplift the race. I'd bet a thousand dollars your Detective is protecting his sister. Or some other nigger that's close to him. You can bet your ass on that one Arnetti!"

"Like I said, Rozen, Rock says maybe. But I'm as sure as you that it's his sister."

"Well then, there's only one thing left to do... It's a definite conflict of interest. Take his ass off the task force ASAP. I don't give a shit what you tell him, but his sister has got to pay. No way is some black bitch gonna kill my only son and not be punished for it. Understood? You are going to resolve this. Put somebody else on it. Make sure they bring her down. Do it right. Do it now!"

"I'm sure I can convince Detective Rock to bring her in.7"

"I don't think you understand, Captain Arnetti. An eye for an eye. She gets what my son got. Look, you think I am not wise to that shit you pulled with Joey. Everybody in the city of Philadelphia knows what his Bronco looked like. No way Mackey steals his jeep at three in the morning and goes joy riding. The rest of the city might be fools, but I sure am not. You fix this problem and you fix it right, and if Sasha's brother gets in the way— look, either they go down or you do! It's your choice."

"Mayor?"

"Captain Arnetti, this is the last time we talk."

. I had finished off the last of my lunch when my phone rang. At first I thought it was a female on the other end. But I never gave any women, except Sasha, my cellular phone number. Then I remembered how high Carlous's voice got when he was excited.

"Only thing I can say is, sit your ass down and listen—"

The conversation I heard blew me away. I told Carlous to call in sick for the next couple of days. I was sure I was going to need his expertise.

Session V

21

Sasha

The summer soaking sun was exactly what I needed to start my day off. Bright. Warm. Soothing to my skin. Feeding my melanin. Making it stronger. It cradled me in its arms and gently rocked me, until I was awake. I had slept quite well. I would get up with the intention of doing what was right. I decided I wasn't going to look into the future. Not try to argue and fuss with the animal inside of me. Not try and figure out its next move. Just live one hour, one minute, one second at a time. Live each instant, I just want to live. Every day I would take as it came to me. I accepted that whatever happens, happens.

I took my time driving to work. Stopped on all the yellows. Drove the speed limit. Ignored the horns of all the 'important' people behind me who were in such a rush to get to wherever they were going. Just chillin'. I walked up the stairs to my office. No elevator for me. Sat back in my chair and smiled. Success hadn't spoiled me, but being a black woman hadn't been a hindrance to my career. I have a wonderful son and a fantastic brother. Money. A nice home, but no man. Maybe one day, I told myself.

I didn't know when my next client would walk in.

Was she going to be a referral, or a walk-in? Or if social services was going to send somebody to me. I never knew. Sometimes I would water my plants, and wait. Wait for the door to open; wait for somebody who needs my help to enter my life. I have a very rewarding job. I love it. While I was celebrating success I heard the door open.

"Hello. Dr. Timms?"

"Yes. Please come in. What can I do for you?"

"My name is Gloria. Gloria Azeem. I took a leave of absence from my job. I'm just getting over a nervous breakdown. My insurance company gave me a list of shrinks, sorry, psychiatrists. I didn't mean to say that."

"No, that's okay, I hear it all the time. In fact my daddy used to say to me, 'Baby, one day you are gonna be the best shrink this city has ever had.' I wanted to be a shrink for as long as I can remember."

"Well, they gave me a list of names. I wanted a woman who was close to my home. I live on Parkside Ave. On the other side of the park. So here I am!"

"Great. Come on in and sit down. Can I get you something to drink?"

"Yes. Coffee. Black."

"So Gloria, you had a nervous breakdown. What caused it?"

"My son, William, was murdered three months ago. To the day, as a matter of fact. He was only fourteen. I just can't get over his death. It haunts me. Every day, I see his screaming face, and I know that he died in pain. My baby suffered. I know that he called for me and I was unable to be there for him. My life is in shambles. Nightmares!"

I put down my cup and went over to Gloria and hugged her. Touch is very important to me. You make a person feel loved and they will be comfortable around you. It's easier to open your heart to someone who you think you know. Someone you can trust.

"Take your time, honey. You have plenty of time. You don't have to rush. Just talk about what makes you feel good for a while. When the time is right, you will find the strength to talk about your son's death. I can only imagine how you feel. I have a twelve year old son myself. At one time in his life he was victimized. But he lived through it. We lived through it. Trust me. Things will get better. Sasha can assure you of that."

"Thank you, Sasha. All I wanted was to be able to wake up in the morning and see my son's face as I remember it. Full of life. Vibrant. Excitable. Ready to take on the world. He was going to be one of America's great leaders one day. He always told me that. Not how I imagined it. Screaming. Crying. Begging for his life. I wasn't there when he died. But when I saw his body I knew that he suffered. He needed his mother and I wasn't there for him."

"It's okay. Gloria, just calm down. Stop crying. It's going to be all right. Listen to me. Do you like to shop?"

"Y-y-yesss."

"Good."

Part of my therapy is doing things that my client likes, and shopping is something that I never get enough of.

"Leave your troubles in my office. Right now, you and

I are going to take on the City of Brotherly Love. Sasha style. Now you have to promise me. Today, not another peep about your son. Let's enjoy this day. Tomorrow will be better. Okay?"

"Sounds great. Sasha. You are a unique woman. One of a kind. I don't know how to thank you."

"No problem, Sugar. Let me just turn on my answering machine and we can get out of here. You like water ice and soft pretzels?"

"I love South Street!"

"Me, too. Let's go."

Gloria and I hit it off quite well. She was around thirty-five years old. About five nine. Tall for the average woman. Like me. Didn't look like a woman who ever had a baby. After I had Demetrius I made it my business to get my flabby ass to stop dragging behind me on the concrete. She must have done the same. It was terrible that she had to undergo the trauma of losing a loved one. This is a mean city when it wants to be. I parked on Fifth Street right off of South. I told Gloria to relax and have a good time.

"I'm sure we can find a couple of outfits to make some heads turn a little harder."

Our conversation proved that we had a lot in common. She had gone to college and majored in psychology for a year, then switched to nursing. She worked at a hospital in West Philadelphia. Loved aerobics, and on and on. I brought us a pair of cross trainers, biker shorts and black Danskin tops. We planned on taking a few classes together when she got back on top.

There was nothing like a nice afternoon walk on South Street. We had pretzels, water ice, grilled chicken sandwiches, soda. Ate like pigs. Spent a couple hundred on clothes. But as we headed back to the car I noticed something on Gloria's face. A smile. Her day went a little better because of me. I couldn't hold back the tears.

"I hope you had a good day, Gloria."

"Sasha, you don't know how much this means to me. I feel so much better. When you grieve, sometimes you forget to breathe! All the air you hold in your lungs is just the hurt and anguish that has built up inside of you over the course of time. Sometimes, no matter how hard I try, I just can't get all of the air out of my lungs. Each day there seems to be so much more hurt. So much more grief. I couldn't breathe ,Sasha. Today, I feel like I got a chance to inhale and exhale freely for the first time in a long time. Thank you."

"Gloria, there is one thing that you have to always remember. If there isn't any air in your lung,s you'll be about ready to die. There has to be a little bit of air in there at all times. That way you will never forget your grief. You won't forget what happened. You won't forget your son."

I took Gloria back to her car. Then, I headed home. We agreed to meet again in two days. It had been a good day for me. I didn't force Gloria to tell me how her son was killed; who killed him? I didn't want to know. Not yet anyway. She caught the animal sleeping! I found out I could get through a day without him disturbing me. I knew that when I heard what happened to her son, that would be another story. Bad news is like an early morning alarm clock to the animal. He jumps up, eyes wide and focuses on every detail. Yeah, it was sleeping that day. I prayed it would stay that way.

Gloria and I met at the plaza outside of my office on Thursday. We walked around and window-shopped before we went inside to talk. I wanted to make sure that she had a clear head, and clear lungs. Talking about the death of a loved one is very difficult. I was hoping to lift her spirits high enough to ease some of her pain in recalling what happened to her boy.

"You have a seat, I'll get us some coffee. Black, right?"

"Right. Thanks Sasha."

"Tell me about your son. Take your time. If you need a break, we can head to the mall."

"Sasha, I am the one supposed to be paying you. You keep running me to the store and I will have to sell my house just to pay my tab."

"Fine. Fine. Just go slow. You'll be fine."

"All right. William was a good boy. Smart. Very, very intelligent. I knew in my heart that one day he would make something special of himself. I knew that he would make his mother proud. He was always at the top of his class, academically. He was in all advanced classes. He always talked of going to Harvard. He was just the opposite of his brother James, my older son. He's 19. To sum up, James, he's just a product of his environment. Street gangs. Dealing drugs. But when I had my nervous breakdown, James took care of the house. He paid all the bills. He took care of everything. In his life of irresponsibility he is a responsible young man. I just wish he would leave that street life alone.

"Now, William, he was a good boy. I was so proud that he was beating the streets. He came to me one day and said that he needed to get a job. He was still a teenager who wanted to have the latest gear just like the rest of his friends. Karl Kani, Used, Nike, whatever was the fashion of the month, he wanted it on his back. When I was in my right state of mind I refused to allow his brother to buy him anything. I had already kicked James out of the house two years before, and I didn't want his negative influence affecting his younger brother.

Carter, that was my boyfriend at the time, had his own video store and offered William a job. That was perfect. William would be doing honest work, plus he would be around a positive male role model who I trusted. That's what I thought at the time. Carter was the opposite of my kid's father. He was a hard working man. Decent. Honest. My husband was a bum who left me damn near before William got out of my belly good. Haven't heard from him since, but that's okay. I rebounded. Well, I had one fine son.

Gloria was overcome with emotion again. The tears started to flow. Seemed like she cried as much as I did. The memory of a dead son was a great weight to bear. I didn't want both of us to sit there crying our eyes out. I had to be strong.

"Are you okay? Take a couple of deeeeep breaths. Breathe in strength. Breath out the hate and anger. You'll feel better."

"Sasha, you are wonderful. The world needs to know about you."

"You think so? Well, maybe they will one day. Maybe the whole world will know about Sasha Timms, one day! Feel better? Good. Please continue."

"Sasha, William was a good boy. Honest to God, he was. Anyway, like I was saying William started working for Carter in his video store. Since he was underage he worked for cash under the table. Swept the front of the store. Dumped the trash. Shit, dirty as the street was, that was a full-time job by itself. But, you know, nothing major. He had a job, and Carter was keeping a few dollars in his pocket.

"I called myself honoring my son's privacy by not asking him how much Carter was paying him. He talked about getting the latest in fashions, but there was no way on this earth he was making the kind of money to afford the things he was bringing into my house. Leather outfits. A pair of sneakers for every day of the week. Brought me a TV for my birthday. Stereo for his room. At first I was so shocked, maybe a bit naive. I was so excited that my son could do for me with responsible earnings. When I popped back to reality I realized that there was no way a fourteen-year-old helper could make that kind of money. I asked William if he was selling drugs, or doing something illegal. He assured me he wasn't. He said he just did whatever Mr. Woods told him to do. Then, he got paid. He said that sometimes Mr. Woods would have him deliver videos to people, get an envelope from them and bring it back. Whenever he did this he said he got an extra bonus from Mr. Woods. He was sometimes making more than a hundred dollars a day.

I confronted Carter:

"Carter, honey, we need to talk."

"What's up, baby?"

"What exactly do you have William doing? I mean he's bringing home a little bit too much money to be a helper. Last night I found six hundred dollars in his underwear drawer. Can you explain that?"

"Baby, I'm just trying to keep some money in the boy's pockets so that he doesn't have to be worrying you for anything. Is anything wrong with that? Huh? Is it?"

"Please, Carter, don't raise your voice to me. I want to understand how my son is making so much money working for you in a video store. Shit, I might need a good-paying job like that myself one day."

"Oh, really?"

"Look, all jokes aside. William says he's making deliveries for you. He said you always give him a bonus. Now what the hell could a fourteen-year-old be delivering that earns him a hundred dollars, besides something illegal? Answer that question."

"Gloria, I love you to death. But you know one of the reasons why I haven't married you yet? Cause you too damn nosey. You ask too many fuckin' questions. Here I am thinking I am doing you and yours a favor by giving the kid some extra cash to enjoy his poor-ass life. Do you thank me? Fuck no! You question my ass. Is that the thanks I get for giving your son a job?"

"Look here, when it concerns my son I get to ask all

the fuckin' questions I want. Now all I want to know is what the hell you got my son delivering? I don't like it. And it's going to stop. If you need a drug runner, I am sure James can recommend someone to you."

"Gloria, I don't have any involvement with drugs. Tell you what. If you don't want William working for me , that's fine. But when I give him his pink slip you make sure you explain to him why you're taking six-hundred American dollars, tax-free mind you, out of his pocket every week. You make sure your nosey ass explains that to your darling little broke-ass boy. Okay? You explain it to him!"

"Six-hundred a week!? Fuck you, Carter. Domino's don't pay twenty dollars a delivery. Whatever the hell you doing-it ain't right, and I don't want William mixed up in it. Don't worry, I will explain everything to William. You! You just get the fuck out of my house. I'll have your junk in a box waiting for you."

"So, Carter left. I thought that would be the last time I had to deal with him. When William got home from work that night he was distraught. I figured he was disappointed about losing his job. I was far off":

"William, I know that you are upset, but I can explain."

"What do you have to explain to me , mom?"

"About why I made Carter stop letting you work for him."

"Believe me, mom, I wouldn't want to spend another second of my life working for him."

"Baby? What happened?"

"Well. When I got to work today, Mr. Woods told me that he would be hiring someone else to do the deliveries. He said that you two broke up and that you didn't want me working for him any more. But he was desperate, he didn't have anybody today, so if I could finish the day he would really appreciate it. Mom, he was putting mad money in my pockets. How could I say no? So I had made about three runs when finally I had to do something that Mr. Woods told me I better not ever do. He told me never ever look inside the packages I was delivering. Anyway, he told me he was going to his club for some supplies, and should be back before I got back. The delivery he gave me this time was across town so I had to catch a cab. Mr. Woods always gave me cab money for long deliveries. He said a smooth young brother like me shouldn't have to ride the bus. When he left I told Melanie that I was going to the bathroom. Said I had to do #2 and would be a while. I opened the package in the back, Mom. It was a video tape. I popped it in the VCR. Mom, I could not believe my eyes. Little kids having sex. I mean young, seven, eight-year-old. Black kids, white kids, Hispanic."

"William, you've got to be kidding me?"

"Cross my heart and hope to die. Well, this was one delivery I wasn't making. I left him a note and came home. What he's doing isn't right, Mom. If I knew what was inside my deliveries I would never have done it. I was making so much easy money though— I didn't think anybody was getting hurt."

"William, you are a smart boy. I love you. Come

here and give me a hug."

"How can anybody treat little kids like that? They didn't look right either. They looked like something was wrong with them."

"Baby, when a person uses children for pornography, they usually drug them up so much that they don't even realize what they are doing. The sad part is these monsters usually kill the children after they're done using them in the films. Carter Woods sure kept his dirt a secret. I would have never believed that he would do anything like this."

"Well, I didn't actually see any kids tied up in the back room. Maybe he's just selling them for someone else."

"I don't know, William. But you hear me and you hear me good. You stay away from Carter. If he comes near you, run, call the police, then call me. I am going to tell the police what's going on. Maybe they can get in there and get enough evidence to lock his ass up!"

"Believe me, I won't go anywhere near him. I'm going to bed. See you tomorrow when you get home from work."

"Goodnight, baby!"

"Goodnight, Mommy!"

"Sasha... Sasha that was the last thing William ever said to me. I leave for work before he gets up to go to school. I stopped in his room on my way out the door, just to look at my little big man before I left. Sprawled across the bed in his boxers. No shirt, thinking he's grown. A nice fresh haircut. You know it's funny? William, he always tried to be so grown, always calling me Mom or Mother. But before he went to bed that night he called me Mommy. It's as if the whole situation scared him. Fear can make you remember how precious childhood is. How having a Mommy to handle all your worries and responsibilities makes life so much easier to bear."

"Gloria, sometimes it feels like the umbilical cord has never been cut. I can feel my boy hanging on to me with all the strength that he has. You ever feel like that?"

"All the time."

"We have to remember that our children, are just that, children. Even when they are teenagers they are still too young to be totally responsible for themselves. They aren't ready to handle real-life situations by themselves. They long for independence, but when they get it, along with a dose of reality, sometimes it scares the shit out of them."

"So true."

"What happened next? You said that, 'Goodnight, Mommy' was the last thing William ever said to you."

"Goodnight, Mommy! Those words will be engraved inside my head until the day I die. I leaned over and kissed his forehead before I left. He kinda half smiled in his sleep. I don't know if it was my kiss or if the boy was just dreaming. I didn't know it would be the last kiss I would ever give him.

"William didn't come home from school that day. I freaked. I called James over and told him to get his cronies in the street and find his brother. About three days later the grapevine got news back to James that they heard somebody saw his brother in a bootleg porno flick. Couple days later they found William's naked body in a Dumpster downtown. He had apparently been beaten to death. I know Carter did it because he closed down his video store. Now he only has his disco. I can't prove a thing. There aren't any records of William ever working for Carter. Also, I found out that Carter is large in the crime world. James is afraid of him. I know James wants to kill him, but he doesn't have the heart. He's not as big time a thug as I thought he was.

"When I went to identify the body, I was not prepared for what I saw. Never in a million years would I have envisioned my baby like that. You could just tell by the look on his face that he suffered when he died. It's almost like I can hear him screaming for me to help him, and I wasn't there to do a blessed thing for William. I can't handle the screams, Sasha. How could Carter do this to my son? When you get to see the naked soul of a person for the first time that's when you really know a person, what they are capable of. Angel or monster— you never know."

I thought to myself... I'm no monster. If Gloria could see inside of my soul she would be surprised. Sure the animal is in there, ugly, waiting to attack. But she would also see a heart full of love, willing to do anything for any one, if it made a bad situation better.

"Gloria, right now I am speechless. Probably for the first time in my life. I don't possess the words right now to tell you anything that could possibly make you feel better. My heart is aching. It's aching because I cannot feel what you're feeling. Don't try to live your entire life all at once. Worrying about what's going to happen tomorrow, or next year. Take life as it comes to you. Live it one hour, one second, one minute at a time. Time is the only thing I can think of that can make it better. And having someone to talk to."

"And maybe a nice round of bullets through Carter's heart. I hate that man, Sasha. He is going to pay for what he did to William. For what he's doing to me right now."

"Honey, I know how you feel. But you have to let the law handle this situation for you. Matter of fact, my brother is a cop. I'll give him a call this evening. Maybe he can help. Tell you what. You go home, get some sleep if you can. We'll talk some more tomorrow. Stop by at eleven-thirty."

"Thanks, Sasha."

In my heart I know that God loves his children more than anything else in this world. With that in mind, I believe that William is in a better place.

"Rock! Hey, big bro, what's happening, stud?"

"I'm fine, Sasha. Killed anybody lately?"

"No smart ass, but I been thinking about it."

"Well, don't think too hard."

"Cecil, I know that you're probably still pissed at me, and I probably don't have any right asking you what I am about to ask you but—"

"Well, don't ask then!"

"One small—"

"Hell no!"

"Teensy weensie—"

"Sasha, kiss my ass!"

"The last time, I promise—"

"Hell no!"

"Small favor."

"Hummmm. No."

"Rock. One of my clients, her son was murdered. Fourteen years old. She thinks her ex-boyfriend killed him. The child was drugged and used for pornographic videos before he was murdered. Help the mother of a child lost. Please."

"I understand tragedy, but do you have to pile the bullshit on so thick?"

"Go to hell, Rock!"

"When did this happen?"

"About three months ago."

"Who is she?"

"Rock, you are the best. You know I love you, don't you?"

"No, I don't know that. Who is she?"

"Gloria Azeem, lives on Parkside Ave. She thinks the man who murdered her son is a guy named Carter Woods. He has a disco in town. Rock, this man has got to be dealt with. You must be proud of me. I am at least giving you the opportunity to take care of this before I do."

"Tell me, sweet princess, what's that remark supposed to mean?"

"Come on, Rock, lighten up. I'm just proud of myself that I haven't done anything to upset you, yet. I thought that you would be proud of me, too."

"Well, Sasha, all I can promise you is that I will go and talk to this Carter Woods. That's the best I can do right now. If the police aren't doing any surveillance on him now, then his hands are probably clean. I'll also ask around and see if anybody has heard of this guy. Who investigated, the routine shit. But I ain't spending a lot of time investigating him when I have— You know I am tied up in more important matters, like what the hell I am going to do about you. Bye!"

"Cecil..."

I knew what that chump was doing. He was challenging me. Since the boy was already dead, and the killer was still living, Rock figured that I would do something about it. He's a slickster. But that's okay. I was going to give him time, not much. But he would have ample opportunity to do the right thing. After that... Tough shit for law and order, and tough shit for Cecil Rock and his problems. Sasha doesn't have time to be put on hold. Especially when the animal wanted blood!!

22

Rock

Baby sis, baby sis. I knew Sasha was hot as hell. She didn't have any reason to be upset with me. She promised me that she was going to at least try to be on her best behavior. Carter Woods. I thought I'd look into it.

23

Sasha

I thought about spending the rest of the evening being mad at my brother. Instead I called Jeanette to check on my son. Demetrius wouldn't say a word into the telephone. Jeanette said he was doing fine. A warm bath and a good night sleep was what I needed. I woke up the next morning feeling refreshed. Invigorated. Work wasn't work for me. I didn't hate the job. What I do is a way of life for me. Hum, was that killing, or counseling?! Gloria got to the office almost the same time as I did. She seemed anxious to talk. That was always a positive sign. Ventilation is a positive step in the healing process.

"Hey, Gloria, come on in. How are you doing today?"

"The thread is taught, but I am not letting go! How you feeling?"

"Good for you. I'm fair. Gloria, I have to be honest with you. My brother said he would go and talk to Carter. He wasn't very optimistic, though. Since Carter checked out clean, it's going to be hard to prove or find anything. The type of low-life that he is, you know he's covering his tracks.

"Rock isn't the only cop in the city, but he's damn good, and he always takes a personal interest in the cases that he is working on. I figured when he heard that a young child was involved, he would be more than happy to help you out. He's gonna look. I just hope Carter rubs him the wrong way."

"Why is that?"

"Because Cecil will take a personal interest in trying to find out all he can about Carter. Especially if he has the slightest inkling that Carter is crooked."

"Sasha, I appreciate the effort. Sure, the police talked to Carter. They questioned him. But any evidence that could have been recovered at the video store was gone. Like I told you earlier, he closed that 'bad boy' down right after he killed my baby. Besides, how many young black boys are killed in this city? Matter of fact, how many are killed in America, and their deaths are ignored? Filed and forgotten."

"Gloria, America might forget about our young black men, but you aren't going to forget about William. Neither will I."

"You're right, Sasha. I'm glad you care."

"Question? Did anyone happen to see William with Carter the day he didn't come home from school?"

"Umm. Well, nobody actually saw him with Carter, but one of his friends saw him get into a black car, possibly a Trooper. Carter owns a black Trooper. They just saw William get in, they never saw the driver of the vehicle. But that's enough evidence for me. My boy was smart, he wouldn't get into a car with somebody that he didn't know. Even though I told him to stay away from Carter, I know that smooth talking bastard probably reassured him it was okay. W-W-William just couldn't see the danger signs enough to resist. I don't know..."

Gloria could barely get her words out.

"You go ahead and cry, honey. Cry right here in Sasha's arms. It's gonna work out. You can trust me on this one!"

All I could do was cradle Gloria in my arms and try not to let too many of my tears fall into her hair. Touch and true emotion were so important to me. I always want my heart to be a part of therapy. I don't want to ever think that I am too important to hug or cry with someone. Gloria probably didn't realize it, but her grief had become my grief. Her desire to put some bullets through Carter's chest were the same desires of the animal. The same desires of Sasha. A monster like Carter didn't deserve anything, except death.

"You feeling better, sugar?"

"Yes, Sasha. Thank you so, so much. You know, this is the first time since William's murder that I could just let it out. When he was killed, James was with me, but I felt like I had to be strong for the both of us. You make me feel— feel like— like family. I appreciate the love that you freely give to me. I feel much better now. Much better."

"My pleasure. Believe me, it's the least I can do. Now finish mopping up the tears so we can talk shrink talk!"

It was good to laugh. Gloria had a smile on her face. That made me feel good. A smile! I needed to interrogate Gloria and not sound like a detective.

"Fire away, Sasha!"

"Tell me more about Carter. No contempt, no bitterness. If possible. Just facts. First, why are you convinced that Carter murdered your son? Don't be offended by the question. I believe you when you say that he did it. I just want you to explain it without malice. That way I get facts. You understand what I'm saying? I can help you deal with your feelings. I think that is where the real pain lies."

"Yes. I understand. It's just so hard to separate the mother fuck— uh, the maniac from the crime. But I will try, okay?"

"Great. Now, why do you believe Carter killed William?"

"My first instinct was to check with the phone company for a number to call to get videos delivered. Hoping it would be the same number as Carter's video store. I knew there wouldn't be an ad for kiddie porn, but I was hoping that there would at least be a delivery video number. No such luck. Next I went through William's room from top to bottom. I was hoping, matter of fact praying hard, that William left something, anything that would give me a clue that would link Carter to the videos. Sasha, would you believe that I found almost fifteen hundred dollars in an envelope under his mattress? On the front it said 'Christmas money for mom's gifts.' Broke my heart. He was always thinking of me. Trying to be the man of the house. Barely stopped peeing the bed and the little man trying his damnedest to take care of his mother. Bless his heart.

"I searched and searched. I was so determined to find

something. I felt if I had something to give to the police, then they might take up a more serious investigation. You would think that cops would take a more sincere interest in a homicide. Especially when a child is involved. They just told me they questioned Carter and that five people confirmed his alibi, that he was in Atlantic City gambling the day before, during and after William's death. Shit, they were probably the five people he had working for him at the video store. I bet those super sleuths didn't even do a background check on the five liars!"

"All right now, Gloria. Remember, leave your heart out of this. Just give me the facts. I know it's difficult. I can help you get over this."

What I really meant was I can take care of this. "...but I need facts. I don't want to give advice on how to handle a situation one way, when it actually happened another."

"Gotcha. Sasha, I spent what seemed like hours, looking for the slightest hint of anything that would help pin Carter to William's murder. At least something that would convince the police. I was already convinced the muth... Sorry, Sasha, I'll control it as best I can." She took a breath, "But I am convinced! Sorry... Okay... anyway... Sasha, I couldn't find a thing. I was so distraught. No clues, no evidence, no jail time. I spent the night in William's room, holding on to his picture of him and his brother. Missing my baby."

"See, Gloria, it works like this. You don't cry, I don't cry, maybe we can get something accomplished. Now pass me the Kleenex and get back to your story!"

"You are one weird lady, Sasha, but I love you anyway! So like the average hard-working, former teenage mother that gets into a crisis, I called my mother. We had a nice long talk. She helped me to stay focused, patient in terms of giving the police a chance to find William's killer or having a chance to prove Carter did it. 'Things will work out. They always do. Don't worry, baby. The police will find William's killer, and make him pay.' Sasha, I have to admit. I wasn't in the mood for any of my mother's super-optimistic enthusiastic speeches. I really wanted her to give me permission to go and kill Carter myself. Couple of days later I had my nervous breakdown. When I got home, I found out that mother had been right, as usual.

I was doing some laundry, William's. Don't ask me why. I mean dead people don't need clean clothes, do they? Anyway, I found a note in his pocket from Carter:

Little man, I had to run to Delaware for a few hours. This delivery is gonna get you a double bonus though. Go to my club on 17th Street. Ask for Zack. He's gonna give you a box to deliver in Yeadon. The address is 4949 Patricia Drive, Yeadon.

C.W.
P.S. This is an important run so whatever you do, don't fuck up! I know I can count on you, little man! Peace

"I found that pot of gold. And I was dammed happy!"

"So did you turn the information over to the police?"

"You did ask me how I knew for certain that Carter

killed my boy, right?"

"Right."

"Well, I wanted to be certain as well. I went out to the address that was on the note. Hoping that maybe the pervert who was buying the videos had an innocent wife or girlfriend at the house and I could get a look at his collection. Sasha, when I got there, a young woman answered the door. How she managed to make it to the door without falling over was a miracle. She must have been using drugs."

"Hi, I have a delivery for Mr. Lewis. Where should I put it?"

"Where the hell is William, our regular. He made the delivery last time. Shit, I ain't about to stuff no hundred dollars in your back pocket. William got a nice ass for such a young boy, I ain't into women. Huh, where he at?"

"Sasha, I had to control myself because I wanted in that house. This woman looked like she could barely stand up straight for more than five minutes without tipping over. Now, I knew how William was getting his bonuses. And the bitch— sorry, the junkie was feeling on my baby's behind. A safe delivery was obviously worth a lot of money to the customer as well as to Carter. Fuckin' Bastard!"

"Miss, last I heard, his mother made him quit. Besides, you can put my tip in my hand, I really don't mind."

"Fine, you little stuck-up bitch. Here's your hundred. Put the shit in the basement by the desk, and

don't fuck with anything while you down there or Cazzie gonna kill you the next time he sees you!"

"Mr. Lewis isn't here?"

"No! He probably out fuckin' around or gettin' me sum mo' shit. Now git out my face. I'ma take this last hit and catch a nap. Yo' black ass better be out of here when I wake up!"

"Found that pot of gold. I stomped halfway down, the steps, put the box down then creeped back to the top. Mamma's eyes were already rolling to the back of her head. I figured she would be out long enough for me to look around the basement for some clues. Girl, I was all jittery and nervous inside. It's not like I was a PI before or anything. But there was kind of an invigorating rush at playing detective. It was exciting. Plus, I was willing to take chances to find out who killed my baby. It was worth the risk to me.

"I started looking around the basement. There was a footlocker sitting in the corner. Locked, of course. Obviously Cazzie wasn't overly secretive about what was in the trunk. I lifted the end and just by chance the key was underneath. When I opened the trunk, I was floored by what I saw. My son on the cover of a magazine, being sodomized by a grown man. His face was nothing more than a stoic picture of disinterest. There's no doubt in my mind that he had enough drugs in him to make him think he could fly!"

I didn't know how Gloria had the stability to recall the events surrounding William's death. She was a strong woman.

"Damn, that's awful. Look, do you want to stop? Are you all right?"

"Sasha, give me two seconds to get myself together. I'll be honest. When I think back to that day, the only emotion that I really have is hate. Hate for Carter and what he did to William."

"Hate is an appropriate emotion to have in this situation. I totally understand. Take your time."

"...So, I see William and I can't believe my eyes. If it weren't for the grace of God I swear, I would have burned down that house on the spot. I needed a clear head though in order to get what I came for. I dashed upstairs as quietly as I could to check on the space cadet. **G.O.N.E.!** Sleeping off her high. Great. I ran back downstairs, fast as I could, I wasn't concerned about being quiet. The footlocker contained all the information I needed to link Carter to my son's death. There was a membership kit. How to purchase the videos. Code words. Tip expectancy, and so on. All written by a low-down son-of-a-bitch named Carter Woods! The more I think about it, I'd been dating this bastard for three years. Carter obviously wasn't his real name. He even had a business card. I never would have suspected that the man I loved, the man I planned on marrying was as sick a bastard as he was."

"I know, honey. Sometimes the person we fall in love with is not the same person we marry. Believe me, I know!"

"There was a pager number on the business card. I called and waited. The phone rang five minutes later. I was numbed by the sound of Carter's voice on the other end. I did my best to imitate Ms. Lewis. Slurring, stuttering, and raspy.

"What can I do for you?"

"Uh, yea, my number is A175 dash zero six."

"Go on."

"Send me, uh, n-n-numbers eighteen and t-tw-twenty six."

"Six o'clock tomorrow. Take care of my delivery boy, okay?"

"Right, sure, bye."

I guess he calls back from a phone booth or a cellular. This way there wouldn't be a way to trace the call back to whereever he makes his films. Plus he doesn't say anything on the phone to incriminate himself. If the line he's using is tapped, there isn't going to be much evidence. If the police raid the disco, all they will find is a bunch of music-happy Negroes sweatin' their asses off! The man is a very talented criminal."

"Without a doubt!"

"I had a friend, Johnny, call the number to request a start-up kit. He gave Carter Cazzie's name as a reference along with a special code number that only Cazzie would know. This way Carter would be certain that the police weren't on to him. The paraphernalia that Carter sent also included a special set of eight digit numbers. If Carter received six numbers instead of eight for an order, he would automatically know that it was a setup. Smart bastard. Smart as hell. Get this, all of this was part of the new members requirements. If this ain't sick—"

"... what is?"

"You got that right. Anyway, about two hours later, this young man brings a box by Johnny's house. We both dished out fifty bucks apiece, just like the instructions said, including a tip for the young entrepreneur. He ran off smiling. I wouldn't allow Johnny to see inside the box. When I got home, everything that Cazzie owned I owned. Along with a free first issue and video. My son was the star of both. Sasha, I don't know what you can do verbally to help me. If I can prove but one thing, it's that Carter exploited my son before he killed him. But you said you wanted facts. Fact. The video speaks for itself. And fact number two, the magazine speaks for itself. Now all of this might not indicate that Carter actually killed my son himself. But he knew that William was into a business where the only way you get out was death. If he didn't do it, he ordered it. Besides, Carter's lifestyle mandates that he die either way, for exploiting children or for killing my son. I know he's guilty of both."

"You have an excellent point. But don't think that words can't help your cause. There is power in words. Especially when they come from Sasha Timms!"

"That's good to know, Sasha. Good to know."

"Let me ask you a question? You ever thought about being a cop? That was quite an impressive piece of investigating you did, and brave, too."

"Naw. Too dangerous. But, you would be surprised to know what a woman will and can do in the midst of anguish and betrayal."

"Not too surprised. What happened next?"

"I called Johnny and asked him to go to the disco and just walk around. Then call back and tell me everything that he saw."

"How did you get this man to do all this running and buying for you and he not ask any questions? I'm sure he wanted some answers."

"We had been friends since— since we were teenagers and went to the junior prom."

"Your first love?"

"My only love. He still loves me, and he'll do anything for me."

"Good for you. Then what happened?"

"Johnny said the upstairs was a bar and disco floor. Crowded as hell. He saw some steps leading downstairs. The bouncer guarding the stairs was about six-five and three-hundred pounds. He asked if he could go downstairs and use the bathroom. The bouncer grabbed Johnny around the throat and yelled something about pissing in the corner. That seemed kind of odd behavior just for asking to use the restroom. Like he was either hiding or protecting something. Johnny got nervous and left. But the info he gave me was enough to convince me. How about you?"

"I'm convinced. I pray that Carter Woods gets what's coming too him. Look, Gloria, you go home now. I want to go over my notes, to enable me to give you the best advice possible. This is about as difficult a situation that I have ever faced. Oh, is his club on 17th off of Spring Garden?"

"Yes. Why?"

"I want to make sure my brother has the right place. I think I have driven past it a couple of times. I never would have figured it to be the home of a child pornographer. Then again, no place would be appropriate."

"Who would, Sasha?"

"The worst kind of pervert out there, Gloria, the pedophile! Oh, can you also give me Carter's home address, please?

"Sure. I'll see you in a couple. Thanks for everything. Gimme a hug to take with me."

"My pleasure. Get some rest, Gloria. We'll talk, for sure."

I had to commend Gloria on her investigative skills. If I didn't know better, I would have sworn she was a PI or cop or something. But I felt her hurt, her pain. I understood why she would go to the lengths that she did, why she would take the risks that she took. I would, and have done the same myself. Humph! I almost wanted to ask her to come with me when I pay Carter Woods a visit. But that could be a bad idea. Everybody who talks about killing isn't always about killing when it's time to actually kill. Last thing I needed was an accomplice who didn't have any courage. Gloria was different though. I almost believed that she might have killed someone in her past, the way her facial expression changed when she described how she wanted to just put bullets through Carter's chest. Eyes wide. Eager. Ready. Nostrils flared. Just a glaze of perspiration on the brow. Edgy. Sitting on the tip of her chair. I started to call her bluff and see if she wanted to go and find Carter right then and smoke his black ass! Heard

Rock using that term during one of his police stories. If she called my bluff though, who knows what would have happened? I decided to give my brother one more chance. I stopped and got some fat-free yogurt on the way home. The animal didn't need a lot on its stomach. If Rock wasn't willing to take the edge off, then I was. You can best believe that, cause Sasha said it!

Next morning the rays hadn't even started soaking me good when the doorbell rang. I hadn't even finished my dream with Denzel. My God! I wondered who could have been at my door so early in the morning. I wasn't exactly ready to take on the world that early.

"Hello, Miss, flowers. Delivery. Please sign here! Thanks. Good-bye!"

"You're welcome."

Well, well, well. What have we here? I wondered. Two-dozen long-stem red and white roses. Now who could these be from:

Sasha, I hope these brighten your morning just as the memory of your smile brightens each moment that I live. Hopefully our paths will be fortunate enough to once again cross.

Earlston Belefont

p.s. I had mentioned you to my big mouth sister (in full detail) who went back yapping about you to one of her aerobics friends. Jeanette Jones, of all people, your best friend. She wouldn't give me your address or number, but she agreed to send these. Enjoy!

As the aroma of those beautiful red and white roses

tickled my nose, I was reminded of that gentle man I met in Columbia, Maryland. Mr. Earlston Belefont. So smooth for such a young man, but once again thoughts of him had to be set aside. I needed to talk to my brother. I hoped he was in a cooperative mood.

"Rock! It's Sasha! You up yet?"

"Well, damn, if I wasn't before..."

"Why are you so grouchy? Have you even looked outside to see how beautiful it is today? The Lord has made us a lovely day, big brother. Something wonderful is bound to happen."

"Sorry I don't share your radiance, Sasha. I had a late night. Busy."

"Rock? Did you think any more about helping Gloria out? I mean personally. I promised her you would help her out. Gloria did a bit of investigating herself. Seems like she has some good clues that could help prove that her ex-boyfriend murdered her son. Do you have a pencil? Write down these addresses to Carter's club and also to his home. Gloria's not positive about the home address but you can at least check it out."

"Sasha? What was your major in college? I, for some strange reason, thought it was psychology or something."

"Criminal Justice!"

"Right. All I'm trying to say is, let the police police and let the counselors counsel."

"Rock, all I'm trying to say is, do your job. Or I will!"

I hated to hang up on my brother. I always viewed that type of act as obnoxious and immature. But I had enough of Cecil's bullshit. It seemed to me like he was tempting me. Trying to see if I would act; break my so-called promise. I loved my brother dearly, but it was obvious, even after our little talk, that he didn't fully understand what was driving me. This evil that rots my gut doesn't understand mind games. It couldn't take time out to be rational, or draw reasonable conclusions. It wants. It gets! I didn't control it; it controlled me! Patience was not an option. Bullshit was not an option. I believed that if Rock acted quickly in rectifying the matter, there would be no prey to be hunted. Therefore the animal would have to go into remission. Instead, he had to play mister hard ass. He was trying me. Not a very good idea.

Then my song came on the radio. Ohhhh, Teddy, Teddy! Sing that song man... 'Lookin' back- over the years. I guess I shedded some tears. Told myself time and time again this time I'm gonna win...' Uhm, uhm, ummm! Damn! That brother can sing. Love TKO! Damn. I loved that song. I remember the first time I heard Teddy sing live. Years ago. He did a wonderful show. Sing it, man...

Revenge! Retribution! Reprisal! Vindication! Doesn't matter. Right or wrong. They all spelled: Sasha was empty on the inside. Something besides my son was missing in my life. Love. Peace of mind. Joy. Companionship. The animal inside of me had consumed damn near everything that was good in my life. I blame Coleman. Why had he betrayed me? There was nothing he could have said to me anyway, especially from the view that I had.

Sasha! Yes, Lord, I started talking to myself. Time for self-pity is over. Time for self-doubting to take a back seat. Happy or sad. Right or wrong. War or peace. There was a person not worthy of even being called a man that had to be dealt with. No mother should have to endure the agony of having a child abducted and exploited in the worse fashion imaginable. No mother should have to see her child as Gloria saw hers. An endless nightmare. Endless. Endless suffering. The screams. How she described them. It's almost as if I could hear them. That so called cop brother of mine had better get his ass in gear, because the animal wasn't going to sit on this one for long.

24

Rock

I couldn't imagine how many years it had been since the Captain was on a stakeout. Bugging offices, watching people. But there he was, sitting outside of Sasha's office, all by himself. Sitting. Looking. Watching. His custom-made van had all the comforts of home. TV, VCR, fridge. Recliner. Bed.

I ran a check on Carter Woods and got the same address Sasha had given me. I sent Carlous there to exterminate, you know, bugs. I knew where his disco was. I needed to be there early, like before his place got too crowed.

When I got to the club there was a Black Trooper double parked in front. This Niggah must have thought he was living in South Philly! I cut him a break and didn't give him a ticket. No time.

Inside was a classy place. Surprised me. I figured it to be a hole. As soon as you walked in there was an ivory-colored bar that stretched halfway across the front room. The bar itself had an intricate design that would have taken me months to figure out. The counter top was covered with glass. Your reflection jumped right out at you. Maybe this was for those who were supposed to be on the wagon. It allowed them to take a good look at themselves as they were drinking away the rent money. Maybe it would give them the strength to push away. The bar stools were black and white with high backs. The padding was so thick you could fall asleep in them. Pictures of all of my favorite jazz artists decorated the walls. Dizzy. Bird. Ella. Miles. Black and white frames, no less.

Right past the bar, running the length of the front room and proceeding into what appeared to be the dance area were small round tables with two chairs at each. Romantic. The tables were black, chairs white. Then I noticed the checkerboard-floor pattern. Black and white! Small plants hung tastefully at the corners of the mirrored ceiling. Larger bamboo plants underneath them on the floor. Clean. Quiet. Damn near empty. But sharp. I liked it, I had to admit to myself.

"Excuse me, I'm Detective Rock. I'm looking for Carter Woods. Where can I find him?"

The bartender seemed rather cool, like nothing ever went wrong in this club. He used one of those pocket walkie-talkies to call Carter.

"Just a sec— Mr. Woods, there's a cop up here."

Up here— was all I needed to hear. That meant he was downstairs. I looked for the stairs. The big ass bouncer wasn't real happy to let me down, but I assured him that unless he moved he was going to get about six new holes in his chest. The stairwell was decorated with more pictures. Some of Philadelphia's most famous celebrities: Dr. J, Patti LaBelle, Grover Washington, Teddy P, Randall Cunningham. No Italians. Ain't that a bitch. Downstairs was as fashionable as upstairs. Another dance area. More tables and chairs. I met Carter at the bottom.

"Carter Woods?"

"You weren't invited down—"

"Look, calm down, brother, I ain't got no major beef with you. I just need to ask you a couple of questions. I know you'd rather talk here than at the precinct. Oh, and I will leave your ass in the lock-up a good fifteen hours before we talk. So, can we talk in your office?"

"Yeah."

"Let's keep this informal. Why don't you go and grab me a brew?"

When he turned to call on his walkie-talkie I stuck a wireless mike underneath the lip of the desk in his office. I had one in place at the bar, too.

"Thanks, man."

"What do you want? I got things to do."

"What can you tell me about William Azeem?"

"William? He used to work for me. He was a great kid. I treated him like a son. I'm sorry things didn't work out between me and his mother— shame how he died."

"His mother seems to think that you had something to do with it."

"Me? Man— shit, I wasn't even in town when it happened. Check the police report. My alibi checked out. Not that I needed one."

"Well, Carter, I know you're busy. Thanks for your time. Sorry to bother you."

The following day I met up with Carlous at his spot on Sixty-third Street. We jumped in his Corolla. He had tape recorders, phone lines, wires, microphones of all sizes, electrical tape, scissors, tools, all kinds of shit, in his back seat.

"Damn, bro— I knew you was into this surveillance shit, but I didn't know it was this heavy."

"Actually it ain't— that heavy. When you said you needed my help though, I got all my stuff together. I wanted to be prepared. Know what I mean?"

"Most definitely. Where to?"

"Just a minute. Let me turn on the transmitter and see where your boy is headed. Looks like he's headed in town. Let's see where we end up."

"Damn, Arnetti didn't waste any time checking out Gloria. He's going to see Carter now. This ought to be an interesting conversation."

"It will be if you got the mikes in the right place."

"Don't you worry, amigo!"

"Fuck you!"

Obviously the captain had been doing some checking up on Sasha and Gloria. He ended up at Carter's bar. We parked in a lot diagonally across the street. We could see in the bar area, but that was about it. Still, our ears captured all that we needed.

"Bartender! Give me a Heiney!"

"Sure, buddy. Help you find something, Officer!"

"That's the problem with these neighborhood bars. You can smell a cop a mile away. Before I can make my hands touch around your fuckin' neck, and in the process squeeze the fuckin' life out of you, I got one question. I know you know the answer, since you know every fuckin' thing else!..."

"Y-Y-Yes-s-s-s-sir-"

"Where is Carter?"

"Downstairs, door on your left, just inside the dance room."

"What color shirt does he have on?"

"Uh...a uh... No...no...he uh, has on a cream colored silk shirt."

"No hard feelings, huh?"

I looked over at Carlous and he looked like he was having the time of his life. All jumpy and excited.

"Damn, Rock, the Captain is cold. He must think he's Dirty Harry or something, huh?"

"Be quiet."

"Hey, big fella."

"H-hello."

"Use your right eye. See this badge?"

"Yes, sir."

"Good. This means that it's okay for you to let me go downstairs. Would you agree?"

"Yeah. I agree."

"Carter Woods?"

"What can I do for?"

"Are you Carter Woods?"

"Yeah. What's up? Quincy already called down and let me know you were coming. Warned me. Humpf! You a bad-ass I-talian, huh?"

"Fuck with me and I'll cut your heart out and mail it

to your momma, boy. Now, Gloria Azeem seems to think that you killed her boy."

"Is that right? Well, the cops done questioned me, when William was first killed. I helped them all I could. But I didn't do it. They said I was clear."

"So tell me. Why does she still think you killed her boy?"

"Well, we broke up a couple of days before he was murdered. See, Gloria hated the fact that I had done more for her son in a few months than she was able to do in his entire life. I guess she was jealous. So, I come home one day, she starts asking me a whole lot of stupid ass questions. I got mad, said some things I shouldn't have, then she told me to fire William and come back the next day for my junk—which, I might add, she had sitting at the corner. By the time I got to it, half the neighborhood was walking around with my shit. By the way, can I file a complaint against her? Can you make her pay for my stuff ?"

"Her son was tortured and murdered. She's paid enough. Wouldn't you agree?"

"Yeah, you're right. So, we split, I fired William. He pops up dead a few days later and she wants to blame me."

"What kind of things did you say?"

"Oh, just how fucking nosey she was. All in my business."

"Did you kill William?"

"Look, Officer—"

"Arnie. Just call me Arnie. You got that?"

"Whatever. Am I under arrest? If not I don't have to

answer any more questions."

From the sound of it, the Captain was beating the shit out of Carter. If folks stopped asking questions, the Captain might have calmed down and been a little nicer.

"Mother fucker, don't you ever question me as long as I let you live. You got that?"

"Yeah man, I got it."

"I hadn't planned on taking this course of action with you. But, you left me with no choice. Now, all I need is some cooperation from you. You get your people in check. I don't want any problems from you or them. Like the next time I come, I want your bartender to have my drink on the counter waiting for me. Listen up. Here, wipe your mouth. I want you to stop all that moaning and groaning and shut the fuck up. Now, Gloria is coming after you."

"How do you know?"

Some people never learned. By the sound of it, I'm sure Arnetti hit Carter with his patented backhand. He gave me lessons on the proper use of a backhand and the effect it has on criminals. 'Hold your gun in the palm of your hand tight, then swing. Man, the force. Turn any bad ass into a pussy, guaranteed.'

"She's coming after you. I know this. Now. Ask your question. I promise I won't hit you."

"Wh-what do you want me to do?"

"Nothing. Not one mother fuckin' thing. Keep doing what you're doing. When the time comes just make sure you duck. By the way, you detestable imitation of a human being. I have a ten-year-old daughter. I should put a bullet in your head right now, you sick mother—But, the problems I have are much bigger than you. That's the only reason I am letting you live. I need to know where you film. Think about your reply. Lie or bullshit me and I kill you on the spot."

"It's over on Wallace. Seventeen-hundred block. Here's the address."

"That's a good boy. Take this card. Go to this address in about two hours. Dentist. He'll fix your teeth for you. That's the least I can do. I know you killed William Azeem. That's not my concern, not right at this minute anyway. Do good and maybe I'll allow you to leave the business with both of your legs still attached to your body. Fuck up... Make sure you get to that dentist. Today!"

I guess everything had come full circle. I couldn't control Sasha. Sasha couldn't control herself. The Mayor wanted revenge. The Captain wanted to save his ass. What about me? Seemed like I was in the middle of all of this shit. With family like Sasha, who needs nuclear war! Diane Reeves sang about her Grandmother and better days. Well, if mine didn't get any better I knew I was bound to crack up. I wasn't looking forward to going to work the next day.

"Rock! Get in here."

I figured Arnetti would be calling me into his office first thing that morning. Even though I am an independent contractor with total autonomy I had a hunch that being in the precinct at first light was a necessity. Sure, right, I didn't have to answer to anyone. I worked alone. Whatever. Times were changing.

"Yes, sir."

"Close the door. Sit down."

"Rock. I hate to tell you this, but the Mayor—

"Rozen. Our distinguished and fearless leader. What about him?"

"Jesus Christ, you would think that at nine o'clock in the morning you wouldn't have to be a smart ass. Can you ever just keep quiet and allow a person to talk?"

"Sorry, sir!"

"I don't know why I have been putting up with your shit for all these years."

I was about a nervous wreck. I didn't know exactly what the Captain was going to say. I did, however, know that he was after baby sis. I didn't like that one bit, but I had to be cool.

"Maybe it's because—"

"Will you please shut the hell up?! Migraine headaches. That's all I get when I am around you, Detective!"

"Sorry. Shall I get you an aspirin?"

"No sit down and shut the fuck up. Please!"

"Yes, sir!"

"Rock. Truth of the matter, we have a conflict of interest that won't allow you to continue on with the task force."

"How so?" I knew what Arnetti was getting at. I wanted to see how much he was willing to tell me. If he was going to give me an abstract warning, maybe a subtle suggestion that I get myself and Sasha out of town. Maybe he was going to proceed with taking her down, and me too if necessary.

"If you're telling me that you are pretty damn sure that Sasha killed Kyle—

"I never said that! Anyway, what's your point?"

"If you think she did it, how can I honestly expect you to bring her in? She's your sister for Christ's sake. Family. You're going to bend every rule a couple of times for as long as necessary until you can get her off. Right?"

"Much the same as you would do for a family member of your own, like Joey for example. Just what is your point, sir?"

Captain Arnetti had this simple-ass look on his face like he was surprised to find out that I would do anything I could to protect my sister. I hated to be the one to tell him, but contrary to popular belief, blacks do stick together. We are loyal to one another. I wanted Sasha to stop killing. I also wanted her to get some help. I thought Captain Arnetti might be able to help.

"Rock, I am taking you off the task force."

"Fuck that. I am in this shit knee-high. I waded in, now give me some time to get out. That's the least you can do. I can't abandon—"

"Sorry."

"What do you mean, sorry?"

"Came from the top."

"The top my ass, you mean the Mayor."

"Like I was trying to tell you earlier, the Mayor feels like you just haven't given us anything sufficient since we put you in charge. We can't justify your existence as a separate entity any longer."

"My existence? You plan on taking me behind a building and putting a bullet in my ear the way you did that pimp about five years ago?"

"You know, that's what I love about you, Rock. Your memory. You don't forget a damn thing, do you?"

"Nightmares, sir. Fucking nightmares. They never leave me. Got so bad I started writing them down."

I wasn't being a smart ass at that moment. I wanted Arnetti to know where I was coming from. If he was going to take me down, he was coming right along with me. Daddy told me a long time ago. 'Cecil, always cover your ass!'

"Not at all, Rock, I would shoot you right here in my office if I ever decided to get rid of you."

"Well, that's comforting to know."

"Once the Mayor found out that Kyle and Coleman were lovers he hit the roof."

"What do you mean, '*Found Out*'? You mean after you told him."

"I had no choice. I couldn't continue to have no answers for him and expect him to remain complacent. Besides, he pissed me the hell off. I had to shut his Irish ass up."

"Oh, so you sell out my sister, sell me out, just to shut him up. Damn, there's a word for your actions, sir."

"What's that?"

At that point, insubordination wasn't the first thing on my mind. Arnetti had broken our bond. I didn't know where this was going to leave me— or Sasha, for that matter.

"Um…That's Fucked Up! Sir!"

"Regardless, I am assigning another officer to the case. I need all the information that you have gathered regarding the other murders you have been investigating. Plus, your investigation has only left you with hypotheses. I need someone who is going to produce results. That's what I need. You're just not getting it done, Detective. Besides, maybe your sister isn't even involved in any of this madness. Just because you suspect someone doesn't make them guilty. Maybe you aren't seeing things clearly because of what Sasha has done in the past. I need somebody who is not going to be swayed one way or the other by what he finds."

"Does my promotion still stand or am I busted back to a meandering street Sergeant?"

"Migraine headaches. There's plenty of detective work that needs to be done around here. Detective."

Well, that was it. Move my ass out of the way. If I got in the way that meant I was somewhere I had no business being. Neat. Smart. Crafty. Fucked-up. We made eye contact right before I left his office. Captain and Detective. Sounds like one of those made-for-TV movies that generally sucked. He knew just like I knew. This shit was far from over. He might have said I was off the case, but I had other intentions. I was going to see this thing through to the end. What I did notice in his eyes was that he was going to do whatever was necessary. He just didn't want me in his way. Maybe he did have a heart. In the end, we would see.

Session VI

25

Sasha

Life in the suburbs was a lot different than life in the city. I envisioned Coleman and myself growing old together in the suburbs. City life, you gotta see it to believe it. Kids of all ages, running around, eating pretzels and water ice. Little kids drinking 'Blue Sky and Pineapple Soda.' The big boys drinking 40's, as Rock would call them. Basketball courts set up on telephone poles with cut-out milk crates, where young men play their version of hoops with determination and skill, fearless of the cars that pass by on their two-lane street that doubles as a basketball court. It must have taken years of practice to be able to swish a round ball through a square crate. Fire hydrants stay uncapped. Everybody takes a dip once in a while, just to cool off. Mothers with their daughters with *their* daughters going to the market. Dragging that metal cart with the bad wheel. Talking about how glad they would be when they got a car. Somebody's always at the bus stop. Bus is never on time. Cops roll in and out of the neighborhoods, stopping long enough to grab a free cheesesteak and some cheese fries. The music of the city wasn't the birds chirping, or the sound of whistling leaves as the summer breeze passes through, but gunshots. At times, fast cars screeching around corners. Rap. Jazz.

Reggae. Conversation. How could you not love it? I could go on for days.

The suburbs, on the other hand, were beautiful, when you're on the outside looking in. Green grass, always well kept. Hardly any trash. Half the time you're so surprised to see some trash that you end up picking it up. See a black man running in the city, you figured he'd either done wrong or about to do wrong. Out here, people running was part of the scenery. Some started with the sunrise. Dedicated, daily regimen. Others waited until the evening to enjoy the night air. Walkers. Joggers with strollers with the big front wheel. Friendly waves from your neighbor across the street.

Living there, on the inside, was empty. Maybe it was just me that was empty. I loved the rosebushes that adorned the front of my house. The Azalea flower bed that runs along the side was absolutely beautiful. The Dogwood tree was blooming. Looked better than the one my neighbor three houses over planted the day after I planted mine. No matter where you went somebody felt compelled to emulate your creativity. The Japanese Maple in the front was as beautiful as I had ever seen. The white rocks that I had used to outline the flower beds accentuated the landscaping quite perfectly.

So there I stood, spraying my roses to keep the beetles out; trimming hedges; kicking little white rocks back in their place; pouring more mulch, gardening, I guess, because everybody else does. After I finished, I grabbed my book and lemonade and sat underneath my Japanese Maple. Read and relax. Touch my soul. Yeah, I was empty on the inside.

Antiquated Journals. Gloria and I had met the author at a book signing while we were out having a good time shopping. After her reading I was sure her book could provide me with spiritual food for my soul. Some 'sister-mamma guidance'! I hoped.

Soon as I got settled and decided to become one with my soul, I noticed a silver convertible Mercedes Benz approaching my house. Initially I didn't recognize the driver, a black man. It was apparent that the brother had good taste. He wasn't selling insurance or Kirbys, that was for sure. Lost? Possibly. Then he smiled.

I said to myself, when I see Jeanette Jones again— I didn't know whether to smack her or hug her. I decided to wait and see how the day turned out.

"Mister Belefont!"

"Miss Timms."

"Mister Belefont."

"Uhm, I was lost. I, ah, took a wrong turn when I was leaving— No good, huh?"

"Nope."

"Was in the neighborhood?"

"Uh-uh."

"Jeane—"

"Who else!?"

"This is the first time I have seen Sunshine under a tree. May I join you?"

"Since you went through all of the trouble to get here."

"Believe me, Sasha, it was no trouble at all. Actually, it was my extreme pleasure to come and see you."

What could I do but smile? Genuine. That was all I could say about this man. Almost perfect. He gave me more attention than I deserved. If he could even fathom what was inside my head, inside me, surely he would be on 95 South. What made him believe that it was okay to lean over and kiss me on the cheek and give me a hug like we were old friends was beyond me. The fact that I reached up and returned his hug and planted a subtle peck on his sweet chocolate skin was totally irrelevant to the way I felt about him.

"...And Jeanette's desire to see you with a good man."

We laughed. For as hard as I tried to stay in control of my emotions, I just couldn't. I didn't want to let my guard down, but what could I do? He just sat there grinning at me. Admiring me with his eyes, those luscious lips. I was almost at his mercy. He was giving me personal time, and wasn't asking anything in return. Earlston made me feel good. Warm. Lov...I wasn't ready for that.

"If it were up to me, Sasha, I could just sit here all day and talk with you. I would really like to get to know you. Let's jump in the car and drive for a while. See where we end up."

"Let me go clean myself up. Even Sunshine gets a little dirty."

I turned and headed for the house. Again I was faced with whether or not to cut my tongue out. Jaws flappin' all the time. I try to stay in control and the tongue ruins it by saying what I am thinking before I have a chance to stop it. I took a peek back at Earlston. He had a white towel in his hand and was busy wiping off the passenger seat of his car. I'm sure it was already clean.

I showed Earlston how to get to Lancaster Ave., told him to make a right and keep straight. The beauty of this section of the suburbs, even if all the lights catch you, still makes a nice ride. From Wynnewood to Ardmore to Villanova we just rode and rode. The winding down of activity on the busy streets was replaced with trees, more trees, and green grass. Tranquillity. Heaven. I didn't resist the 'Sand Man' when he came and carried me off to sleep. I was startled at the sound of my door opening. Earlston had parked somewhere that I had never been. Maybe a place called Utopia.

Before I could argue, or resist, Earlston lifted me into his arms and carried me to a spot under a big oak tree that had a picnic lunch set up. He wrapped his coat around me. He didn't look strong enough to carry me. Maybe I was still sleep. I wasn't. A cool breeze was blowing through the air. We were high up in this place that I did not know. The sun was setting. I didn't know how long we had been there, really didn't care either. I was snuggled in his chest. His arms wrapped around me. He must have had the picnic basket in the trunk. Confident brother. How did he know I loved a good Chef's salad? How did he know I would be home? How'd he know I would agree to come with him? I could stay here— for days.

I hated saying good-bye, but it wasn't a fairy tale. True life. The animal may sleep sometimes, but it never goes away. I would have loved entertaining Earlston, but Carter Woods was on my mind. I had to catch up with that smart-ass Cecil and see if he was going to do what needed to be done.

Our lips met each others' cheeks. We hugged. Earlston Belefont drove off. He gave me a card with the most enchanting words. He wrote it himself.

Sasha, Guess what? I thought that I saw something beautiful today. Maybe it was the sun setting on the Philadelphia skyline. Perfect. A sight worth seeing throughout eternity. Or maybe it was a newborn baby, innocent, pure. I kept looking. Intrigued at its flawlessness, I looked harder, a diamond, maybe, but I wasn't sure. I squinted, strained my eyes, to get a better look. Sunshine in the shade. As I approached your home I realized that it was you! And then I smiled. I had found Eden!

Earlston

He made me feel alive. Loved. That big mouth of mine invited him back soon. Just wait for my call next time, it said. If I didn't have a tongue, I thought, could I still do the job?

I figured it was time to talk with my brother. It was time for Rock to do what he did best. Or I would be forced to do what I do.

"Hey, Sasha, come on in. What are you doing ringing the doorbell? Lost your key?"

"No, I just wanted to give you some privacy for a change. I get tired of walking in on you and your female acquaintances."

"Isn't that considerate, for a change. Turning over a new leaf?"

"Bright yellow and red, spanking brand new."

Boy that promotion must have come with a raise, and an interior decorator. Cecil had new furniture. I couldn't believe my eyes: Royal blue leather sofa and love seat, glass cube coffee table with matching end tables, ivory chess set on one end table, metallic backgammon set on the other, lovely flower centerpiece on the coffe table. Cecil hadn't brought furniture in about ten years. Good for him.

"How are ya'?"

"Still struggling. Yourself?"

"To be honest, I'm a little on the edge. If you know what I mean."

"Sasha, I don't have the slightest idea what you mean. Besides, if I started thinking like you I probably would want to shoot myself. Know what I mean?"

"You live your life as a smart ass and you're surely going to die that way, too. Asshole. Move out my way so I can sit down on your new sofa. And please bring me something to drink."

Cecil had a way about him that made him so endearing. You loved to love him and sometimes you hated the fact that you loved him.

"How's this, Ma'am? A nice, refreshing glass of iced tea. Anything else, your highness?"

"Please, Cecil, sit down. And yes, there is something else you can get for me. Carter Woods in a body bag."

"Sasha? Don't tell me the only reason that you came over here was to bother me about Carter."

"Well, not exactly. I wanted to see how you were doing. Haven't seen you in a couple of days."

"Bullshit."

"I did want to see you. You are my brother whom I love very dearly."

"More shit."

"And, I wanted to see what you were going to do about Carter."

"Sure you right!"

"You do the worst *Barry White* imitation I have ever heard, you know that?"

"Whatever. Sasha, I told you before, let the police police!' Remember?"

"That's besides the point, big brother. I told you before that I got something inside of me that is dying of thirst. The only thing that quenches that thirst is the blood of the perpetrator."

"Jesus Christ, now you're turning into a vampire, huh? What the hell is going to happen next, you going to turn into a big black bat and go bite Carter on the neck?"

"No, I'm going to take this chair and hit you over your damn head!"

"Sure you riiiggghhhttt?"

As hard as I tried to be angry, to stay mad, it just wasn't working. Cecil is about as simple as the day is long. I was trying to convey to him how serious this problem was for me to handle. He just kept playing games, like he's been doing for as long as I can remember.

"Listen, Barry..."

"You listen, Sasha. I am going to take care of this problem. I have to run. Bad guys to catch. Lock up when you leave."

"You have to leave?"

"Promise me you will give me some time."

"Twenty minutes, then I move in for the kill!"

"I guess my smart mouth is rubbing off on you, huh?"

"Just a little. I'll see you later. Work fast, big guy! Work fast."

I'm sure that Cecil didn't hear me suggest that he work fast. He was damn near in his car before I could finish what I was saying. Guess I'll chill here for a while. Watch some Oprah.

26

Rock

Parkside Ave. West Philly. Not a bad part of the city. Actually it was kind of nice. Parkside ran right into Fairmount Park. The Robin Hood Dell Amphitheater was up the hill. Kelly's pool, man talk about wall-to-wall kids. Must have been a thousand of them in that pool. And the daredevils who ran top speed off the platform at least thirty feet in the air, looking like they were gonna crash for sure into the wall, only to miss by a few inches, and land feet first in the water. Everybody below watching, excited, with their mouths open, or eyes closed. Too scared to look. Tennis courts. Barbecue pits. The Cornucopia, the main club we used to party at back in the day. And, of course, Gloria Azeem. She was the best thing about Parkside Ave. If I was gonna take care of this mess, it was going to be through her.

She had a nice row house. Fresh paint. A little gate. Flower bed. Cute. No doorbell. I hated using my knuckles. I rapped on the old wooden door. Of course, I hit right in the crease and earned another set of busted knuckles.

"Hello, Ms. Azeem, my name is Detective Cecil Rock. May I speak with you for a few minutes, please?"

"Detective Rock! Sasha's brother? Please, please,

come right in, have a seat."

The first thing that impressed me about the interior of her house was I couldn't find a speck of dirt anywhere. Her taste in elegant furnishings was more than evident. I resisted the desire to look outside and make sure that I was in the same neighborhood. Very well-kept woman, also. Probably an aerobics junkie, just like Sasha.

"Can I get you something to drink, Detective?"

"Please call me Rock. And some water would be fine. Thanks."

She returned with a pitcher of iced tea and some pretzels. I guess she knew I was watching my weight.

"Sasha told me that you would come. She said you were her favorite brother. That you had a soft heart for a tragic story."

"Actually, her only brother, but I do want to help you. What happened to your son was terrible."

"My son was fourteen when Carter Woods killed him. I still can't believe that he's dead."

"Do you have any proof, anything concrete that I can use to at least bring him back in for questioning? Maybe hold him for a couple of days, and beat a confess— Excuse me, coerce, or make that convince him to confess to me that he killed your son."

"Rock. Carter isn't a dummy. He closed down that video store where William worked right after he killed him. He knew that I wouldn't rest until I found my son's killer."

"Nothing, huh?"

"Not really, just some pictures of my son that I got

from some guy who bought a membership."

"How did you get them?"

"Well, I found a note that Carter had given to William. A delivery that he wanted him to make. I went to the address. Luckily, the woman who answered was high out of her head. She wasn't coherent, that's for sure. I told her I had a delivery for her. She bitched about me not being William, and waved me down the steps. I found a complete membership kit in the basement."

"Incredible."

"Did what I had to do."

"Anything else?"

"Um...just a phone number for new enrollment. But nothing that can be traced directly to Carter. But, rest assured, I know that bastard killed my son. Sufficient evidence or not. If you can't help, that's fine. If I have to kill that son of a bitch myself then that's what I will do. But he is going to pay!"

Immediately I had thoughts of a vigilante murderess menacing the streets of Philadelphia, and she went by the name of Sasha Timms. Now Gloria. Two Sasha's. Two monsters. I needed some aspirin, and a miracle. I prayed, *'Lord, help me nail this bastard before Gloria does, please? I'll go to church.'*

And hallelujah! A phone number! In my mind, all I could say was, sure you right! Gloria talked about, that's all she found. All I needed from Gloria was a sense of urgency and a little bit of trust. With my luck— I'll keep my fingers crossed anyway.

"Let me ask you, how is your relationship with

Sasha?"

"Sasha? Oh, it's great. She was tremendous in helping me deal with William's death. I have to admit though, she has an unorthodox brand of therapy. One minute we're sitting in her office crying our eyes out, the next we're headed downtown to do some shopping, eating and talking about everything except my problems. What I learned from her was that life goes on. You have to live. Have a desire to live, then go out and do it. Live that is. Sure, when the dust settles and I get back home, my mind goes back to my son, but it isn't as hard. I know that I can get on with my life and function. That was something that I couldn't do before I met Sasha. She's wonderful."

"Sounds like you two established quite a strong relationship in a short time."

"We sure did. That's my girl!"

"If the situation were reversed, would you be willing to help her?"

"What do you mean?"

"I mean, if Sasha was in trouble, would you be willing to help her out?"

"Yes, of course. Well, is she in trouble?"

"Sort of."

"I got her back, Rock."

"I really don't want to get into too many details, but I might need a favor from you. It doesn't involve much."

"What do you need me to do?"

"For the next two days, could you be home to answer the telephone between six and eight?"

"Sure. I get off work at three-thirty. I usually get

home around four-fifteen, four-thirty. That shouldn't be a problem."

"Great. I appreciate your time. Talk to you soon."

"Look, Detective, I should be the one thanking you. You be careful, and watch out for my girl."

"Yes, Ma'am, and please, call me Rock."

"Okay. Rock. Talk to you later."

"Good-bye."

I had to move fast. I called my best friend up, who else, the only Spanish-speaking brother I knew.

"Carlous! Que' pasa, man?"

"Nada! What the hell you want? Oh yeah, how is your sister?"

"Yo, brother, you ready to move into the big time? Be my Robin. My Tonto. My..."

"What the hell do you need?"

"Take notes if you have to. I don't have a lot of time."

"Gotcha!"

"You got any cash? Say around two hundred?"

"Yeah, but it's for my rent."

"Great, then we can use it. I'll pay you back if things don't work out."

"Like how you paid me back the hundred you borrowed from me twelve years ago."

"I had your money last week but you weren't home when I stopped by."

"You a trip, Cecil."

"Call me Cecil again and I will come to that dump you call an apartment and arrest your black ass."

"Then who you gonna git to play Tonto?"

"Point. Now, stop complaining about the money and listen up. I want you to call this number at three o'clock tomorrow. Wait for a package to arrive. Whatever you do, don't open it. You don't want to see what's inside."

"What's inside?"

"Tell you over wings, cool?"

"Cool! Continue."

"Whatever the delivery person asks for, pay it. No bitching and complaining like you usually do when you have to spend money. No questions. Just pay the sucker. I'll be waiting right outside. Flash your lights in your living room as soon as he walks down the steps."

"That's it?"

"That's it."

"Piece of cake."

"Carlous, it's a piece of cake as long as you don't fuck up. I'm counting on you like I never have before."

"Don't worry, Dog, I won't let you down."

"My Nigguh! Talk to you tomorrow."

Carlous lived on Sixty-Third Street right past the fire station. The house that he lived in was enormous. It would have been a mansion for any one family. I guess that's why the owner turned it into six apartments. I parked on the opposite side of the street and down about twenty feet from his building. I had a nice angle. I could still see his living room window and not be so close that someone coming to his house would know that I was watching.

I don't know how Carter did it. He managed to find another minor, about William's age to deliver his filth.

His Used Jeans outfit was two sizes too big. Even though his pants hung well below his ass, he didn't bother to pull them up, and obviously didn't care. His haircut was fresh, and his Air Jordans didn't have a speck of dirt on them. He must have been reaping the benefits of his labor. It was around four. The kid jumped off the bus carrying a box that looked like it weighed maybe eight or ten pounds. I almost slept on him on his way out. I caught the light in Carlous's window. That's one good thing about those old houses. Lots of trees, and dark as hell, even in the day time. The youngster hailed a cab, jumped in, and settled in the back with the demeanor of a successful businessman. He looked satisfied with the business trans- action he just completed. The cab headed down Sixty- Third Street towards the South West section of the city. Made a left on Chestnut, made every light. Didn't even speed. Following the cab was easy. As he headed toward the park I decided to make my move. I put on my red light and pulled the cab over.

"Yo, Cabby. What's up?"

"Was cool teel now, why you hangin' onto me? I know I didn't buss no rule."

"I know you didn't, Pops. I want to holler at the youngin' in the back seat. If it's okay with you."

"Do whucha want, but the meters runnin' all night, and all day!"

This brother looked old enough to have started Yellow Cab. He had about a thousand maps in the front seat, half a sandwich, maybe ten Snickers wrappers, soda cans all over the floor, black and yellow silk or imitation silk print shirt, jeans that probably were blue at one time, now had a hue of black. What I thought were even blacker patches on his jeans were actually two old, dark, crusty knees, trying to make it through another day of driving. The black skin that was taunt on his face depicted about sixty years of a hard life. Scotch tape held the clasps together on his Eagles cap that was decorated with about twenty pins: Flags, eagles, peace symbols. The pins helped to cover up about twenty years of dirt on the cap that was so old the Eagles wings had fallen off!

"How' ya doing back there, young man?"

"Whatup!"

"My name's Detective Cecil Rock. What they call you, youngblood?"

"Why? I didn't do nuttin'."

"I didn't say that you did. I just want to know your name."

"Ahmed. Ahmed Myers."

"Well, Ahmed, I need to speak with you. Your boss, the one you make deliveries for, asked me to talk to you. Would you please step out of the cab?"

"Cabby! Have a nice day. Hey....Ah-mmmmmmmed!

Just what the hell I needed. The kid took off in a huff. Arms pumping and knees rising. One thing for sure I wasn't about to catch him on foot. My corns were hurting bad enough already. I jumped in the car kind of mad. I might run his ass over. He covered about fifty yards by the time I got moving. Trouble was he was cutting across the Parkway towards the Art Museum. If he got up by Pennsylvania Avenue before I could cut him off, I might

lose him. There were too many one-way small-ass streets
to drive through safely. I was about fifteen yards behind
him but he made it to Pennsylvania Ave. I jumped out of
the car and took off on foot. He saw me chugging after
him, made a sharp right and headed up towards Spring
Garden. Maybe all those miles I put in running in my
heyday would give me the stamina to keep up after this
punk. Maybe not. It seemed like the harder I ran, the
smaller he got. He ran and ran and ran. He looked like a
sprinter. I wasn't going to let him get away though. As we
headed down Spring Garden towards the community college I noticed a mountain bike parked on the sidewalk. A
young man was sitting on the steps with a helmet in his
hands talking to a young lady. I would have to stop by and
thank him later. One big jump and I mounted the bike in
full stride before the dude had time to notice or respond.

"I'm a cop, I'll bring it right back!"

Ahmed was becoming larger and larger as I peddled
with all of my might. All he had to do was jump in some
water and my tri-athletic career would be underway. Each
time he turned to see how far I was behind him, his eyes
got bigger, and his gait quickened. I was close. Just as he
was about to make a sharp right turn down another street
I dove head first and rode him to the pavement. The hard
concrete was the only cushion for our fall. I thought he
was going to pass out from the weight of my body coming
down on him. He screamed as though he just lost a leg or
something. I didn't think I weighed that much. He rolled
over, mad and tired, and insisted that I get the 'fuck' off
of him.

"Calm down, little brother."

"Man, just get the hell off of me. Damn!"

"You all right?"

"Yeah. You have to be fine, since I cushioned your fall. What do you want with me anyway?"

"F-first, you're going to pay for a cab back to my car."

I had to stop talking and get my breath.

"Then I'm going to take you home. You're on house arrest. If you so much as move from your house you're going to jail. Also, I am going to tell your mother that you have been delivering child pornography video tapes for Carter Woods for large tips. How's that, Mr. Big-time?"

"Bullshit. Ain't hardly no fuckin' kids on dem tapes."

"Look, he's already killed one boy about your age who found out about what he was doing. I'm going to take you home. Don't pick up the phone. Don't try to call him. Just stay in the house for the rest of the day. When this is over, get yourself a job at Domino's or something. A real delivery job. Okay?"

"You saw the tapes?"

"Sure did. If you don't want to go to jail— Look kid, just tell me where you live so I can get you off the streets. I will take care of Carter myself."

"He's a sick mother—"

"Watch your mouth. I'm sure you don't talk like that around your mother."

"Yeah, yeah— hey! Why do I have to pay for the cab?"

"Because you're the one out here doing *Michael Johnson* on a bad day, that's why. Besides, I know you got a pocket full of dirty money. Might as well spend it on something useful."

Since we had only covered about four blocks, the cab cost Ahmed four bucks. A dollar-sixty to sit down and two-forty to get us back to my car. The Cabby tried to stick us for an extra buck for having two passengers. I assured him that Ahmed would be more than willing to pay the extra fee, plus tip. The Cabby took Ahmed's ten spot and headed off to find his next fare. Ahmed didn't live too far from Gloria. When I asked him if he knew William Azeem he shook his head no. I didn't believe him. I think he believed William screwed up. That's why he got killed. Like he ratted and deserved to die the way he did. His mother assured me that Ahmed wouldn't be any trouble anytime soon.

My plan was for one pornographic delivery person to come up missing. Make Carter Woods a little restless, wondering if his time was winding up. Time for phase two.

"Hello, Gloria. It's Detective Rock, glad you're home."

"Hi. It's no bother. I was anxious about your phone call. I'm ready for Carter to get his. How are you doing?"

"Good!"

I detailed the plan to Gloria. I was positive she wasn't going to screw up.

"...And remember, Gloria, feel what you're saying. Be convincing. I trust you'll do fine."

I tried to reassure her as best I could. I wanted her to be as relaxed as possible when she made that crucial phone call.

"Yes. And call you as soon as I hang up, right?"

"Right. Say what you have to say and get off the phone."

"Yes, sir."

"Bye."

I knew if she could pull this off it would allow me the opportunity to see everything in my life clearly. With my luck... maybe today it's going to change.

"Hello. Yes, my name is Gloria Azeem. May I speak with Detective Cecil Rock, please?"

"He's not in."

"Well, may I have his superior officer, his Captain or whoever is in charge of the task force that Detective Rock is on?"

"Hold on, please."

"Hello, this is Captain Arnetti. How may I help you?"

"Please, sir, I am desperate. My name is Gloria Azeem. I need to speak with Detective Rock as soon as possible. Do you know how I can get in touch with him?"

"Azeem. Wasn't your son murdered a little while ago?"

"Yes, he was. How did you know?"

"I am the Captain, Ma'am."

"Well that's simply wonderful to hear, but I really need to speak with him right now."

"Miss. Please. Slow down. Detective Rock isn't in right now. Maybe I can be of some assistance to you."

"No. No. I really need to speak with him personally.

It's about his sister Sasha."

"Sasha? Sasha Timms? What about? Look, I have known Detective Rock for many years. I practically raised him in the police department. If there is some type of emergency involving his sister— well, he's like family to me. I can undoubtedly be of some assistance. Tell me, what's the problem?"

"Captain, does he trust you? I mean, maybe I should speak with him personally."

"Gloria, I'll be honest with you. Rock and I are as close as two men could be. Like I said before, he's like my son. Talk to me. I can help."

"Okay— all right. After William was killed I had a nervous breakdown. I went to see Sasha for therapy. She was wonderful. We went shop—"

"Shopping? I hate to interrupt, but?"

"Sorry, I didn't mean to rattle on so. Well, I told Sasha about William's death and how I suspected Carter Woods to be the killer. Well, now Sasha feels like she needs to vindicate my son's murder herself."

"How so?"

"She called me up sounding crazed and nervous. She said she can't sit still any longer while Carter walks the streets. She said she kidnapped the delivery person and she forced him to tell her where Carter makes his films. She said when the sun sets, she's going to move in and cut his heart out."

"Miss Azeem, I know you want to help, but your story sounds a bit unreal. How does she plan on cutting Carter's heart out?"

"She's sort of an expert in karate. She's skilled in several weapons. And she sounded just a little over the edge. I believe her. Captain Arnetti, she sounded very serious, like she could actually kill him. I'm just afraid for her."

"Don't you worry, Ms. Azeem, I'll get a car over there to stop her. Thanks for your information."

"Any time."

I figured if I lit a little fire under the Captain's ass he would get moving. I knew he would want to be at Carter's when Sasha got there. Kinda liven up the party. I planned on crashing myself.

"Detective Rock?"

"Gloria. How'd it go?"

"I think he bought it. He sounded overly concerned about helping you and your sister. He was very convincing as far as his love for you. He said he raised you like a son in the police department. Is that true?"

"Yes it is. To a degree anyway."

"Detective, why did you need me to call the Captain, is Sasha really going after Carter?"

"Sasha will be fine. Gloria, I appreciate all of your help. In the morning, get up, read the newspaper, and have a wonderful day. Pray that this situation ends without..."

"I get the point, Rock."

"William is gone, but we are gonna fix some things that are broke. Thanks for your help."

"Thank you, and God bless."

It was time to move my ass. Big brother needed to be

watching!

Carlous met me at my house and we picked up the Captain's van headed in the direction of Carter's disco. His home address wasn't too far away. I was sure that's where he was headed. I was glad I had the Orkin man, make that Carlous the imitation Orkin man, stop by Carter's place. A coupon for a free extermination and a report of some deceased termites always gets him inside. When we got close enough to see, Arnetti was already at the front door talking on the intercom.

"Who is it?"

"Open the door, Carter, you got me standing out here in this fucked-up neighborhood, looking like the next victim for a stick-up."

"Didn't know you would get here so soon. My bad. C-c-come on in, Arnie. Can I get you something to drink?"

"Sure, you get me a drink. While you're at it, fix yourself one. Oh, try to relax. I'm not here for you."

"Cool man, anything you say."

Carlous told me that by the looks of Carter's place he was making money on top of money. All at the expense of children. I wasn't impressed with his good taste. I hated him because of how he obtained his wealth. This kind of money wasn't worth having. I was starting to hate Captain Arnetti, too.

"Here you are, Arnie."

"Thanks. So, you have quite a place here. What kind of work do you do?"

"I own a club, couple of video sto—"

"Come on now, boy, tell me how you got the money

to furnish this place. Your home is baaaaad, brother!"

"Look, man, you come here to rag my ass or to fucking get Gloria off my back? If you gonna kick my ass again for asking questions, well then do it. I know you didn't come over here to get better acquainted and this ain't the lifestyles of the rich and famous. You know how I fucking make my money. Shit, you a cop, I'm sure you done dipped your hands in a few pots your damn self. I already got an envelope ready for you, here! I know the shakedown is coming."

"You's a smart boy, Carter. Very smart. Tell you what, we'll sit here and wait— for 'it' to happen. But don't you ever sound off at me again, or I'll kill you quicker than I can knock the teeth out of your black-ass mouth. You got that?"

"Yeah, man, I got it. We gonna sit here and chill. Just sit here."

"Question? All your people accounted for today? Any problems?"

"Huh?"

"If I have to repeat myself, it's gonna be a long evening for you. Get the answer right, too."

"Accounted for? Oh, naw. Matter of fact, a delivery boy didn't check back in after his last delivery. I figured he went downtown to spend some of the money he made. That's all. No big deal."

"No big deal! The kid works for you. Goes home early, and it's no big deal. I figure, that's got to concern you just a little."

"Actually, I was madder than a mother fucker that

the little punk didn't check back in. But hell, he was only running about an hour and a half late, then you called. Wasn't no use worrying about him. After his last delivery I usually cut him loose anyway. Besides, I didn't want to keep *the man* waiting. Now, that's something to be concerned about."

"Like I said before, Carter. You a smart boy. Guess what?"

"What?"

"Word got back to me that Gloria kidnapped your delivery boy. Said she's starting at the bottom and working her way to the top. Says she's going to extinguish your business with or without the help of the police."

"Ain't that a bitch. Her son winds up dead, and she's losing her mind. Then she turns around and fucks with somebody else's kid."

"Who the fuck are you to talk? She's doing the same damn thing that you are. Only thing is at least she's trying to do good. I'm sure she isn't going to harm that boy."

Breaking and entering. Bustin' my way into this fool's crib. I had sat in the car long enough. I moved around to the other side of the building. As I peered through the rear window I caught just a glimpse of Captain Arnetti talking with Carter Woods, pacing the room. Must be lecturing him. That's how he did when he was screaming on me. Cap' seemed to be pretty cool, relaxed. Carter was edgy, anticipating the arrival of somebody.

I made my way down the stairs to the lower level of his apartment. A small yellow light barely illuminated the ten- by-twenty foot area that probably served as a dance floor at parties. There was a double window with a metal grate across. Cheap bastard. The lock was broke off. He just had the grate sitting in the hinges, giving the appearance of security. Too busy filming kids to get it fixed. And what was I saying about my luck? I slid the grate off and leaned it against the wall.

The window was locked. Damn! What would McGyver do in this situation? Got it: *I took a bullet out of my pocket. Opened the housing. Dumped out the gunpowder. Ah-hah! Perfect. A smooth stone conveniently left next to the window. I used the stone to sharpen the edge of the bullet. Then I needed a handle. Something to grip the bullet. I searched around the dimly lit area. In luck! A hammer with a forked end. Then I just needed something to force the bullet into the opening. Hey, use the stone, dummy. Perfect. Done. Homemade glass cutter. Gently I carved a fist-sized hole…*

What do I do? I'm not McGyver. I took the butt of my gun and tapped a hole in the glass. Luckily, the entire pane didn't break. The glass that hit the floor seemed loud enough to wake the dead in Carter's hollow-sounding basement. I unlocked the window and climbed inside the apartment. I'm sure they heard me upstairs. They knew I was coming. The Captain was expecting Sasha. Surely he wasn't expecting the Rock. Felt like Batman. No. Superman. No. Captain Ameri— I should have felt like watching my ass before I got myself killed.

There was one door in the basement, another room. I looked in, had to make sure nobody snuck up behind me. I almost lost my lunch, dinner and last week's pizza. Pictures all over the walls. Kids, fucked up. He's a sick son-of-a-bitch. A bed, camera, on a tripod, sex paraphernalia. Sick shit. Mother— I got work to do. At least the room was empty. One closet. Nobody was hiding in there either. Covering my ass. I creeped up the steps real slow, wished I could say quietly, but it was an old house. Old wood. Plus, that cheesesteak didn't help my weight any either. I hated that creek-creek sound steps always made whenever you were trying to be sneaky or quiet. I still moved real slow.

"Damn, Arnie, what you gonna do? You gonna stop her?"

Carter should have known now wasn't the time to be asking questions. The Captain smacked him across the back of his head with his gun. Carter groaned and fell face forward on the rug. Arnetti grabbed him by the back of the shirt, trying to pull Carter to his knees. Choking him in the process.

"Get on your knees, mother fucker. The time is now. Don't move and don't open your mouth."

Petrified. Laceration in the back of the head. Confused. Carter had no choice but to comply. As he groped for a steady hand, Arnetti continued to pull on his collar. Spit dropped from Carter's mouth. He finally got his hands firm on the floor and managed to push himself to his knees. With a groan, he arched his back and raised upright. Arnetti placed the muzzle of his gun against Carter's chest. You could take the man out of the Mob, but I guess you couldn't take the Mob out the man.

"Don't move! Ms. Timms. Is that you? Please, come join us."

I slithered closer to the top of the stairs I looked up at the wall ahead of me. My shadow was visible. I was sure the Captain could see it too. I inched and inched. Slow. Deliberate. Cunning, I must say. As the top of my head, then hairline, then forehead, then eyebrows, then eyelids and then, finally, my eyes made their way even with the floor, and then slightly above it, I could see the Captain standing over Carter.

"Ms. Timms. We've been waiting for you."

27

Sasha

"Sasha, you poor thing, where were you while all this was going on?"

"It gets deeper, Doc."

I called Gloria to see if Rock had been by to see her yet. I was growing both impatient and exasperated with his attitude.

"Hey, Gloria, how you doin', girl?"

"Sasha. Good to hear your voice. I'm okay."

"Good. Look, I was just calling to see if my brother had gotten in touch with you."

"Matter of fact, he did."

"Really, is he going to help you? What did he say?"

"Actually, he gave me the impression that you needed help."

"Oh. How so?"

Gloria sounded a little anxious to me. I switched over to the cordless telephone and sat on the sofa. I guess I'm naturally more comfortable talking on a sofa.

"He didn't say. He just asked me how our sessions were, if we were friends."

"What else?"

"If you were ever in trouble and needed help, would I be willing to help you?"

"What did you say?"

"What do you think I said? Of course. Sasha, after all you've done for me, I would be willing to do anything to help you out."

"Thanks Gloria. I appreciate knowing that."

"Sasha, are you in some kind of trouble?"

"No. Why? What exactly did Rock say?"

"It's not what he said, it's what he asked me to do."

"Which was?"

"He had me call the police department and ask for him, even though he wasn't there. Then I was to talk to Captain Arnetti."

"Is that it?"

"Not exactly."

"Gloria! You're making me crazy!"

"Okay, sorry. Well, then I told the Captain that you had lost it. I mean mentally. That you were taking William's death pretty hard. You had kidnapped Carter Woods' delivery boy and you were going after Carter next."

"Where did all of this come from?"

"Rock. Your brother told me to do this. He said to sound frantic. To feel every word that I was saying. Sasha, what the hell is going on? Are you in trouble?"

Cecil. Mr. Detective. I knew what he was up to. He was going to try and wrap the whole matter up by himself. What I couldn't figure out was why he needed the Captain to be there. Then danger signs started popping into my head.

"No, honey, I'm not in trouble, but my brother might be. Did he say anything to you about where he was going? An address or anything?"

"Yes, he did. He told me to tell the Captain that you were going to go to Seventeenth and Wallace to find Carter Woods and kill him."

"Thanks, Gloria. How come you didn't call me?"

"I did. Have you checked your messages in the last hour? I've been calling you every fifteen minutes."

"Oh, I'm not home. Look, Gloria, thanks for everything. I'll talk to you later."

"Sasha, be careful. I never wanted you to get so—"

"Sweetheart. Everything is fine. The sun is going to shine brightly tomorrow."

Fine! There was no way Gloria could understand everything that was going on. I had to find Cecil's journal. Since he was ten years old, Cecil had kept a journal of every important event that had taken place in his life. He had to have taken notes about what his plans were. I hoped. Every drawer, with or without a handle, I pulled open. Junk, love letters, more junk. Nothing. Bedroom. Closet. Dresser. Under mattress. Nada! Zilch. Not a God-blessed thing. No journal. As I was tearing apart his desk, furious, damn near frantic, I was mad at myself for even getting my brother involved in the first place. As far as I was concerned he was in above his head. I was more than qualified to do all the killing that needed to be done, for myself, by myself. Damn. This man had more books than the damn library. No journal. I was just about to leave. Take my chances down at Seventeenth and Wallace when all of a sudden I was catapulted into the twentieth century. Home computer. Bingo. On. Check. Flipping, scrolling. Come on. Come on. Windows already booted. Great. Let's see. Where does he write? Word! Why not. Files. Open. Sasha.doc. Hell, I don't want to read that one. Budget.doc. Nope. Bahamas, Momdad, Resume, 'dot d-o-c! This was getting frustrating. Why did he scramble the files? Where in the hell could it be? He's about one secretive individual. Live alone and still hiding shit. Didn't trust a soul. Shit. Files, files, which one?. Let's see. Where is it? Could this be. Hum. Let's see. Betray.doc, initiated yesterday. Jackpot.

Who would betray Cecil Rock? None other than his very own Captain:

Today is a sad day in my police career. My man Carlous, full-time janitor, parttime wannabe detective dropped a wireless mike in Arnetti's office. We overheard the Mayor demanding that Arnetti take care of my baby sis. If I got in the way, me too. I can't believe this shit. After all of these years on the force, it finally boils down to this. Either the Captain saves his ass or his career is through. If he has to betray me, our trust, then that's what he'll do. For some reason, naive I guess, I figured he would come to me and suggest we try to figure this thing out. The Mayor really reamed the Captain's ass. The Captain busted the Mayor's groove by telling him that his son was fucking Coleman Timms, a black man, and my brother-in-law, up the ass when he got killed. Said that, I, (sold my ass right out), might think that my sis-

*ter was behind the killings. I never actually said that, but I
guess he added it up on his own. He didn't even try to protect her. He wasn't going to give me any more time to figure
out how to help her. I can't see her behind bars. I can't let
that happen, no matter how fucked-up in the head she is. All
she needs is some help. Psychiatric! I got to flush this shit
out. Get the Captain to think Sasha is coming after Carter
Woods. He'll move. See if he's really going to take her out. I
can't believe...*

I didn't even want to read the rest. I had to get over
there fast. Cecil was in trouble. He's too trusting. He
believed that the Captain could have been reasoned
with. He believed that the Captain was going to do right.
Ask me, that man was going to save his own ass, and get
rid of anything that stood in his way, including his own
detective. Seventeenth and Wallace. I knew the neighborhood.

28

Rock

My legs had started to ache standing so rigid and still on those stairs. Arnetti still didn't know that it wasn't Sasha. He was going to make a move. He had to. I inched a little more. I guess he wasn't willing to wait until he could see me. The sound of the gun going off confirmed everything that I didn't want to believe about Captain Arnetti. He was going to eliminate all the problems in his life. Poor Carter. Executed. Ain't that a bitch?

"See what you've just done, Ms. Timms?"

"Captain?"

"Huh? Rock! What the fuck are you doing here?"

"That's what I should be asking you. Why are you calling for my sister? Were you expecting her?"

"Rock, you shouldn't be here."

"No, sir, you're wrong on that one. This is exactly where I need to be."

"Put your gun away, Detective. You know as well as I do this piece of shit deserved to die. It's all over."

"It'll be over when you explain to me why you were calling for my sister. And what you meant by 'See what you've done!' Then it'll be over. Sir!"

"Oh that. I can explain."

My old partner Judy got shot once. She told me that when you experience a traumatic event in your life, everything happens in slow motion. As I blinked, my eyelids were raising real slow-like. The Captain's arm, the one that still had the 9-millimeter attached to it swung towards me. I tried to react. My arm rose towards him. I squeezed. It was too late. It's almost like I could see the bullet coming right at me. Turning and turning, slowly. Right at my chest. Dodge left. Duck. Do something, anything except get shot. I made what I thought was a gallant attempt to get out of the way. Actually, all I had time to do was tense the muscles in my chest. The only thing that I could do in a fraction of a second. This bullet is going to rip me apart, I thought. When it hit me there was pain like none that I had ever experienced in my life. My vest wasn't working. Like a giant oak I fell backward. **TIMBER!**

The steps were unkind to me as I tumbled back. Head, shoulders, back, knees, elbows, neck. Every part of me that was most sensitive to pain seemed to find a corner or edge of this hardwood staircase. Unkind. Painful. Agony that was climaxed by a hole in my body, torn open by a former friend. I felt the muzzle of a gun in the back of my head. My role model wasn't quite through with me yet.

"I didn't want things to turn out like this, Rock. Now you're gonna die. Sorry to say it. Fast or slow, it's up to you. Tell me where your sister is and I'll let you lay here and bleed to death. Don't cooperate and I'll put a bullet through your skull."

"Captain?"

"Yea."

"Suck my d—..."

That's all I remember. I didn't know if I died or if Captain Arnetti shot me again or I just passed out.

29

Sasha

I hit Wallace in about twelve minutes. Problem was, I didn't know which house. They all had secured entrances. Most of the mailboxes didn't have any names on them. Just numbers. I happened to glance across the street and noticed Rock's Honda. I knew he wouldn't park in front of the house. A little farther down I noticed a conversion van. Fancy. Expensive. It seemed out of place; didn't quite look like it fit in the neighborhood. Then I heard it. A sound that never sounded so numbing when I was the one who made it. A gunshot. It came from about two houses down.

I climbed the fence in between the two houses where I thought I heard the gunshot. I was fearing the worst, that my brother had been shot. My knees buckled with the sound of the second gunshot. One of the windows was wide open, that's where the noise was coming form. I was horrified at the sight. Rock was face down. Blood everywhere. I eased back into the shadow of the alley when the Captain put his gun to Rock's head. I could still see some, but I heard everything.

"I didn't want things to turn out like this, Rock. Now you're gonna die. Sorry to say it. Fast or slow, it's up to you. Tell me where your sister is and I'll let you lay here and bleed

to death. Don't cooperate and I'll put a bullet through your skull."

Rock raised his head just a little, ready to tell him to fuck off or something. His eyes, those beautiful, brown loving eyes of my big brother, the brother that had been there for me my entire life, those eyes looked up for a miracle. Savior! Not me. I'll just consider myself his guardian angel. His eyes met mine. I couldn't move, otherwise I would end up with a bullet in me, too. I'll never understand my brother. He had a maniac standing over him with a gun at his head and he still found time to wink at me. Then he mouthed something. What was he trying to say...v...v...van? That's it. The van. It belonged to the Captain. Then he moaned the last words I thought I would ever hear out of his mouth.

"Captain?"

"Yeah?"

"Suck my d—"

His head dropped to the floor. Arnetti, cold and uncaring, rose to leave. I made a beeline for the fence and said two prayers. The first was for the life of my brother. The second was that the Captain did like every cop on every television show in America. They leave their car door open. My second prayer was answered. All kinds of surveillance equipment. He probably had been following me for all I knew. I sat in the easy chair that he had in the back seat. I turned around so that I was facing the back door.

When the bastard jumped into the front seat I couldn't believe my ears. He was whistling. No tune that I was familiar with, but whistling. He just shot my brother, and for all I knew Carter Woods, but he deserved it, and this mother— was whistling. I slid the weapon from out of the pouch that I carried. The Sai. One of my favorite weapons that I learned to use quite well during my Martial Arts training. The Sai is about twelve inches long, thin, round and blunt on the end. It also has a similar shaped prong on each side attached at the handle. It looked like the letter 'M' with two short legs. The beauty of my personal Sai was that its once blunt end was sharpened, for the occasion. Just as Arnetti put the key in the ignition I turned around. Our eyes met in his rearview mirror. Before he could flex even one muscle I had wrapped my left forearm around his forehead and forced his head hard against the back of the seat. Cops are fast. Sure, he had his hand on his gun. He might have even thought about shooting me. But the pain that interrupted his thought process was too overwhelming. I shoved the Sai deep into his ear until the short prongs were wedged into his skull. Shoot, my brother, you get your brains scrambled. You die... but quick.

I pulled the Sai out and he fell into the passenger seat real easy. A large envelope fell out of his jacket, full of money. Dirty money, Carter's money. The Captain either took a bribe or he was working with him. Either way, he got caught, by me.

I rushed back to the basement to see about Rock. I felt his body. The best warm I had ever felt in my life. He was still alive. I ran upstairs and searched for a dead, child-abusing patsy. There were two gunshots and the

Captain was whistling. He probably guessed he had two kills and was about to go and make the third. Carter was on the floor, dead. A very large hole in his chest. Close-range kill, no doubt. I put the Sai in his dead hands. I sure am going to miss my Sai. I had to get big bro to a hospital.

I had to be strong for my brother. I had to. When I reached the bottom step, I fell to his side. Rolled him on his back. He was still alive, but barely conscious. I stroked the bald head of my big brother. He had the most perfectly round head. No bumps. No hair. Just— I wasn't ready to be alone. He had to be okay. I tore open his shirt to see the wound. I had to stop the bleeding. If I could see through the tears, maybe I could help. If I could have stopped shaking, maybe I could have done something.

"Cecil? Cecil? Can you hear me? I have to get you to a hospital, fast."

"S-S-Sasha- where's Arnetti? Did you get him?"

"S-s-shhh. Don't talk. I need to get you to a hospital."

Rock grabbed my hand so that I could feel his vest.. Luckily for him he had it on. The bullet hit him on the shoulder. There was plenty of blood, but I knew he'd live.

"Dammit, Rock. He's in the van. He's dead. He shot you, what was I supposed to do? Rock, your Captain had an envelope with about twenty-thousand dollars worth of one-hundred dollar bills in his jacket. He must have gotten the money from Carter. Is that a trip or what?"

"Twenty-grand, huh? I guess the Captain got a little too caught up in his work this time."

"He got caught all right."

"Carter?"

"Dead. Look, I used my Sai on the Captain, then put it in Carter's dead hands. Perfect setup. Now, I have to get you out of here."

30

Rock

I was elated for the first time about one of Sasha's kills. In my head my report was almost complete. Let's see: *Information was leaked to Captain Arnetti that Carter Woods was a child pornographer who could be bought. The Captain decided to start his retirement fund early and take care of Carter himself. He blackmailed Carter Woods for twenty grand. That way Carter could continue his pornography business. Carter gave the Captain the money, but decided to kill him before he could get away. I coincidentally showed up at the same time because of information obtained from Gloria Azeem. I was too late to stop Carter from killing the Captain. Carter shot me in the shoulder with the Captain's gun. When he came over to finish me off, I tripped him, we struggled, fought over the Captain's gun. Fortunately I got it from him. He grabbed the Sai, but luckily I got off one round that hit him squarely in the chest.*

"Sasha, this is what you're going to do, but first help me back upstairs...

31

Sasha

Here I was trying to save the life of my brother. He had blood all over him, had to be in excruciating pain. He could barely move, and in no position to be giving orders, but, that's exactly what he was doing.

"I can't believe you're lying here half dead, and losing blood, and you are going to tell me what to do."

With the little strength that he had left, Rock reached up and placed his finger over my lips. Although his face was etched with pain, his eyes were soothing and reassuring to me.

"Baby girl, you wipe those tears and listen up. I want you to go to the corner and call the police. Tell them you heard gunshots, you think somebody has been shot. Make sure you tell them to send an ambulance. Give them the address. Then—"

"Why, Rock? Why? I can't leave you like this. No, I won't..."

"Sasha Timms! Calm down. The bullet went through my shoulder. If it had hit a major artery I'd be dead by now. There is a brown envelope in the glove compartment of my Jaguar..."

"Rock!"

"S-sorry. My Honda. You take that letter and you mail it to the Mayor for me. Okay, baby girl? Can you do that, please?"

"Okay, Cecil. You hold on."

I called the police just like I was instructed to do. The contents of the envelope would be a nice treat for the Mayor. Rock let O'Grady know that he had a tape of him and Arnetti's conversation about the Mayor's desire to have me taken care of, and Rock, if he got in the way. Rock also included a small novel's worth of misconduct by Captain Arnetti. Payoffs. Murder. Extortion. Rock even insinuated that the Mayor had knowledge of Arnetti's despicable conduct. He also assured the Mayor that there would never be any mention of the real way his son died. I added to the note:

> *Dear Rozen,*
>
> *Detective Cecil Rock wanted me to inform you that your esteemed Captain Arnetti had an envelope with about twenty-thousand dollars on his person when he found him dead. Obviously ,some sort of payoff from Carter Woods, a child pornographer. I wanted to extend my condolences to you in regards to the death of your son Kyle. I want you to know that I lost a husband and my son lost his father on that day.*
>
> *Sasha*

Timms

There was a mailbox on the corner. I dropped the letter inside. Doublechecked to make sure that it dropped in. I pulled off my black gloves, covered with blood, and shoved them into the pockets of the bloody windbreaker I was wearing on top of my jacket. I pulled the jacket off and stuffed the entire thing, blood and all, inside of the pocket which doubled as a pouch. Zipped it shut, fastened the elastic strap and slung the pouch over my shoulder. Ready for disposal in a nice trashcan fire. Then, I waited. Five minutes late,r three police cars arrived. One minute later an ambulance. They carried my brother out on a stretcher. He was still alive. Carter and Arnetti left in those cute little black suitcases.

I headed for home. I heard the news on the radio about ten minutes later:

Captain Vincent Arnetti was brutally murdered by Carter Woods, a child pornographer in North Philadelphia. Woods, in turn ,was shot to death by another officer, Detective Cecil Rock, who happened to arrive on the scene a few minutes too late to save his Captain. Detective Rock was also wounded. There will be more details pending an investigation.

Final Session

33

Sasha's Way

"Lord, have mercy."

"Cecil says that you are an excellent psychiatrist. Is that all you have to say?"

"Sweet Jesus."

"Doctor Evelyn Davis, are you getting the Holy Ghost or something?"

"Forgive me, Doctor Sasha Timms. There just aren't any words that I can say at this time. How long was Cecil in the hospital?"

"They sent him home the next day. I stayed with him for an entire week. The big baby had me running and jumping the whole time like I was his personal private-duty nurse."

"Really?"

"Yes. I loved every minute of it."

"I'm sure you did."

"Look, Evelyn, I don't mean to be rude, but I have had about enough of this office to last me a lifetime. I want to go and see my son."

"Honey, your brother was absolutely right, you need help—"

"Well, you know what, Sugar? I've been seeing you for three weeks, and I feel better than I have since—

since all of this madness started. All I needed was a chance to vent. You allowed me to let it go. I am truly grateful."

"I guess I should say you're welcome? But, let's meet a few more times to see how the animal inside is doing."

"Okay, but—"

"No *but*, Sasha!"

"May I have a week off?

"Sure. See you in seven."

"Thanks, Evelyn."

"Mister Earlston Belefont, very good to see you."

"You're late, young lady. I've been sitting out here for over an hour. You told me to be here in three hours and I was. What were you doing in there all of this time?"

"Sugar, I just had to get some things off of my chest. That's all. Look, hang a right at the corner and then follow the signs for 95 South. I want to see my baby."

"Sasha?"

"Yes."

"I have something I want to say to you."

"Earlston, I have had a trying day. Maybe later. Okay?"

"Fine then, I won't say it. It really didn't apply to you anyway."

"Don't push your luck, buddy."

"Then listen up, my Queen."

"Earlston, you look so serious."

"Please don't interrupt anymore:"

It's funny, I knew it was you the first time I saw you

I knew
The way your hair laid so delicately on your shoulders
I knew, it was you
casually dressed, confident stride,
Your face reminded me of a Regal Woman
prideful, assured, with a touch of arrogance
I knew
The first time we talked you seemed
more interested in insults than compliments
I wondered why I was even with you
then I realized. I remembered,
I knew
We talked a little more, laughed, hugged
you apologized for being contemptuous
I wanted to keep in touch, call, talk, visit
you said 'No'
But deep down inside I wasn't worried
because I knew
although your best intentions were replaced with
mild sarcasm, I endured
I did my best to stay on your good side
never splintering the fragile shield that
encompassed your personal space
Because I knew that one day, you would call, and say
'I'm sorry,' or 'I need you,' or simply
'Please come as soon as you can'
And I did, because I knew
just like the first time that I saw you
That one day, the woman that
captivated my heart…

the woman who I know has a remarkable
level of brillance
Would one day

Be
My Friend!

"Earlston, put the car in park."

"Here?"

"Yes. I want to taste those luscious lips. So sweet. So soft. So warm. So mine!"

"MA'AM! SIR! DO YOU MIND PAYING THE TOLL FIRST AND FINISH YOUR KISSING ON THE SIDE OF THE ROAD OR SOMETHING! YOU'RE HOLDING UP MY LINE!"

"This isn't a fairy tale, it's My Story... My Life... My Way... Sasha's Way!"